CW00761874

STORMY WATERS AT HARBOUR HOUSE

FENELLA J. MILLER

Boldwood

First published in Great Britain in 2025 by Boldwood Books Ltd.

Copyright © Fenella J. Miller, 2025

Cover Design by Colin Thomas

Cover Images: Colin Thomas and Alamy

A CIP catalogue record for this book is available from the British Library.

Paperback ISBN 978-1-80549-301-3

Large Print ISBN 978-1-80549-299-3

Hardback ISBN 978-1-80549-300-6

Ebook ISBN 978-1-80549-303-7

Kindle ISBN 978-1-80549-302-0

Audio CD ISBN 978-1-80549-294-8

MP3 CD ISBN 978-1-80549-295-5

Digital audio download ISBN 978-1-80549-297-9

This book is printed on certified sustainable paper. Boldwood Books is dedicated to putting sustainability at the heart of our business. For more information please visit https://www.boldwoodbooks.com/about-us/sustainability/

Boldwood Books Ltd, 23 Bowerdean Street, London, SW6 3TN

www.boldwoodbooks.com

For Lizzie Lane (Jean Goodhind) for her unfailing support and encouragement, a fellow Boldie, and my companion on numerous 'writing retreats'.

1

FEBRUARY 1940

Something dragged Emily from her contented sleep. It was dark. The house was silent apart from the rhythmic purring of Ginger, who was snuggled down beside her. Her heart was pounding. Was it an air raid? Were the horrible Germans going to start bombing them? Then she slowly relaxed as the wail of the siren wasn't echoing over the village in the darkness.

'Did you hear anything, Ginger?' She didn't want to sit up as her bedroom was dark and freezing. Fires weren't allowed upstairs unless you were ill. The cat continued to purr and Emily flopped back into the warmth and safety of her blankets, satisfied that there was nothing going on. If her cat didn't stir, then things must be fine. Since she'd been attacked last year by Pete, the nasty evacuee they'd taken in, Ginger had become her constant companion; he'd saved her life and now considered that she needed his protection.

She smiled as she slid back under the feather eiderdown she'd been given for Christmas. This kept her lovely and warm as long as she stayed under the covers. Mummy hadn't liked Ginger when they'd first come to live in this old house last summer, but even she loved him now. Emily's brother George was a bit miffed as initially Ginger had preferred him, but he had Sammy, an evacuee from London, as a friend now so it was only fair that Ginger was hers.

There was no school today as the air-raid shelter in the grounds of her school in Colchester hadn't been finished. All the girls had been told to remain at home and were expected to continue their lessons independently. The very good thing about this was that she'd been spending a couple of days a week at the farm looking after the Peterson children and being paid with extra rations for her family.

Her parents agreed that she was learning more important things than schoolwork such as being responsible and discovering how a busy mixed farm worked. Emily loved the three children but being outside in the yard feeding the chickens, collecting the eggs and helping in the dairy was even more exciting, especially when Jimmy Peterson was there to explain things to her. He was fourteen now and always walked her home if she left in the dark as he had done right from her first visit last year.

George and Sammy still had to trudge through the thick snow to catch the train to their prep school in Lexden Road every morning. Both boys were nine and according to Mrs Bates were growing like weeds.

Emily couldn't tell what time it was in the blackness; even if it was dawn, the heavy blackout curtains kept even a glimmer of light from coming into the room.

She sighed, wriggled and plumped up her pillow – much to the annoyance of the cat – and tried to go back to sleep. After a while, she gave up and decided to get up. If she put on her warm woolly dressing gown and slippers, she'd be fine. Being awake had made her want to use the WC, which was downstairs. Her torch was on the bedside table and she flicked it on before searching for her things.

'Are you coming, Ginger? I'm going to make myself a mug of hot milk. I'll find you something too if you come.'

Talking to the cat was silly but all the family did it, even Mummy. As Emily quietly opened the door, the cat thumped onto the rug next to the bed and padded over to her. He wound himself around her legs and she reached down to stroke his head.

'Thank you. I don't like being downstairs in the dark on my own.'

'You won't have to be, sweetheart; your mother's having the baby,' Daddy said as he came out of their bedroom right at that exact moment.

'Golly, you're dressed. Is she all right?'

Mummy answered from the bedroom. 'I'm tickety-boo, darling, but if you're up, I'd love a mug of cocoa and a piece of cake if there's any left from supper.'

'I'll do that. It must have been Daddy getting dressed that woke me.' Her father had already raced down the stairs, unlocked the front door and slammed it behind him. 'Is he fetching Nurse Symonds or Dr Cousins?'

'The midwife, Emily, but the doctor's only next door if I did need him, which is very unlikely.'

Reassured by Mummy's cheerful voice, Emily dashed downstairs, closely followed by Ginger. The old-fashioned kitchen range that supplied the hot water for baths, washing up and so on was always alight. She knew how to riddle it and get it burning bright enough to put a saucepan or kettle on the top.

Nancy, Mrs Bates's daughter, had told her in confidence that having a baby needed a lot of hot water. She wasn't exactly sure what the water was for but thought it likely the baby and the mother would need a nice wash. Maybe it would be a good idea to put on the kettle and all the saucepans. She wasn't supposed to light the lovely new gas stove, so Daddy would have to do that when he got home. But eleven years was old enough to do this in her opinion, so she decided to risk it.

The window in the scullery banged as Ginger went out. She hoped he didn't return with a live mouse or, even worse, a rat. Dead ones weren't so bad; she'd collected several bodies and tossed them into the rubbish bin without feeling sick.

By the time the front door slammed open again, she'd made the cocoa and every saucepan was full of water and heating up. She braced herself for Daddy's angry reaction when he saw she'd disobeyed and lit the gas rings.

'Well done, sweetheart. I hoped you'd get things started. I see you've mastered the gas stove. Don't let the boys see you doing it. They're still too young to be trusted with matches and gas.'

Emily glowed at his praise. 'The cocoa's ready and so are the slices of cake.'

'Good. I'll take it up. Would you stay down here and supervise? Nurse Symonds said she'll need warm, clean towels as well. Can you sort that out too?'

'Of course I can. I'll let the midwife in when she arrives.'

He snatched up the tray and vanished. It wasn't like her daddy to be so flustered. Maybe having a baby wasn't as easy as Mummy had told her.

There was a loud knock on not the front door but the back. It hadn't taken the nurse long to get here. She hurried into the icy passage and unbolted and unlocked the door. Standing outside wasn't Nurse Symonds but Nancy Bates. What was she doing here?

* * *

Nancy Bates had dressed in a hurry after Mr Roby had woken them up. Nancy's dad had gone down and explained that her mum wasn't well so Nancy would be coming to help out instead. The factory where she worked was closed for few days as the pipes had frozen and the two big iron stoves had packed up as well. It was too cold to sew military uniforms in that big old building even if they were essential to the war effort.

She'd been doing a bit of child minding of a weekend since Mrs Roby had been told to rest by the doc. Mum and the other ladies who worked for the new family helped out during the week but Mr Roby sometimes needed help on a Saturday and Sunday, too. The extra cash was going in her savings account at the post office. Nancy was putting this away to buy items for her bottom drawer as even if she didn't marry her boyfriend, Dan, she'd marry someone in the next year or so. She wanted her own home, to not have to share with her three younger brothers in the tiny two-up, two-down cottage at the other end of Alma Street.

Mum said seventeen was far too young to be thinking of getting married. To be honest, Nancy agreed, but as neither of her parents would allow her to join one of the services then marriage was the only option. She'd quite like to be a WREN, or a WAAF but didn't want to be in the army. She spent all day sewing the hideous khaki uniforms for those girls.

Dan's half-brother Reggie had been sent to a remand centre after breaking into Harbour House last October and she'd almost broken up with him then. But he'd been as shocked as she was and so she'd decided to remain his girlfriend. He was the best-looking young man in Wivenhoe. She wasn't quite sure if she was still with him because every other girl envied her or because she was a little bit in love with him.

Dan was a fisherman, three years older than her, but wanted to enlist in the navy. He'd look a treat in blue and having him away would probably suit her better. He wanted to take things further and she didn't; now wasn't the time to be bringing babies into the world and especially not unwanted ones.

Doreen Harper, her best friend, was walking out with a soldier from Colchester barracks and the way they were carrying on, Nancy thought they would very likely have no choice but to get married.

It was only a minute from her home to Harbour House and she banged on the back door and was surprised to see Emily in the doorway. Quickly, she explained why she'd come and not her mum and the girl smiled.

'Daddy has left me in charge of hot water and warm towels. I was just going to get some from the linen cupboard and put them on the airer in front of the range.'

Nancy nodded. Emily seemed much older than her years and she wasn't surprised Mr Roby was trusting her to take care of this.

'If you're going to be down here, why don't you nip upstairs and get dressed properly? I'll watch the water.'

'Actually, I'm warmer in my pyjamas and dressing gown, thank you.'

'Shall I make a pot of tea? I expect everyone will want a cuppa later on.' It seemed a bit off asking a child for instructions but if Mr Roby was happy to leave his daughter in charge then it wasn't her business to complain.

Emily didn't answer and dashed off, making her long plait bounce, to fetch the towels.

Nancy was just pouring the boiling water over the leaves

when there was a loud knock on the front door. It would be the midwife.

She waited a moment to see if Emily came to answer it, but when she didn't, Nancy did. It was Nurse Symonds.

'Good evening, or should I say good morning as it's after midnight. Nancy Bates, isn't it? I delivered all your brothers.'

'I know, my mum told me. She thinks the world of you. Is it snowing again?'

This was a daft question as the jolly nurse was covered in it.

''Fraid so. Would you be a dear and hang my cloak up so it will be dry when I leave?'

There was no need to tell her where to go as she rushed up the stairs, her ample backside bouncing underneath her smart navy uniform, her big leather bag held in front of her like a trophy.

Later, Emily insisted on taking the tray of tea up herself and came back looking upset. 'What's wrong, love?'

'I can hear Mummy crying and I don't like it.'

'Never mind, it's not called labour for nothing. You should have heard my mum screaming when she had my brothers. I reckon they heard her over the river in Rowhedge.'

Emily smiled and looked a bit happier. 'I heard the nurse telling Daddy to leave but he refused.'

'Crikey, I wondered where he was. The blokes don't hang around in the room as a rule. My dad was off to the pub and left me to look after the others. There's a big gap between me and them.'

'Oh, why's that?'

'My mum lost a couple of babies early on.' As soon as she

said this, Nancy regretted it. Emily was too young to hear about miscarriages.

The girl, yet again, surprised her.

'My mummy might have lost this baby; that's why she had to stay in bed and why Daddy carried her up and down stairs for ages.'

'I'd forgotten about that. What do you hope to have: a sister or a brother?'

'A sister, of course, then there'll be two of each in this family. Mummy and Daddy are trying to persuade Sammy's mother to give him up so they can adopt him.'

'I'm not surprised; the little lad even looks like a Roby with his dark hair and that. He could be a twin to your George.'

'That's why we want to keep him. He's part of the family and speaks like all of us now. He's doing really well now he's attending the prep school at the Colchester Royal Grammar School. His teacher thinks he'll get a scholarship like George when he's old enough.'

This was a sore point for Nancy as she'd passed the exam but hadn't been able to go because the uniform and other things were too expensive. For some reason, she told Emily and the girl was upset for her.

'I knew you were intelligent. Mrs Bates thinks you shouldn't be working as a seamstress in that old factory but doing something better. You could learn to be a typist and work in an office, couldn't you?'

'I could, and if I've got regular work here then I might give it a go and leave the factory.' She'd quietly moved across the kitchen and shut the door so any yelling from upstairs wouldn't be heard. She hoped the boys were sound sleepers.

'Daddy has a typewriter; I'm sure he'd let you practise on it if you're working here. I'd like to learn too. Better than doing lessons whilst I'm stuck at home.'

Emily yelped and Nancy slopped her tea on the floor as the boys erupted into the kitchen. Both were white faced and in tears.

'Someone's killing Mummy,' George sobbed and fell into his sister's arms. Nancy hugged Sammy and tried to explain.

'It's painful having a baby. Screaming helps the mother and gets the baby out quicker.'

George stopped crying, sniffed and wiped his snotty nose on his pyjama sleeve. 'She's not dying? I was so worried when I heard her. I'm glad I can't have a baby.'

Sammy wiped his face on her jumper before speaking. 'How does a baby get out, Nancy?'

Emily was as interested in this answer as the two little boys. Nancy turned red, and didn't know how to explain it. She had to tell them something. 'Girls are made differently to boys and have a special place where babies can come out when they're ready.'

Emily nodded. 'But how do they get in there in the first place?'

Nancy was stumped, not sure how to explain without being rude, but to her astonishment, Sammy piped up.

'Pete told me about that. The man puts his...'

She thanked God that Mr Roby walked in before Sammy could continue.

'I've come to tell you that you have a baby sister. The midwife said it was an easy delivery and you can come and meet her in the morning.'

Emily squealed and threw herself into his arms. 'I'm so pleased it's a girl. What are you going to call her?'

'We can't decide. We thought the three of you could each

make a list of ten names and we'll do the same. The ones that appear the most on our lists will be what we call her.'

Poor bloke looked shattered and accepted a mug of tea gratefully. He grinned at Nancy and raised his mug.

'Elizabeth's tired but remarkably happy considering what she's just been through. I'll take a tray up to her and the midwife.' He turned to the children. 'Go to bed now; the excitement's over. We'll exchange lists at breakfast tomorrow.'

'Will Mummy come down?' Emily asked.

'No, a new mother has to rest for ten days at least. However, you'll be able to go in and see her. Chop-chop, you three. Off to bed now.' He hugged each of them. 'Absolutely no talking. Straight into bed and asleep. Is that clear?'

Emily flew upstairs, elated that she had a baby sister and that Mummy and the little one were both very well. Daddy's suggestion that they choose the names as a family was a wonderful one. She already had a few ideas but wouldn't write them down until the morning. When he spoke like that, you just had to do exactly as he said.

She thought she was far too excited to sleep but as soon as she fell into bed, she yawned and her eyes closed on their own. As she drifted off, she wondered what Sammy had been going to say. She intended to ask him when she got the chance.

2

Nancy was tempted to sleep on the sofa in the Robys' sitting room but thought this might not be approved of. She wasn't going to go home and disturb her three brothers so would have to sleep in her dad's chair in the kitchen.

The house was quiet, the midwife long gone, the children asleep and as far as she knew, so was the new arrival and her parents.

It hadn't taken long to wash up and make sure the kitchen was spotless. Then she laid up the long, scrubbed pine table in the kitchen ready for breakfast and also got a tray ready for Mrs Roby. If she was lucky enough to be offered work here for the next few weeks, she needed to make a good impression.

She was just checking the black kitchen range had enough fuel to keep burning until she returned in a few hours when Mr Roby came in – he was in his pyjamas and dressing gown.

'Good, Elizabeth and I thought it made sense for you to stay here tonight. I've dumped some bedding on the sofa. You can pop home in the morning if you need to when your brothers are at school. I hope Molly's feeling better soon.'

'Thank you, that's very kind of you.'

He didn't say goodnight but that wasn't surprising as he was in bare feet and they must have been perished.

Nancy slept surprisingly well and woke at exactly half past six. She had an infallible method of waking herself that didn't involve an alarm clock. She banged her head the same number of times as the hour that she wanted to wake up and for some strange reason, always opened her eyes at exactly the time she wanted.

There was no sound from upstairs, not even a wail of a newborn baby. The sitting-room fire was alight, the kitchen warm and welcoming and Nancy was confident she had everything as it should be for when the family eventually came down.

Nurse Symonds turned up before the children woke.

'Good morning, Nancy. I'll show myself up,' the midwife said cheerfully.

'I'm just about to take a tray of tea to Mr and Mrs Roby. I just took them up a jug of hot water and left it outside the door. I knocked and asked how they were, and he said that everything was fine. Mother and baby both sleeping.'

'Splendid. I'll send Mr Roby down whilst I see to mother and infant.'

Emily arrived next, looking sleepy, which wasn't surprising as she'd only been in bed for a few hours.

'Morning, Nancy. I didn't hear my sister crying at all. Do you want to see my list of names?'

'Names?'

The girl explained that everyone in the house was involved in selecting the name for the new arrival.

'Go on then, show me what you've written.'

'I'll read them out to you. Sarah, Jennifer, Verena, Grace, Sylvia, Lily, Ruth, Amanda, Cynthia and Margaret. What do you think?'

'I like them all. I hope the boys don't put something silly down.'

'If they do then it won't be on my list or my mummy's and daddy's.'

* * *

The boys tumbled into the room more excited about the fresh fall of snow than naming the baby. They gobbled down their porridge and toast, put on their overcoats and wellington boots, gloves, hats and scarves, eager to go into the front garden and build a snowman.

'Leave your lists on the table, boys, then Daddy can take them up with mine to show Mummy later on.'

'We only made one list,' George said as he rushed off. 'We couldn't think of any other names.'

Emily frowned. 'The lists were supposed to be written in secret.'

'Never mind, Emily. I don't suppose boys are that interested in naming a baby.'

'Do you think I can meet my sister soon? Daddy said it would be this morning.'

'I reckon it'll be after the midwife has gone and your mum has had her breakfast. Listen, I just heard the front door bang,' Nancy said. 'I think the nurse must have gone.'

Mr Roby walked in smiling and hugged his daughter. 'If you'd be kind enough to take the tray, Nancy, I'll eat down here.' He pulled out a chair after helping himself to porridge from the pot on the range. 'Do you have the lists of names, sweetheart?' He didn't look at them put pushed them into his jacket pocket. 'I saw the boys in the garden; probably better the baby isn't overwhelmed by all three of you on the first visit. I'll take you up as soon as I've eaten.'

Nancy admired the tiny infant and congratulated Mrs Roby, who looked radiant, and not at all tired. She left Mrs Roby and her new baby and headed back to the stairs. She paused at the window to look at the boys, who were playing outside, and was shocked to see Dan, her boyfriend, striding up the snowy path. What did he want?

Despite her worry at his unexpected arrival, she smiled. He was so handsome. Tall, with broad shoulders and dark hair curling over his collar. But it was his smouldering blue eyes that made her heart race. No wonder all the girls fancied him.

She hurried down and opened the door before he could knock and alert the family to the fact she was receiving a personal call during working hours.

'Sorry to intrude, love, but I needed to speak to you. Your mum said you wouldn't be home until later this afternoon.'

'I can't be out here for long. I've got breakfast to clear and lunch to make.'

He smiled, his teeth white against his skin. All fishermen were sunburnt from being out in all weathers. 'How's the nipper and the mum?'

'Smashing, thanks for asking. Now, quickly before the boys want to know why you're here.'

'I just wanted to tell you I'm not joining the Royal Navy after all; I'm going to be mate on a Thames barge. Less rules and I can leave when I want.'

She smiled. 'Couldn't that have waited until this afternoon when we're going to the social up the road?'

'No, I'm leaving first thing tomorrow. The owner of the barge at Brightlingsea runs goods down the coast. Wooden hulled, so less likely to be blown up by a mine.'

She shook her head. 'Then I still don't know why I'm standing out here freezing to death when you could have told me this later.'

His smile blazed and he reached out to take her hands. 'Will you marry me, Nancy Bates?'

Marriage? Nancy hadn't been expecting a proposal, wasn't even sure she wanted to marry him or anyone.

'Don't be daft, Dan; my parents wouldn't let me, and we need their permission until I'm twenty-one.'

'Not right now, but maybe next year when you're nineteen. I've rented a nice little cottage at Brightlingsea and I'll do it up so it's ready for you when we marry. Now I'm a mate, I can afford my own place.'

She'd intended to refuse, to send him away with a smile but he was so nice, so kind and loved her so much she couldn't hurt his feelings.

'All right, I'll be engaged to you but no talk of marriage until next year. You'll have to square it with my dad, but I warn you that he's likely to hit the roof.'

He glanced across at the boys, who were too busy building snowmen to take any notice of them and before she could escape, he drew her into his arms and kissed her. His lips were hard, icy, but heat still flooded through her body.

Dan strolled away, well pleased with his visit. All he had to do now was convince Nancy's dad, Bert, that getting engaged wasn't the same as getting married. If he laid it on a bit thick, mentioned how much more dangerous it would be for him sailing a barge up and down the Thames estuary, the bloke might be okay.

He couldn't bang on Bert's door for another hour at least so headed down Station Road to his own home to tell his mum. His stepfather was a nasty bit of work and Dan avoided all contact with him if possible. This was the real reason he'd taken the job in Brightlingsea and rented the dilapidated cottage. He now had a place of his own and need only come to Wivenhoe to see Nancy.

No one used the front door, nor the front room; everyone went round the back. His two younger brothers weren't as bad as the little bastard, Reggie, who'd attempted to rob the Robys last October. Still, they were no angels and were always in some sort of trouble.

'Morning, Dan. Ta for clearing away all the snow; saved me a job this morning,' Sid Smith, who lived next door, called out from behind his kitchen window.

'No trouble. How's Gladys today?' Sid's missus was always poorly with something or other. They had no kiddies and Sid doted on her.

'Not too bad, ta, but I'm not letting her out in this weather. Brass monkeys, ain't it?'

'Perishing.' Dan decided to tell Sid his news. 'I've just got engaged to Nancy Bates, and I'm leaving Wivenhoe tomorrow to be mate on a red sail berthed at Brightlingsea.'

'Good for you, son. She's a lovely girl and you'll do all right with her. You going to be living down there, then?'

Dan nodded. 'I am: got a cottage to do up ready for Nancy when we get married.'

He smiled at his neighbour but frowned when he saw his own home was in darkness.

* * *

The blackouts were still drawn. The house silent. He'd expected his mum to be up even if no one else was. Dan put the kettle on, then let some light into the house. The kitchen was long and narrow, but good enough. They spent most of their time in the middle room where they ate and sat. There was always a bit of a fire in there.

There was an outhouse in the backyard, also a coal shed, and he stopped to fill up the hod waiting beside the shed door. He wasn't that fond of his mum, but she worked hard and had to put up with Bill, who was too old to be called up, more's the pity. The miserable old sod worked over the river in Rowhedge Ironworks. He earned decent money but Mum didn't get much of it. Most was spent in one of the many pubs in the village. Dan had only remained at home to help out with the housekeeping.

Dan had got the fire going in the middle room by the time Mum pushed open the door to the stairs and stepped down, still half-asleep.

'Morning, son. I don't suppose you've got a spare fag for your old mum?'

'No, sorry, I don't smoke, you know that. You smoke too much; that cough wouldn't be as bad if you cut down a bit.'

He'd no idea if smoking was harmful but he was quite certain that there'd be more on the table if she didn't fork out on a packet of Woodbines every day.

'That ain't true; smoking's good for the chest. Stands to reason, don't it; the government wouldn't be giving fags to soldiers if it was harmful.'

Her stringy, grey-streaked brown hair was still in metal curlers, roughly covered by a faded, cotton headscarf tied in a turban. Her feet were in her old felt slippers but she'd yet to don her wraparound apron which hung on a hook in the kitchen; apart from that, she was fully dressed.

She scowled at him. 'Shove over, I'll get them meself. The tobacconist will be open now.'

'Mum, you can't go out like that. If you must have cigarettes then I'll get them. I was about to make the tea and the porridge is ready, the bread cut for toast. I need to tell you something, but it can wait 'til I get back.'

'If it's that you're buggering off to Brightlingsea, then you don't need to bother. It's all over the village that you're not on the *Jolly Sally* no more.'

Dan sighed. You couldn't keep anything quiet in Wivenhoe.

'Right. I won't be long. I want three bits of toast and some of that dripping on it,' he called as he snatched up his donkey jacket and shrugged into it. He'd not bothered to remove his heavy boots; Bill and the boys didn't, so why should he?

The tobacconist was opposite the Greyhound pub, only a couple of minutes from the house. There were few folk about so early and his were the first feet to make imprints in the newly fallen snow. With a packet of ten Woodbines in his pocket, he hurried back, keeping his head down as the wind blowing up from the river was bitter. None of the fishing boats would be out today: too dangerous.

Barges, having no engines, sailed when it was blowing hard; a blizzard wouldn't keep them in harbour as long as the tide and the wind was right. Those ships toing and froing across the Atlantic sailed in convoys escorted by fighters and frigates. This didn't stop the bloody U-boats from sinking lots of them, though.

His mum was waiting at the back door and held out her hand as he stepped in.

'Give us a chance, why don't you? Let me get my coat off first.'

He draped his snow-sprinkled jacket over the back of a chair in front of the fire, sat down, before dipping into his coat pocket and handing over the fags.

'Only ten? I wanted twenty. How am I going to manage without what you pay me for your board and lodging?'

'Bill will have to give you more housekeeping. If he didn't spend half his wages at the pub, you'd have plenty.'

Something heavy hit him on the back of the head and he was knocked forward, almost sliding off the chair.

'Mind your lip, you little bugger. What I do with me own money in me own house is none of your bloody business.'

Dan surged to his feet and turned to face his attacker. He was half a head taller, broader and twenty years younger. Bill had knocked him about for the last time.

Dan's fist clenched and he lashed out. The punch sent Bill staggering back and he ricocheted off the wall and slid down, ending on his arse, blood dripping down his chin from his broken nose.

Mum was screaming. There was a clatter on the stairs and his two half-brothers burst into the room. This could only get worse. Time to leave. His ditty bag was already packed and waiting in the coal shed. He'd half-expected things to end this way.

He nodded at Bill, who wisely made no attempt to get up and continue the fight. 'You had that coming, old man. If I hear you're knocking my mum about, not giving her any housekeeping, I'll be back to finish the job. Got that?'

The man nodded. Point made and understood. Dan ignored the boys, there was no love lost between them, and smiled apologetically at his tearful mum.

'Sorry, but I told him what would happen if he hit me again. Take care, Mum. Goodbye.'

This time, he paused long enough to wrap his muffler around his neck and pull his woolly hat over his ears before leaving his family home for the last time. He'd never willingly return. That part of his life was done. He was on his own now.

He deliberately didn't look at Sid's window; he didn't intend to stop and explain what the ruckus had been about. With his belongings slung over his shoulder, he headed for Alma Street and his talk – most likely a confrontation – with a man he admired and hoped would eventually be his father-in-law.

* * *

Emily wasn't as impressed with her baby sister as she'd expected. She made cooing noises and smiled a lot but her heart wasn't in it. Mummy didn't seem to notice but Daddy was watching her closely.

'Shall we compare the lists, sweetheart? We need to have a name for this new arrival.'

Daddy sat on the big bed and she sat on a stool close to him. He smiled.

'Look, there are two that are on all our lists. Our youngest daughter is either Grace Margaret or Margaret Grace; which do you prefer, darling?'

Mummy laughed. 'Grace Margaret is perfect. The first is a lovely old-fashioned name and the second is the name of one of the princesses. I think registering her birth will have to wait until the weather improves, though.'

'Mrs Cousins has asked me to look after her daughter, Claire, when she starts at my school. I'll enjoy the responsibility. A few months ago, I was being taken to the High School by an older girl and now I'm going to be doing the same for little Claire.'

'At least you'll have the boys with you most days. I'm so proud of you children being able to travel into Colchester and out on your own. You'd never have done that if we'd stayed in London. And hopefully we'll hear from your school that the shelter's finished,' Daddy said.

The boys had had to become independent when Greyfriars had closed until the air-raid shelter could be completed. They'd adapted really well and when she eventually went back to school and had to take Claire, she wouldn't have to worry about being in charge of three children.

Emily carefully returned the stool to the corner so no one would trip over it and was just leaving when Daddy called her.

'I'll be down in a minute. I thought we could join the boys and see if we can build a bigger snowman than them?'

Her spirits lifted. 'Oh, goody, that will be such fun. I'll be putting on my outdoor things and then go out and tell the boys it's a competition.'

* * *

After an hour, the excitement of doing something with Daddy had turned into misery. Her fingers were frozen, there was snow down her neck, and she couldn't feel her toes. Even with thick socks inside her wellingtons, they were still frozen solid.

'I'm going in, Daddy; I'm too cold.'

'The boys and I will be in in a few minutes. Can you ask Nancy to fill some hot water bottles and make a big pot of tea?'

'I'll do that,' she said though chattering teeth. How her brothers had remained out here for two hours, she'd no idea. Boys must be a lot tougher than girls.

It took her ages to thaw out, but George and Sammy had recovered as soon as they'd put on dry clothes and drunk a large mug of tea. Nothing seemed to bother Daddy.

He joined her in the sitting room where she was struggling with her knitting. She so wanted to be able to make something useful for the sailors but like her mummy, this essential skill appeared beyond her. At least she could sew really well, which was something to be proud of.

'Don't bother with that, Emily; let someone else use the wool. You're just mangling it.'

'I am, Daddy, but I hate to give up.'

He flopped next to her on the long, comfy sofa. 'Don't be worried that Grace doesn't look very interesting. She's still recovering from her arrival, and all newborns look somewhat squashed and unappealing.'

'Were George and I like that too?'

'You certainly were and look what a handsome pair you are now.'

3

Nancy was enjoying her weekend working at Harbour House but so far, there'd been no mention of a permanent position. Therefore, she'd have to continue working at the sewing factory when it opened. The Robys already employed her mum as cook and housekeeper, Betty as the daily woman and Enid came in on a Monday to do the washing; perhaps they didn't need her help after all.

She was worried she wouldn't get the afternoon off to go to the village social at the old boys' school up the High Street and Dan would be disappointed. Enid was working extra hours today because of the baby and Nancy mentioned this to her. To her surprise, she smiled.

'You take an hour to see your young fellow, Nancy; I can manage on my own. I might be old but I'm not useless.'

'That would be lovely, thanks, Enid.'

Enid was a widow, had no children, and took care of her mother-in-law who must be in her nineties. Small wonder Enid was often snappy and unhelpful. Her unexpected kindness touched Nancy and she decided to share her news with her.

'I've just got engaged to Dan; you're the first person I've told. He's going to speak to my dad this morning. I hope he doesn't get his head bitten off.'

'He's a nice lad. Always helpful, calls in sometimes to give me a hand with things. I know Molly thinks he's not good enough for you, but she likes him well enough; she just wants you to be happy.'

'We're not thinking about marrying until late next year. I'll be nineteen then and more than old enough to set up my own home. Mum was married at eighteen.'

'I heard he's giving up fishing and joining a ship that sails from Brightlingsea. You'll not be seeing much of him now, will you?' Enid straightened the cup and saucer on Mrs Roby's tray. 'Take this up before it gets cold.'

The old Enid was back, giving orders. Enid's job was to do the heavy work, Betty did the daily cleaning, Mum was in charge of the house. This meant that as far as Nancy was concerned, she was here in her mum's place which meant that she was the one to give orders.

Nancy nodded. 'I'm going. Please have the tray for the sitting room ready for when I come down, Enid.'

From the banging and clattering that followed her up the passageway, Enid hadn't taken kindly to being told what to do by a seventeen-year-old.

Mr Roby had willingly given his permission for Nancy to spend an hour in the dining room with Dan and she was waiting for him to arrive and tell her what her dad had said. She was watching from the window and saw him opening the front gate. He glanced up and smiled. A rush of relief engulfed her. Things must have gone all right with Dad. She ran to the front door and opened it as he arrived on the porch.

'I'm sorry, Dan, I can't go to the social, but you can come in for an hour.'

He grinned. 'That'll have to do. I've got a lot to tell you. I'm leaving this afternoon now, not on Monday.'

He dumped his ditty bag in a corner and kicked the door shut. Then he took her hands and pulled her close. 'Your dad gave us his blessing. We can be wed September next year. I love you, Nancy Bates, and this is the best day of my life.'

She should have said it back but the words wouldn't come. Instead, she stood on tiptoe and kissed him. His arms tightened and for a few heady moments, she forgot where she was and almost forgot her good intentions. Luckily, he remained a gentleman and gently pushed her away.

'Next September can't come soon enough for me, love. Crikey, is that for us?' He pointed to the pot of tea and warm scones on the table and beamed.

'It is. Emily brought them down from the farm and they heated up a treat in the oven. There's also cream, actual butter and jam to go with them.'

She'd not eaten lunch so she could enjoy afternoon tea with him. They ate every crumb and emptied the teapot before they settled back in front of the fire. Sitting on two hard wooden chairs wasn't very comfortable or romantic but being close together in front of the fire was really nice.

'Why are you leaving today, Dan?'

He told her about the argument, fight really, at his house and she shuddered. 'That Bill's a nasty bit of work. I'm glad you're not living there any more. I know we won't see each other so much but I can catch the train when the weather's fine and you can do the same. If my dad approves of us being engaged, then we can meet at home or in one of the hotels.'

He swore and she flinched. She'd never heard him use bad language before. 'Sorry, that slipped out. There's something really important I've not said.'

'It had better be good after that.'

He stood up and dug into his trouser pocket. 'Here, my love. I didn't want to put this on your finger until it was official.'

With a shy smile, he dropped to one knee and held out a pretty green leather ring box. 'Will you marry me, Nancy Bates, and make me the happiest man in Essex?'

'Go on with you, you didn't have to do that. I've said I'll marry you. Get up, you big dafty.'

Instead of doing that, he grabbed her hands and tumbled her down to the floor with him. He flicked open the box and she gasped.

'It's beautiful. Where did you get such an expensive ring?' She regretted her words when his smile vanished.

'I didn't steal it if that's what you're thinking.'

'I'm sorry, I didn't mean that. It's just such a valuable ring.' She pulled it from the box and held it up to the firelight. The diamond sparkled; the setting and ring were real gold. 'I didn't want you to spend all your savings on a ring. We need as much money as we can save for our new home.'

Finally, he relaxed. 'It was my grandmother's on my father's side. He gave it to me just before he passed. I've had it hidden in the coal shed for years. I knew one day, I'd find the girl I wanted to marry and would give it to her.'

'Thank you, I love it, but if I let anyone at the factory see it on my finger, I'm worried it'll be stolen. Mum has a gold chain; maybe she'll let me borrow it so I can wear it around my neck until next year.'

'Wear it for now. Let me see if it fits.'

She held out her left hand and he slipped it over the knuckle of her ring finger. It was the perfect size. She scrambled onto his lap and they kissed until she heard the clock strike in the hall.

'You have to go now. Write to me, Dan, and I'd reply if I knew where to send a letter. I'm going to miss you.'

'Not as much as I'll miss you. The owner said I'll usually be away for ten days, then have a couple of days ashore before sailing again. I'll come back and get a bed at The Grosvenor or Falcon hotel for a couple of nights.'

He was already pulling on his heavy navy coat and pushing his feet back into his boots. She handed him his scarf and hat and they hugged, and he was gone. He didn't look round.

She wasn't sure when she'd see him again and watched him trudge off to catch the train. She rubbed her eyes, cross with herself for crying. There was a war on, and everyone had to be strong and do their duty. She prayed he'd not be torpedoed and drown as was happening to far too many merchant seamen.

And Brightlingsea was only a short train ride away, easy enough to visit him. It wasn't as if he was going to be living on the other side of the county.

Dan crossed the bridge in a hurry to the downside of the platform and arrived just in time to scramble into a carriage. The guard blew his whistle, waved his flag and the train steamed out on its way to Brightlingsea. The points had to be changed to allow them to leave the main line which went on to Clacton and this slowed things down a bit.

He was always a little nervous when they arrived at Alresford Creek – somehow, the bridge didn't seem robust enough to carry the large engine and the following carriages. They trundled across safely and picked up speed and arrived at the station a short while later.

He hefted his ditty bag on his shoulder, then lowered the window in order to lean out and turn the handle to open the carriage door. He'd travelled on his own – hardly surprising on a Saturday. Weekdays, there would be students and schoolchildren, businessmen and housewives going to Colchester, Chelmsford or London and in the summer, day trippers would make the journey. That wouldn't happen any more as now there was a war on, the beaches had been mined and weren't open to visitors.

Dan wouldn't be sailing, obviously, until Monday. Tomorrow, he was to learn how to sail a Thames barge. There was more to this than going out to sea in a powered fishing boat. He had a lot to absorb but was confident it wouldn't take him long to become proficient, although it would likely be a couple of years before he was offered a position as skipper on one of them. Being mate was good enough for him at the moment.

Sailing a barge was just part of it; learning how to navigate the estuary was another. He'd been a seaman since he'd left school six years ago, could sail safely down the coast, the North Sea and the Atlantic but it was Brightlingsea to Yarmouth that he wasn't familiar with.

A Thames barge was a flat-bottomed vessel and could sail in rivers and shallow water that bigger crafts couldn't. They had no keel but two lee-boards which could be lowered and raised on either side to give stability to the boat. You had to be skilled to sail a barge in and out of a harbour safely and he was well aware how much he had to understand before being promoted to skipper. He wasn't entirely ignorant of sailing ships as he'd summered a couple of times before he left school as a deckhand on the racing yachts that had once berthed at Wivenhoe.

These barges were an ancient design and had been sailing up and down rivers for hundreds of years, also along the coast and the bigger ones even went to France. They could carry a massive amount of cargo in and out of small ports and didn't require precious fuel as they were entirely wind powered. Another benefit was that they only required two crew members, although having three made for a safer and easier trip.

The wind was bitter, blowing inland down the estuary from the sea. There was nothing worse for a sailor than being out on the water in a blizzard. Dan prayed the weather would improve by Monday.

The cottage he'd taken a long lease on wasn't habitable even in the best of weather, so he'd got lodgings with the skipper of the *Lady Beth*. Dan hoped he was going to take his place when Percy Jackson, the current skipper and owner, retired.

The cottage was close to the yard, at the far end of the terrace. He hammered on the door, knowing that a polite knock wouldn't be heard over the howling wind. The door opened and a tiny, grey-haired woman with very few teeth beamed and beckoned him in.

'Come on in, son. My Percy's not back from the pub but he'll be here soon for his tea. Take your things up to your room – it's on the left of the stairs. No fire upstairs, but the chimney breast keeps it lovely and warm.'

'Ta, thanks for taking me in.'

Whilst she rearranged the blackout curtain, which also acted as an efficient draught excluder, Dan unlaced his boots and dropped them into the wooden box next to the front door. There were pegs for his donkey jacket and oilskins and he quickly hung these up.

He was more than satisfied with his new accommodation. It might be small, but it had everything he needed to be comfortable. There was even a Bible next to the bed in case he had the urge to read the good word. It was certainly warmer, cleaner and more to his taste than the attic space he'd occupied all his life in Station Road.

* * *

Dan was expecting to be asked to accompany his skipper and his wife to the Presbyterian chapel they attended and was relieved he wasn't required to.

'No need to go to church today, lad; too much for you to learn before tomorrow,' Percy said with a knowing wink.

'I'm glad; I'm not a churchgoer. I've not set foot in one since a funeral last year.'

'Only high days and holidays for me, lad; the missus don't mind as long as I turn up Christmas and Easter.'

'That's good to know. Thank you for giving me this opportunity. I'll not let you down.'

'I know you won't, lad; I'd not have offered you the position otherwise.'

They wrapped up well and headed for the harbour. Dan noticed that the shipyards they walked past seemed to be overrun by naval blokes. Since the outbreak of war, every ship had to get routing instructions from the Admiralty, everything was now controlled by the navy, but as a fisherman, he'd scarcely seen the bloke from the Naval Control Service at Wivenhoe. Things seemed to be different down here.

'Why's the navy so blooming interested in somewhere as small and insignificant as Brightlingsea?'

'Don't talk to me about them idiots. Most of them don't

know one end of a boat from another; they've been dragged out of offices and suchlike, sent down here to tell us what to do.' Percy grinned. 'Mostly, we ignore them. If we didn't, we'd mostly not get anything done.'

'Fair enough. Nod and smile, collect the necessary paperwork, and that's the ticket. Where are we loading tomorrow?' Dan asked as they approached what was going to be his new berth.

'Grain from Ipswich to London. Everything we need is on board. We're all set to sail. I've got a youngster as well as you – he's cook and bottle washer.'

Lady Beth was bobbing up and down in the waves. Dan had been impressed the first time he'd seen her, but he'd only had an inspection of the outside. Now he went down into the cabin.

'Crikey, it's smart in here. I didn't expect it to be so big and so warm. Where do I sleep?'

'Don't worry, lad, your bunk's cosy too. Captain kips in here. That's when we get chance to sleep. Not often when we're at sea, that's for sure.'

'I'm used to that. But then we were rarely out more than twenty-four hours. It'll be different living on board and I'm looking forward to it.'

'Right, that's enough chin wagging. I know it's bleeding cold but by the end of today, I expect you to know the name of every sail, every sprit, every item on this barge.'

* * *

Emily was intending to spend all day Monday at the farm and was busy sorting and washing the freshly collected eggs, not so many of them now as there had been, but still lots to do. Jimmy poked his head in the shed door.

'Your brothers are outside, Emily; you've got to go home.'

Her stomach flip-flopped. Had something bad happened at home?

He grinned. 'Don't look so worried; your school called. Your mum wants you back to get ready to go in the morning.'

'That's a relief. They must have finally finished building the air-raid shelter for us to hide in if there are any bombs dropped in Colchester.'

Talking about air raids made her feel guilty that none of them were wearing their gas mask around their necks. No one on the farm bothered and the boys only put them on when they were going to school.

They were breaking the law by leaving them at home and if one of the ARP wardens caught them, they'd be in trouble.

George and Sammy were talking to Mr Peterson and seemed for once to be actually listening. She waved to them but they didn't see her. George and Sammy should have both been at school so what were they doing at the farm?

She kept to the path swept in the snow that crossed the farmyard and headed for the boys. Her brother heard her crunching behind him and turned.

'We got sent home, Emily; our teacher's ill and there's no one to look after us as there's two others off already. We got a train home at lunchtime. Mummy sent us up to get you.'

The boys raced off, sliding on the patches of ice they found and yelling and laughing. She followed and was tempted to copy them, but she wasn't any good at that sort of thing and would probably fall over.

They decided to cut down Queen Street which, being a steep hill, gave them the chance to skid most of the way to the track that led to the railway crossing. Just as they got to the crossing, a huge train steamed past, covering them with soot.

'That's going to Clacton, Emily,' Sammy yelled over the racket. 'The engine taking the train to Brightlingsea's smaller.'

'Daddy said I can take you there in the Easter holidays. I'm old enough to look after you now.'

George, on hearing this, turned and beamed. 'I suppose that now you're helping with the children and doing jobs on the farm, looking after us will be easy-peasy.'

Sammy was listening to the conversation. 'I've never seen the sea. Is there any at Brightlingsea?'

George shoved him playfully and Sammy lost his footing and fell backwards in the snow-covered hedge. They were wet and cold but giggling by the time he was pulled out.

'Sorry, Sammy, I didn't mean to knock you over. I was just excited at the thought of going to Brightlingsea again. It was really good and we had fish and chips for lunch and ate them out of the newspaper.'

'Course you did; what else would you eat them out of? It'll be a real treat going to the seaside.'

'It will be a lovely day out. Sammy; you'll want to see the shipyards and the Thames barges,' Emily said.

The boys weren't allowed to cross the railway line on their own and waited whilst she opened the gate and looked in both directions. The line was clear.

'Come on, let's cross. Don't run; the planks are really slippery.'

4

Nancy was forced to return to work in the clothing factory the following morning as the burst pipe had been repaired. As always, her best friend Doreen called round at five minutes to eight so that they arrived at work at exactly eight o'clock.

'Congratulations, Nancy, you've got the best-looking bloke in Wivenhoe as your fiancé.'

'Thank you, we won't be getting married this year but I'm pleased to be engaged. Did you know that he's going to be mate on a barge?'

'I heard that. Better than going out into the North Sea and catching sardines and that,' her friend said as they joined the queue of chattering women waiting to punch their cards. Everybody was wearing work overalls, had their hair tied up in turbans and were hanging up their overcoats whilst moaning about the cold.

'It's bleeding perishing in here,' Doris said as she stomped off up the stairs to her position at one of the benches on the first floor.

'Taters is what it is,' Gladys moaned as she followed her friend.

Nancy and Doreen worked at the first bench in the downstairs space. The cast-iron anthracite stove at the other end was supposed to heat the entire room but only those sitting a couple of yards from it got any benefit.

The disgusting toilet was by the exit door so not only were those working at this bench freezing cold; they also got the stench from the WC.

'Good thing it's so cold; it's blooming awful sitting here in the summer,' Doreen said as she pulled down the metal lever on the wall that sent the power to their bench.

The wooden stools they sat on were uncomfortable and offered no support. By the end of a long day – they finished at six – she'd have a stiff back and a sore backside. Nancy would much rather be working at Harbour House than in this dreadful place.

Today, she'd be making pockets and sleeves for army coats. It was piecework: they got paid for what they did, not by the hour. Often, the girls on her bench would sing to keep up their spirits up but today, it was too cold. Their breath steamed in front of them.

'I wish I was on the press, Nancy, then I'd be warm even if I wasn't making as much money,' Doreen said as the needle of her machine whirred in and out of the fabric.

'It's soul-destroying work, but we get a decent amount in our wage packets on Saturday,' she replied.

The women put a few pennies into a kitty and took it in turns to buy sweets – but since rationing had come in last month, these weren't available so they had to make do with broken biscuits. Mr Moore's shop opposite the High Street end of Alma Street always seemed to have some for the girls to buy.

They didn't get any breaks and had to ask forewoman permission to use the WC. Any eating was also done at their bench. Nancy had worked here since she'd left school three years ago and was considered an expert seamstress and was usually given the complicated things to do.

The finishers stitched everything together and she often did that, but not today. When she'd finished her quota, she had to log it in the book. This was how the forewoman knew what they'd done and how much they should be paid.

Doreen nudged her and grinned. Nancy watched as her friend entered more than she'd actually completed. One of these days, this deception would be discovered and then she'd get the sack.

Once they were safely outside in the freezing-cold darkness, Nancy grabbed her arm. 'I wish you wouldn't do that; I don't want you to be dismissed. Having you next to me is what makes working there just about bearable.'

'I don't care; I'm going to join up. I'm going to Colchester after we finish on Saturday to put my name down.'

'My parents won't allow me to sign up or I'd do it too. How did you persuade your mum?' Doreen's dad was an invalid as he'd been poisoned by mustard gas in the last war.

'One less mouth to feed and I'll still give her most of my wages. Mabel signed up last weekend and was told she'd have to wait several weeks to get her papers. I'm going to make as much money as I can before I leave.'

'Just be careful not to be in the family way; you can't join up if you're expecting.'

'I've just got my monthlies, don't worry. My Johnny's being posted so I won't see him again until he gets leave.'

Doreen lived in The Folly just down by the river so said goodnight and Nancy slithered down the narrow passage to the back of her own home. She'd miss her friend when she went but was relieved she wouldn't have to worry about Doreen getting into trouble.

The kitchen was lovely and warm. Her three brothers were sitting at the table playing dominoes. There was no sign of their mum or dad.

'What's up, boys?'

Dave looked up briefly. 'Dad's in the Black Boy and Mum's round to Auntie Ethel's. Uncle Stan's been taken poorly again.'

'Right, I'll get the tea served and put theirs in the oven to keep warm.'

This information just received grunts from the three of them and she shrugged and smiled; she was used to being ignored by her little brothers. Mum had everything ready; all she had to do was strain the potatoes, cook the cabbage and dish out the rabbit stew.

'Okay, put the dominoes away; I'm going to serve.'

With some friendly grumbling, her brothers tossed the dominoes into the wooden box as they began to eat. Afterwards, the three of them had returned to their game, the washing up was done but still Nancy's parents weren't back. She kept glancing at the clock and as it inched towards seven, she decided to find out what was holding them up.

'Boys, behave yourselves for a bit; I'm going to nip around to Auntie Ethel's and see what's what. I won't be a tick.'

She still had on her thick, woolly socks so just pushed her feet into her rubber boots, hoping her toes didn't freeze. Her heavy work overalls were warm and with her scarf wrapped around her head and neck over the top of her thick coat, she reckoned she'd be fine.

Auntie Ethel lived in a terraced cottage in Anglesea Road,

not far if she cut down Hamilton Road and up Brook Street. The back gate was in Paget Road and that's where she'd go.

As she crunched up to the Brewery Tavern and Yachtsman's Arms, she heard the men laughing and glasses clanking. She wasn't going in any pub to look for her dad; women didn't go in those places on their own and only into the saloon bar if she had a man to escort her.

Her heart was pounding by the time she opened the back gate to her aunt and uncle's house and it wasn't just from hurrying. Auntie Ethel was Mum's older sister and had never been blessed with kiddies of her own. Therefore, she'd lavished her love on the four of them.

She walked past the outside privy, unsurprised that the path from this to the back door hadn't been cleared. Not a glimmer of light showed anywhere – even though there'd been no bombs dropped so far, folk took the rules regarding the blackout seriously. She knocked loudly on the back door and then opened it and slipped inside.

She blinked for a few minutes in the brightness and then called out. 'Mum, Auntie Ethel, it's me, Nancy. I've just come to see if there's anything I can do.'

Why was the house so quiet? Surely she should be able to hear voices? As in all cottages like this one, the stairs were shut off from the middle room by a door. This was closed so that must be why she couldn't hear anyone.

There was a small fire burning in the central grate and the old range in the kitchen kept that warm enough. She pulled open the stair door, her fingers clenched on the handle. Auntie Ethel sounded upset and Mum seemed to be comforting her.

With dragging feet, Nancy walked up to join them. She'd never seen a body and braced herself to see Uncle Stan's mortal remains laid out in the back bedroom. Mum and her aunt were in the front with the door closed. She decided to pay her last respects to the man she loved almost as much as her dad. He was far too young to have passed away, not yet fifty, she didn't think.

She stiffened her spine and stepped into the bedroom.

'Evening, Nancy love. Didn't expect to see you tonight,' Uncle Stan said from his bed.

'I thought you were dead,' she managed to say before her legs gave way and she collapsed on the chair by the dressing table.

'Just a bit poorly: usual tummy trouble. I'll be right as ninepence in the morning.'

Nancy's head was spinning. 'Mum didn't come home so I came round to see what was holding her up. When I heard Auntie Ethel crying, I feared the worst.'

He laughed. 'Tears of happiness, love; we've come into a fair bit of money. A relative she never met has left her their entire estate. Never heard of the bloke and don't know why he never left your mum nothing. I'm not exactly sure, but there's a house, shop and a few hundred pounds in the bank.'

Nancy stared at him. 'I can't believe it. Does that mean you and Auntie will be moving away from Wivenhoe?'

'The shop's in Head Street, Colchester. We don't even know whether it's a tobacconist, haberdashers or an ironmonger. Imagine living just a few miles away and we none of us never knew.'

'How exciting – excuse me, please, Uncle Stan, I'm going next door for a bit.'

He chuckled, sounding and looking better than she'd ever seen him. Nothing like a small fortune to cheer you up.

She tapped on the bedroom door and immediately, it opened. 'Goodness me, Nancy, I'm so sorry; I didn't mean to drag you out to look for me,' Mum said with an apologetic smile.

'I'm so pleased for you, Auntie Ethel, especially as I thought that Uncle Stan had died when I heard you up here. I can't tell you the turn it gave me step in his bedroom and see him hale and hearty.'

It was another twenty minutes before Nancy and her mum eventually left the small cottage. Auntie Ethel had promised to divide the inheritance between the family, not keep it all for herself.

'I don't understand where your dad is, love; he never stays for more than half an hour as a rule.'

'He's probably home now. I can't wait to see his face when you tell him the news,' Nancy said.

They slithered their way back in the treacherous conditions and Nancy was relieved to arrive in Alma Street unscathed. Twice, her mum had had to grab onto her arm in order to remain on her feet.

The boys were still happily playing at the table but now it was a noisy game of snap. The oldest, Jim, looked up.

'Dad's not back. I reckon his tea is dried out by now. Is Uncle Stan all right then?'

'He's fine, son. I'll put the wireless on and give you a bit of entertainment to go with your cards.'

Nancy kept her coat and boots on. 'I'll go down the Black Boy and see what's what, Mum. It's not like him to be gone so long.'

'You do that, love. I'll put the kettle on.' Mum sounded cheerful but Nancy knew she was as worried as she was.

Luckily, her brothers, all being under ten, didn't worry about missing adults. As long as they got their tea on time, they were content.

Her nose was running and she couldn't feel her fingers but it wasn't far to the pub which was at the end of the street she lived in on the hill next to the café.

If it was high tide, there might well be river water right up to the doors. It often flooded down near the Colne, but it never came up as far as Alma Street, thank God. Of course, no lights were allowed to show inside the pub, but she expected to hear the sound of voices, often a fiddle paying and sea shanties being sung, but it was eerily quiet.

She banged on the first door, the one that led to the lower bar, but got no answer. Puzzled, she walked the few paces to the steps that led to the upper bar. She banged again and this time, there was movement.

She heard the door opening and slid in behind the blackout curtain and then pulled it shut behind her.

The place was deserted. Just the landlord's wife, Violet, looking worried. 'There's a fire in Husk's yard. The men have gone down there to put it out. Your pa's with them. He said to tell you not to worry, he'll be back when he can.'

'We'd be able to see the flames if it was a bad one. Can't smell anything either. Our ARP will be tearing his hair out if he sees the faintest glimmer of light. Imagine what he'll be like when there's actually any bombs being dropped,' Nancy said. 'I was just up that way and didn't hear or see a thing.'

'There's not much going on down that yard nowadays. Reckon the Admiralty will take it over soon enough,' Violet said.

'We're going to need as many ships as possible to defeat those blooming Germans. I'll be getting home then; my mum will be worrying.'

Nancy paused and looked down the hill towards the shipyard. Now she knew what she was listening for, she heard men's voices and the clanking of what she thought were probably buckets. They'd be able to form a chain to the river as it was high tide. But there was not even a flicker of red to indicate there was anything serious going on in the more or less abandoned shipyard. Satisfied her dad wasn't in any danger, she scurried back to the warmth and comfort of her home to tell her mum.

* * *

Emily had heard the baby crying during the night but turned over and put her head under the blankets. Poor Daddy would be kept awake and he was the one who'd got to go to work in the morning. Mummy didn't have to get up and would be able to get lots of lovely sleep.

When she went to bed, she took her knickers and vest with her and put them under the pillow so they'd be toasty warm in the morning. She was really good at taking off her nightie and putting on her underwear whilst she was still under the covers.

Nobody spent much time in their bedrooms any more as quite often there was ice on the inside of the window. Baby Grace would have a fire as she had to be kept warm. Emily didn't know a lot about babies but she did know that.

Sammy had told her how a baby was started inside a mummy, but it all seemed very unlikely and silly to her. She did know both parents were involved somehow and that babies didn't come from under a gooseberry bush or delivered by storks.

She was dressed and downstairs in minutes. They now washed in the scullery where they could collect hot water from the range in the kitchen. Mrs Bates called it a lick and a promise and Emily liked that way of explaining a quick wash.

Bath night wasn't too bad as there was always a lovely fire in the little room off the scullery. The large tin bath was filled up with far more than five inches as Daddy had said that as all three of them were going to use it, they weren't breaking any rules.

They took it in turns to go first – she wasn't sure whether having fresh, hot clean water but only being allowed to stay in the bath for a few minutes was better than being the last in the water when it was cooler and dirtier but you could stay in as long as you liked.

'Morning, Emily. I'll have the porridge done in a jiffy,' Mrs Bates said cheerfully.

'Good morning, Mrs Bates. Is there any hot water in the scullery?'

'Course there is, love. Your dad's washed and shaved already. He's tickled pink by the new arrival.'

'We all are. She's not very interesting yet but my mummy says in a few weeks, she'll be smiling and looking at us.'

Emily dashed through to the scullery. It was always much warmer at this end of Harbour House because the range was on all the time. Also, the little laundry room with the huge copper that was filled and heated on a Monday was right next to the scullery.

They only had a fire in the sitting room so that was where they sat in the evening. Her homework was now done in the kitchen and she liked being in there with no distractions from the boys. They did their work in the sitting room so Daddy could supervise them. Since she'd changed class halfway through her first term, she now liked her school. It was such a shame she could only play with the good friends she'd made during school time, though.

Also travelling with her brothers made it all more fun. The boys caught a bus to their school and all she had to do was take them to the right stop. She collected them in the afternoon as well.

She smiled as she washed her face, hastily brushed her teeth and plaited her hair. If she had friends who lived in the village then she wouldn't be spending so much time at the farm. The three children were a delight to take care of and the extra treats that Mrs Peterson gave her every now and again made her feel as if she was truly contributing to the family.

Farming was so interesting that Emily hoped that she'd be able to study agriculture one day if she was able to attend a university. Daddy had told her not many girls went but he'd make sure she got a place if that's what she wanted.

But what she really liked was being escorted home by Jimmy – he'd just had his fourteenth birthday and was officially a man but treated her as an equal. She knew that once it was light enough to walk home without a torch then she'd have to do it on her own. Jimmy was working a full day on the farm and it really wasn't fair on him to give up half an hour to escort her.

5

Nancy returned to work the following morning, eager to share the excitement of the previous night.

'Well, I never! Your family will be too posh for us to speak to now,' Doreen said as she hugged her.

'It won't make any difference to us – it's my Uncle Stan and Auntie Ethel who inherited a small fortune. They don't even know what their shop sells. My dad got home covered in ash but the men put the fire out easily enough. The nightwatchman had gone home to get some supper apparently. He's got the sack and it serves him right.'

Nancy's thoughts kept drifting away from her work and twice, she nearly machined her finger to the fabric. Doreen snorted with laughter.

'What's wrong with you? The forewoman will dock your wages if you get blood on them pockets you're sewing,' Doreen said.

'I know, I'm just wondering how Dan's getting on. Being mate on a Thames barge is a bit different from doing the same on a fishing boat. So many fishing boats have been sunk by the

German U-boats, I suppose I should be grateful he's not doing that now.'

'He's a survivor; he'll not get blown out of the water. I'll be dancing at your wedding next year, don't you worry,' Doreen said as she collected the items she'd finished and took them to the bench where they were needed.

Nancy concentrated on her work, trying not to think about Dan getting blown up. And the more she sewed, the more money she'd make. Doreen had a habit of doing something really dangerous most evenings, not dangerous in that she could be hurt but that she could get fired.

True enough, at ten minutes before clocking off time, Doreen checked that the forewoman was upstairs and then crept over and moved the hands of the big clock forward five minutes. Doreen had done this several times before and so far had been undetected.

The girls knew what had happened but nobody said anything as they all were grateful to finish a few minutes early. Nancy hurried home, arriving half an hour before her mum did, and got the tea started. Dad got home much earlier as there wasn't much they could do at the upstream shipyard after dark because of the blackout.

'Evening, love,' Dad said from his comfy seat by the range. 'Put the kettle on; I'm parched.'

She loved him, he was a good father and provider, but sometimes she had to bite back an angry answer. She'd been working just as hard as him and for longer hours so why didn't he get off his backside and put the kettle on for himself? He'd been home for at least an hour.

'Give me a chance, Dad; let me get my coat off.'

He didn't answer as he was already immersed in the sports page of the newspaper. Not that there was a lot of sport to read about as most of the men had been conscripted. There were still more or less professional football matches being played where there were enough men available. Any football was enough to enthral her dad.

Her brothers were sitting at the table as usual playing Snakes and Ladders. She was saving up to buy them the new board game that everyone was talking about called Monopoly. It would be a joint birthday present as the boys all had birthdays over the summer.

Mum came in and hugged her. 'You're such a good girl; I don't know how I'll manage without you when you get married next year.'

'Maybe you could get the boys to help,' Nancy answered with a smile.

'Now that would be something. That Mr Roby's a one-off helping out the way he does. Even Dr Cousins, who's an absolute gem, doesn't help out with domestic things. I don't suppose you've had time to sit down since you got home. I'll take over.'

Nancy joined the boys. 'You've got to put this away in a few minutes and one of you can lay the table. If you take it in turns, you'd only have to help out every few days.'

'Dad don't do nothing in the house – he says it's women's work. So we ain't doing nothing neither,' the oldest of the three, Jim, said belligerently.

Nancy took a breath to tick him off but her dad got there first. 'None of that lip, boy, or I'll tan your arse. You'll do as you're told and it don't matter who tells you. Got that clear?'

Her brother scowled and muttered an apology but didn't mean it. The younger boys, Harry and Mike, were on their feet and the table was cleared in seconds. Dad had returned to his paper but Mum took over.

Without warning, she reached out and slapped Jim hard

across the back of his legs. He yelped and had the tablecloth and cutlery on the table before Mum could smack him again.

Nancy was puzzled as this was the first time Jim had ever talked back like that. She doubted he'd do it again. If he did then it would be she that slapped him – she was an adult and quite capable of sorting out bad behaviour from a ten-year-old.

The next morning, it was still below freezing but at least the sun was trying to come out. Doreen was her usual jolly self and they joined the other women at the door to clock in. Nancy was just about to push her card down when the forewoman appeared from the office. 'I need to speak to you and Doreen right now. Follow me.'

Doreen grabbed Nancy's elbow. 'She knows about the clock. I can't get the sack; it's my money what's keeping us going.'

'Don't worry, I'll take the blame. My family's doing all right at the moment so if anyone's getting the sack, it can be me.'

Ten minutes later, with just a couple of pounds in her pocket, Nancy was unemployed. She hadn't expected things to escalate so quickly. Mum would know the best place to ask for work. Nancy had a horrible suspicion she'd have to join the girls in the canning factory and she really didn't want to do that. You had to slosh about in ankle-deep water half the time and came home stinking of fish.

Mrs Roby would still be confined to bed, Mr Roby would be at work, and the children would be at school, so nobody would know that she'd called in at Harbour House uninvited, but she needed to speak to her mum. She met the huge ginger cat in the back garden – more a yard really with outbuildings – but with room to hang the laundry in the summer and a big apple tree.

'Good morning, lovely boy, are you pleased to see me? I thought cats slept most of the time. Don't know why you're wandering about the streets.'

The cat purred and walked in and out of her legs with his tail erect. She leaned down and stroked him. Talking to an animal was daft but it'd cheered her up. He followed her through the back gate to the back door which opened into the passageway between the scullery, laundry room and the kitchen.

She didn't knock – she didn't want Mrs Roby to hear and her bedroom was directly above. Nancy opened the door, the cat stalked in and she followed.

'Mum, it's me. Can I come in?' She didn't call out until she'd closed the door behind her.

Her mum appeared in the passageway, her hands floury and with a smudge on her nose.

'Crikey, what are you doing here? What's wrong?'

Nancy remained where she was, not sure she'd be as welcome when her mother knew what had happened. Before she could explain, she was beckoned in.

'Enid's slipped and broken her ankle, silly moo. I don't suppose you can stop a bit and help out? Betty's got the flu so we really need someone else.'

Nancy laughed and flung her arms around her. 'I've just been given the push; I didn't do anything, it was Doreen, but I couldn't let her lose her job. Will I get paid if I stay and help?'

'You certainly will, Mr Roby asked me to find somebody temporary. I'm having to keep an eye on the boys as well as do everything else. You're an absolute godsend.'

'Look, I can't work here dressed in these overalls. I'll run home and change into something more suitable. I won't be long. Whatever you want me to do can wait ten minutes.'

Nancy skidded out of the house and tore around to their

cottage. She tossed her overalls into the laundry basket, delighted that she'd never have to wear them again. Things couldn't have worked out better for her. She was quite happy to be there doing the cleaning in the morning until Betty came back and even doing the laundry and heavy work would be preferable to the sewing factory. She hoped the Robys would ask her to stay all day and help with the baby and the children.

* * *

Everything worked out as if it was meant to be. Nancy couldn't believe her luck. She'd wanted to work at Harbour House and now she had more or less a permanent position.

Her wages were the same as the best she'd ever made slaving away in that horrible sewing factory and now she was working in a lovely house with a lovely family doing something she was good at.

* * *

Emily came home from school at the beginning of the week to discover that Nancy had replaced Enid and she couldn't be happier. Nancy was more like a big sister and she could talk to her about things she didn't want to bother her mummy with. What was even better was that Nancy was here this weekend to help out and would be doing this until Mummy got up again.

'When will my mummy be able to come down and do things with us again? Is baby Grace going to be upstairs all the time or will she come down as well?'

'People like your mum are expected to stay in bed for more than a week after having a baby – ordinary folk are up and about within a day or two. Your mum isn't ill; she's just getting a nice rest. I don't reckon she or your dad get much sleep with a new baby in the room.'

'I think you're right, Nancy; I often hear my daddy walking about and I hear the baby crying sometimes. I'm going to tell you something that I know I shouldn't say. I'm really glad that Enid isn't working here any more and so are my brothers. We didn't like her very much.'

'I know you shouldn't say that, but I'm glad that I'm here instead of her. Enid never had children of her own and I think that makes a difference to a woman,' Nancy replied.

The boys were in the sitting room playing marbles, Daddy spent most of his time upstairs with Mummy and the baby, so if Nancy hadn't been here, Emily would have been on her own when she wasn't at the farm helping out.

'I finished my homework now; is there anything I can do for you?'

'If you wouldn't mind taking up this tray to your mum and dad, that'd be a big help. I'm doing a lovely Sunday dinner and I'm about to put the Yorkshires in.'

'Are we having beef? I don't really like that, especially when it's all red and bloody,' Emily said.

'No, a smashing roast chicken. I think it's nice to have Yorkshires with any roast, don't you?'

Emily didn't really have an opinion on the subject but was thrilled to be asked as it made her feel grown-up. 'I'd like to eat Yorkshires with golden syrup on them. Could we have that for dessert?'

'I reckon if there's any left over, you and the boys could have them for tea. That bowl of cracked eggs you brought back from the farm yesterday meant I've been able to make plenty of batter.'

Emily ran to the sitting room first and told the boys that if they wanted a drink and a biscuit to keep them going until lunchtime, it was in the kitchen. George looked up, and for the first time, she realised just how like Daddy he was.

'Thanks, we'll be along in a minute. There's going to be a marbles competition in the school hall next week and we want to be really good so we win lots of marbles from other people.'

'Goodness, I'm surprised that boys are allowed to play that indoors.'

Sammy grinned. 'Not just boys, Emmy; girls can play them as well.'

How Sammy knew this, as there were no girls at the prep school, was a mystery. Maybe he played marbles with girls when he was out at the weekends.

Emily was a bit shocked by this. She just nodded and smiled and thought she'd ask Nancy what she thought when she got back to the kitchen.

Daddy was waiting at the top of the stairs. He looked thinner but so happy, she didn't mind that she wasn't seeing much of him at the moment.

'Thank you, sweetheart. I don't know what we'd do without you. Have you finished your homework?'

'I have, Daddy, and now I'm helping Nancy with the lunch. We've got roast chicken with Yorkshire puddings. I can't wait, can you?'

'Sounds delicious – I'll give the tray to your mother and then will join you at the table.'

Mummy was up, not dressed but in her dressing gown and stretched out on the daybed; the baby was sleeping in the rocking cradle beside her. 'We've not had Yorkshire puddings since we came to Harbour House last year. What a treat and it really doesn't matter that we're not having beef. Are the boys behaving themselves?'

'They're practising for a marbles tournament, Mummy.'

'How splendid, much better than getting into trouble like some of the local boys are; Mrs Cousins told me about it.'

Emily had a quick peep into the cradle as it was expected of her and then skipped down the stairs, eager to ask Nancy about girls playing marbles. She hitched herself onto the chair out of the way of the range and the smart gas cooker and waited until Nancy was free to talk.

'Can I ask you something? Mummy said it's all right to talk about personal things as long as it's to another woman.'

Nancy looked a bit taken aback but nodded. 'Go ahead, love, I'm listening.'

'I'm worried that if girls were allowed to play in a marbles tournament that when they're bending down in their frocks and skirts, they're going to be showing their knickers to everybody.'

Nancy laughed. 'I expect they'd be told to tuck their skirts into the legs of their knickers. It won't be any different to wearing shorts really and you wore those all last summer, didn't you?'

Relieved that her worries had been unnecessary, Emily took a deep breath. 'Can I ask you something else about knickers?'

'Go on then, what's bothering you?'

'Well, it's more my vest than my knickers. I'm getting really plump in my chest and my vest's too tight and I don't want to bother Mummy about it.'

'Oh, I see.' Nancy looked a bit uncomfortable then she smiled. 'I expect your mum would tell you all this but she's a bit busy at the moment. Do you know that a girl's body changes when she gets older?'

'Taller, you mean?'

'Yes, but you also get bosoms so when you're grown-up and

have a baby, you can feed them with milk like your mum's doing your baby sister.'

'Bosoms? You mean like yours? Sticking out? I'm not sure I want to have any of those.'

'I'm sorry, love, you don't have a choice. I tell you what, I'll speak to my mum and ask her to speak to yours. How about that?'

Emily nodded. 'That's so kind of you. I do need new vests. Will I have to wear one of those things with two cups that I've seen hanging on the rack in the laundry sometimes?'

'A brassiere, that's what it's called. Mostly, we call them bras for short. All women have to wear them. It just shows that you're growing up fast – that you'll soon be a woman yourself. I'm not surprised; I reckon you've grown a couple of inches since last summer.'

There were other girls in her class, Monica particularly, who were beginning to look quite different. Maybe she'd be the best person to ask what else was going to change. Emily didn't want to talk about personal things with her mummy. She didn't know why, Mummy was a much nicer person since they'd moved to Wivenhoe, but with the new baby to look after, there didn't seem to be much time for anything else.

'As it's going to be such a wonderful Sunday lunch, do you think we should have it in the dining room?'

'Too blooming cold in there and Mr Roby won't want us to use up the precious coal. Emily, why don't you get one of the pretty tablecloths and lay this table just as if it was in the dining room?'

Emily beamed. 'Goody, I can make it look special. I'm going into the dining room to get the best china and silver cutlery. We've got eight of everything and we only need five.'

The table looked lovely, like for a celebration meal, and she knew the family would appreciate her effort. The tray for upstairs was also special as she didn't want Mummy to miss out.

'There, I'm done. Do you want me to get the boys to wash their hands?' Emily asked Nancy, who was a bit red-faced and bothered.

'You do that, love. I'll get the soup in the dishes and put them on the table. The bread rolls don't look as good as the ones my mum makes but not too bad.'

* * *

Daddy couldn't believe his eyes when he saw the kitchen. He'd hugged Emily and told her how proud he was of her then dashed off with the tray but didn't linger upstairs as he usually did.

Everything about that lunchtime was marvellous. Nancy had cooked it perfectly and the Yorkshire puddings were crisp and golden just as they should be. Emily offered to help with the washing up but Nancy refused.

'No, you've done more than enough, ta. I didn't expect to sit down with you and eat and that's thanks enough. You go on into the sitting room with your brothers.'

'I will. I'm so glad you're working here.' Emily paused at the door and giggled. 'I won't be playing marbles with the boys, though.'

6

Dan clambered on and off the barge that first day in Brightlingsea, learned how to raise and lower the mainsail, to name every item on the boat and list their uses. They didn't stop for lunch. If he was frozen, so tired and stiff he could barely function, how was Percy still on his feet?

Skippering a fishing boat with an engine and no sail was easier than sailing in a Thames barge with her vast, red sails and only the wind and the tide to help you. At Wivenhoe, he'd helped to dock his boat on the concrete hard next to the railway line perfectly even in the worst of weathers. Having a motor made things so much simpler. He smiled; at least now he wouldn't be unloading his catch into crates and transferring them to the train. Those that took their catch to this hard knew it'd be in London at Billingsgate a couple of hours after landing.

Finally, at dusk, the skipper called it a day. 'Right, lad, we're off to eat and get warm then we can have a look at the paperwork. I reckon you've done well. Won't know if you'll be good enough to take over from me next year until I see how you go when we're afloat.'

'Ta, I've done my best. I can't wait to see her under sail,' Dan replied.

Even with his oilskins over his donkey coat and thick trousers on, the cold had penetrated to his very marrow. Dan's fingers scarcely functioned when he eventually stepped inside and had to bend to unlace his boots. Fishermen and sailors were a tough breed; a bit of cold was second nature to them. He'd waited until Percy had sorted himself out before ducking under the low lintel and going into the cottage himself.

Boots off, coats hung up, he padded into the kitchen in his socks to thaw out. Mrs Jackson handed him a giant enamelled mug brim-full of piping-hot tea.

'You sit by the table, son; get that down you and you'll feel just the ticket.'

Dan was incapable of speech and just nodded as he threaded his numb fingers around the welcome warmth of the mug. Percy had pride of place by the range and was doing the same. He had a padded wooden rocking chair and was slowly moving back and forth. The old man glanced at him and nodded.

There was a thick vegetable soup, followed by an even more delicious rabbit stew for dinner. Dan wolfed it down and still had room for the baked apple and custard that appeared afterwards. The meal had been washed down with two more mugs of tea.

'That was the best meal I've ever had, Mrs Jackson: a real lifesaver,' Dan said as he licked his spoon.

'Go on with you, son, just a regular supper. I never serve fish – I reckon you get more than enough of it on board.'

On a fishing boat, this was true, but he doubted anyone put a line or a net out on the vessel he'd be sailing in. Whilst Mrs

Jackson cleared the table and took everything into the scullery, Percy stood up.

'I'm going to fetch the maps, not that I use them; I know the coast from Yarmouth to Kent like the back of me hand. There's also the damned forms we have to fill in for the navy. You need to know how to do those.' Percy shuffled off to fetch the papers and Dan pushed himself upright.

The outhouse was attached to the scullery – an earth closet which had to be dug out once a week by the night soil men – so he didn't need to find his coat and boots to use it.

He staggered up to bed at ten o'clock. Percy and his wife had gone up an hour ago, but he'd wanted to allow them to settle before he followed. He'd used the time to wash and shave so he didn't have to do it in the morning. He'd not bothered to unpack his bag so all he had to do was grab it and take it down first thing.

* * *

Ten days living on board a barge wasn't as bad as Dan had expected. His bunk was comfortable, the food decent and the youngster, Fred, was nimble and knowledgeable. He was also a good enough cook.

By the time he returned to Brightlingsea, Dan was certain he'd acquitted himself well. As Percy was not just the skipper but also the owner of the *Lady Beth*, he didn't have to give half of the money to anyone. This meant Dan received a good wage for his ten days of hard work.

'You've got three days before our next job, lad; we've to pick up a load of barley from Ipswich and take it to Colchester. I'll drop you off at Wivenhoe on the way back from that one if you like,' Percy said.

'That's good. I'll get off now and catch the train. I saw it steaming towards the station a few minutes ago. Thank Mrs Jackson for me, won't you?'

Dan slung his bag over his shoulder and took off at a run. If he missed this one, there'd not be another for hours. He couldn't wait to see Nancy again. He'd sent her a postcard from Ipswich telling her he'd be back to visit soon but you never knew how long a trip would take. The wind dictated everything on a Thames barge.

He jogged into the station in plenty of time. The engine had to be turned and then shunted to the rear of the carriages. The driver would then jump out and reattach it. This time, there were several passengers waiting to alight. Dan didn't feel sociable so huddled into his muffler and kept his eyes firmly on the train.

He wanted to think about the girl he loved. He wished he'd got a gift for her, and wondered if anything exciting had happened whilst he'd been at sea.

The train rocked and shuddered as it moved slowly over the bridge that spanned Alresford Creek – Dan could hear the movement of the timbers beneath him and couldn't help thinking crossing this expanse of water in a heavy train was more dangerous than most things he did.

They steamed into Wivenhoe station on time and he disembarked. As there was no guard at the gate to snip his ticket, he put it back in his pocket for next time. Before he went in search of his beloved girl, he needed to find himself a room for a couple of nights.

The Grosvenor Hotel on the corner of Station Road was bigger than the Falcon which was beside the church and he was confident he'd get accommodation in one or the other. Back in the day when there'd been pleasure yachts in the river, owned by the rich folk from London, he'd have been lucky to get a bed but those grand folks had all gone now. It was war work and fishing only down on the quay.

He decided to try the Falcon Hotel first and he had to hammer on the door to get a response as it was too early for the place to be open and they probably didn't have any residents, it being the middle of winter. Eventually, Norman, the landlord answered looking disgruntled.

'What the hell are you doing banging on my door at this time of the morning? What do you want?'

Dan knew him well and took no notice of his grumpy greeting. 'I need somewhere to stay for two nights – can you put me up?'

Norman's expression changed. 'I heard you had a punch-up with that miserable old sod – good for you. You're welcome here any time. Come along in; it's bleeding cold as I've not lit any fires as yet.'

'Ta. If you don't mind, I'll just dump my ditty bag and then I'm going to look for my fiancée. I'm hoping she can nip out for a bit as she's on piecework.'

'She ain't at the sewing factory no more; got the push the other week. She landed on her feet all right as she's now full time at Harbour House. Life of Riley compared to working in that sweatshop.'

'Then I'll go there. The Robys are good people – they won't object if I call in for a bit.'

It was mid-week so it wasn't likely Nancy would have any time off but she wouldn't be working evenings so they could spend those together at least.

'Can I bring her for a bit of grub tonight? We could have a game of skittles and shove halfpenny too.'

'My Jenny will rustle something up for you, don't you worry.

There's a darts match tonight – you're playing. We might even win with you on our side.'

'Fair enough. Nancy can cheer me on.'

He sniffed the air like a dog as he stepped out – it was something seamen did to test the wind; it was definitely warmer so a change in the weather was likely. The weather had turned really nasty over a week ago and he'd near frozen to death going to Ipswich and back. It was the twenty-first, nearer the beginning of March than the beginning of February, so it blooming well should be warmer.

Sailing on a Thames barge wouldn't be pleasant until April but if his nose was telling him correctly, at least there wouldn't be a blizzard and gale-force winds on his next trip this Saturday.

Nancy was loving her new job and working with her mum made it even better. The children were well behaved – you wouldn't know that Sammy wasn't an actual Roby – and now that Mrs Roby was taking an interest, the house felt normal. Having the baby downstairs was a treat, although Nancy was worried about the lack of curiosity from the older children, especially Emily. She was a lovely girl, got on well with all her family, but for some reason preferred to spend time at the Peterson farm rather than at Harbour House.

Nancy had just finished clearing the breakfast and was doing last night's washing up when she glanced out of the scullery window and saw Dan come in through the back gate.

He looked different somehow – more confident, even more handsome. She dropped the cutlery she was drying and shouted through to the kitchen where Mum was making her shopping list before she went out.

'Dan's here. Can I invite him in?'

'Mrs Roby told me she'd no objection to him visiting. If he doesn't get in your way, then I've no objection either.'

Nancy hadn't waited to be given permission as the back door was already open. He increased his pace and was almost running when he arrived, he snatched her up and swung her around as if she weighed nothing at all.

'I'm that pleased to see you. Ten days is the longest we've been apart since we started walking out,' he said as he put her down while still keeping his arms firmly around her.

'I've missed you and I loved your postcard. Nobody's ever sent me one of those before. We've both got new jobs now and can save up for when we wed next year. Quick, shut the door; we're letting the cold in.'

He kicked it shut and his hold tightened and she was thoroughly kissed and loved every moment of it.

'That's enough of that, you two; I'll not have any shenanigans in this house if you don't mind,' Mum said from behind them.

Dan didn't let her go but looked up and grinned at her mum. 'Just one kiss – we're engaged, Mrs Bates, so that's allowed, isn't it?'

Mum smiled. 'There's kisses and kisses, Dan, and I don't want to see any more of that sort. Come in, take your boots and coat off and you can help my Nancy finish the washing up whilst I'm round the shops.'

Nancy told Dan to lean against the laundry wall and keep out of her way. 'I'll get on quicker without you next to me. No shenanigans, remember.'

Whilst she hurried through the remainder of her morning chores, he told her about his life on a sailing barge. She listened with interest and was glad that she didn't have to do what he did for a living.

'I love it, Nancy, hard work but more skilled and I reckon it's far less dangerous than with all those mines and U-boats floating about where I was fishing before. I'm surprised none of the boats from Wivenhoe have been blown up or sunk so far.'

'I've been thinking about that and something my dad told me has got me worried. He said that all sailors are now considered part of naval reserve and could be called into the actual navy. Is that true?'

''Fraid so, love, but I don't think it'll happen to me. Percy reckons sailormen, that's what we're known as, like fishermen, are too valuable.' He stepped away from the wall, his expression intent. 'How long will your mum be out?'

She giggled. 'It doesn't matter how long she's out; behave yourself. I've lost one job already and I don't want to lose this one because Mrs Roby walks in on us doing something we shouldn't be doing when I'm at work.'

He sighed dramatically. 'There's always this evening. I've got a room at the Falcon for two nights and Norman's missus is making us some supper. I've got to play in a darts match but there'll be other wives and girlfriends there so you won't be the only one.'

'I like the sound of that. I've not been out of the house since you left. I've got so much to tell you but it'll have to wait. I've to make elevenses in a minute and take it into the sitting room. I suppose you'll want a cup of tea, too.'

'Never said no to a cuppa in my life. Have you heard anything about my mum since I've been gone?'

'Nothing at all, sorry. There's been a bit of bad news for my friend Doreen. Her fellow's been posted to Africa. Mind you, she doesn't seem all that bothered.'

Dan nodded. 'She's got a bit of a reputation, is a bit free and easy if you know what I mean. I reckon she'll soon have another bloke in tow.'

'Well, you're wrong there, Dan Brooks, as she's expecting her call-up papers any day. She's joined the army. I'm going to miss her but if I hadn't got this job, I'd have done the same.'

'I don't want you joining anything, love; you're my future wife and I'd not be happy having you away from here.'

Nancy bristled and put her hands on her hips like her mother did when she was cross with her dad. 'I'll have you know that what I do isn't your concern. We might be engaged but we're not married and the way you're talking makes me think that maybe we never will be.'

His eyes widened and he looked so stricken, she regretted having been so vehement.

'I'm sorry, I just meant that I can make up my own mind. When we marry, I suppose things will be different, but I'm not the sort of girl to be bossed about. If you want someone like that then you've made the wrong choice.'

'I want you; I've always wanted you. I've never even looked at another girl since you were out of pigtails five years ago. I love you, Nancy Bates, and if you have to be the one who wears the trousers in order to agree to marry me then I'm happy.'

Nancy laughed out loud. 'Go on with you, I know you better than that. You're a bloke and will want your own way, want waiting on hand and foot like my dad, but I'm not going to be a doormat. As long as we've got that clear then everything's tickety-boo.'

Fortunately, the kettle whistled on the hob before he could react. From his expression, he'd intended to kiss her and that really wasn't right when she was at work, however much she might want him to.

She took the tea and biscuits on a carefully laid tray into the sitting room and Mrs Roby greeted her with a smile.

'Is that your young man I heard in the kitchen with you, Nancy? How is he enjoying being a barge man? Horribly cold at the moment, I'd have thought.'

'He loves it, Mrs Roby, and I think he's safer on one of them than he would be fishing in a boat with an engine. We're lucky to both have such good jobs.'

'Indeed you are, my dear, and we consider ourselves lucky to have you and your mother working here. How long is your young man remaining in Wivenhoe for this visit?'

'Two nights, and he's staying at the Falcon. Is there anything else you need?'

Mrs Roby shook her head with a smile, then leaned over and adjusted the blanket on the baby before picking up her cup. Maybe both parents were so besotted with the new arrival, they weren't taking much notice of the other three.

Nancy decided that whilst she was looking after the children, she'd make a real effort to take an interest in their lives so they didn't feel left out. She was about to return to the kitchen when she remembered she'd still not asked Mrs Roby about Emily's vests.

'Excuse me, Mrs Roby, but could I speak to you about something that's not really any of my business?'

Her employer raised her eyebrows and nodded. 'Go on, Nancy, you have my full attention.'

'Well, it's like this. Emily told me that her vests are getting too tight. She's developing up there and will be needing support soon.'

Mrs Roby was staring at her as if she was talking gobbledygook. Nancy wished she'd never mentioned it.

'I'm sorry, I'm just the cleaner and nursemaid; it's really not my concern.'

'No, I was just surprised that my daughter spoke to you about this. I've been so involved with Grace that I've not really given enough time to her or the boys. I intend to remedy that. Thank you so much for bringing it to my attention.'

Nancy thought that sort of speech deserved a curtsy as Mrs Roby had sounded more like the lady of the manor than the wife of someone living at Harbour House.

'I'll get on then, Mrs Roby.'

'Of course, and I can assure you that you're far more than a cleaner or nursemaid to us. You're a valued and much-loved employee.'

Nancy walked away smiling, thinking she could have asked for a rise after that but she was already well paid and wasn't going to take advantage.

Dan had poured her a mug of tea – the delicate china was only used by the family – and had found the tin of biscuits in the pantry.

'Is it all right for us to have a few of these or are they just for the family?'

'We can have what we want within reason apart from the coffee. That's just for Mr and Mrs Roby. He had to go to London the other week and came back pleased as punch that he'd managed to find a couple of tins of real coffee.'

'I prefer tea but do enjoy a nice mug of cocoa as long as it's made with milk and has plenty of sugar in it,' Dan said as he pushed the mug across the table to her.

'I can't spend long with you; I've got to do the upstairs now. Mr Roby said that there might be a gentleman from London, another man from the Admiralty, coming to stay soon and the room that Pete used to have needs to be got ready for him.'

Nancy smiled. She loved sitting in the warm kitchen talking to Dan. There might be a war on but right now, she was happy.

7

Emily was frantic. The five-year-old she escorted to and from Colchester Girls' High School every day was missing. Claire always waited for her in the little entrance hall that led to the junior section of Greyfriars House. Emily's lessons finished at roughly the same time so up until now, there'd been absolutely no problems. But today, Felicity, a girl in her class, had fainted and by the time the ambulance had come, they'd been late coming out.

She'd searched the big school, the grounds and even outside on the street where she was quite certain Claire wouldn't have gone. Nobody had seen her and, in her school uniform, the little felt hat on her head and her satchel over one shoulder and her gas mask over the other, she'd have been easy to see.

Emily returned to speak to the teacher whose class Claire was in – it was the youngest group of girls: the five to six-year-olds. There wasn't a single prep school child on the premises as they'd all been collected by nannies, grannies or their mummies. Emily knew they'd already missed the train they were supposed to be on, and she didn't know when the next one was. Hopefully, there might be a Brightlingsea train as that stopped at Wivenhoe too.

'Miss Bennett, I've looked everywhere; do we have to call the police?'

The teacher, an elderly woman with grey hair and pebble spectacles, was trying hard not to cry. 'I'll be dismissed from my position over this, Emily. I've never lost a pupil before.'

'It's not your fault, ma'am; Claire should have stayed where she was told even though I was a few minutes late this evening.' Something else occurred to her. Why weren't the other teachers helping with the search? Was Miss Bennett so worried about her position that she hadn't told anybody Claire was missing?

'Have you asked the other teachers to check their class-rooms?' She knew a pupil in the lower fourth shouldn't be questioning a teacher the way she was, even one as bumbling and inefficient as Miss Bennett.

The old lady sniffed and blew her nose on a little white cotton square with lace all around it. Emily thought it was a useless sort of handkerchief.

As she didn't answer her question and she didn't like to push the point, she tried another tack. 'I'm going to tell the school secretary. She'll know what to do.'

Miss Bennett shook her head, dislodging her glasses so they slipped down her nose. 'You can't do that because today I didn't actually take Claire myself to where she has to wait for you. She went on her own so I don't know if she got there.'

Emily almost stamped her foot. The one place they hadn't looked was in the prep school itself. 'Then she could be in here somewhere. Have you looked in all the cupboards?'

'I looked in this classroom, of course I did, but I haven't looked anywhere else. Why would I?'

Emily forced a smile. 'Shall we look in all the other class-rooms now, Miss Bennett?'

She was still puzzled about the absence of the other teachers but that wasn't her concern – finding the little girl as soon as possible was more important.

She didn't wait to be given permission but ran off to begin looking on her own. Her stomach was churning, she wanted the loo, but that would have to wait until Claire had been found.

After opening and shutting doors in the adjacent classroom, she decided on a new approach. Perhaps Claire had realised she was in big trouble and was now deliberately staying out of sight.

'Claire, sweetheart, you're not in any trouble but you do need to come out as we've missed the train. I'll give your mummy and mine a call on the telephone so they know that everything's all right. I'll tell them about Felicity who fainted in my classroom which made us both miss the train.'

She was standing in the passageway between the other three rooms. She was quite certain if Claire was in one of them then she'd be able to hear her calling out. Daddy always called her sweetheart and that made her feel safe and loved and she hoped it did the same for the missing child.

She tried again, almost certain she'd heard a faint scuffle in the classroom behind her. 'Darling Claire, if you hurry, we might have time to go in the bakers and buy a sticky bun if they've got one and then we can eat it in the ladies' room at St Botolph's station whilst we wait for the next train.'

Then a little hand was pushed into hers. 'Hello, Emily. I was bored and went to look in the other rooms because the teachers had gone to a meeting. Then I was scared I'd be in trouble so I hid under a desk.'

Emily dropped to her knees to hug the little girl, who was in tears and had wet her knickers. 'Never mind, I've found you now. Do you have your spare knickers in your satchel?'

Claire nodded and was clean and dry in seconds. Emily wasn't quite sure what to do with the soiled pants so rolled them up and tossed them into the nearest wastepaper basket. She was sure that Mrs Cousins, being the doctor's wife, would have plenty of spare ones at home.

'Come on, let's tell Miss Bennett I found you. This can be our little secret; we don't have to tell anyone that you got lost in another classroom. All they have to know is that I was late because a girl in my class fainted and that's why we missed the train.'

'I love you, Emily. I wish you were my sister,' Claire said and hand in hand, they hurried back to find Miss Bennett. To Emily's astonishment, the teacher had now vanished.

'I don't know where she is, but we can go to the secretary's office and ask her to make the telephone call. Don't look so worried; everything is going to be tickety-boo.'

The secretary didn't question Emily's explanation and agreed at once to make the telephone call. 'Off you go. If you're lucky, there'll be another train fairly soon.'

* * *

With Claire skipping along beside her chattering non-stop, her usual happy self, her previous worries gone, Emily headed down Queen Street, glad that it was now a little lighter and they could see quite well without torches.

The bakers was about to close but when the kind lady behind the counter heard what had happened, she smiled sympathetically.

'You poor little things. I'll find you something you can nibble on whilst you wait. I bet your mums must have been really worried when you didn't turn up at the right time.'

They left the shop with a bulging brown paper bag stuffed full with a selection of leftover buns and cakes. The lady had told them this was an order that hadn't been collected and as nothing must be wasted nowadays, she was happy to sell it to them. It had taken all the pennies Emily carried in her purse for emergencies but was worth every one of them.

There was no fire in the ladies' waiting room and it was colder inside than out so they went into the ticket office where there was a small fire for a man who worked there.

'Excuse me, sir, would you mind very much if we sat in here? And please could you tell us when the next train to Wivenhoe will be coming as we missed the other one and our mummies are going to be very worried about us,' she said with her sweetest smile.

'Go on with you, ducks; you sit on that bench there. I've just made a nice pot of tea and I'll pour one out for you to share, how does that sound?'

'That sounds absolutely spiffing,' Emily said, loving the fact that she was able to use this strange phrase for the first time. 'The lady at the bakers has just sold us a bag of cakes. There are far too many just for us. Would you like one?'

Half an hour later, pleasantly full of cakes and tea, they were escorted by the guard to the train that had just steamed in. Emily had left the remaining cakes with the kind man in the ticket office as he deserved them.

It was quite dark when they clambered over the bridge that spanned the railway and allowed those on the down platform to exit the station. She still didn't like walking in the dark, even though she knew exactly where she was going.

'There you are, like two little lost orphans in the storm.

Come along, let's get you home,' the doctor said. Claire's father had come to meet them, which made their adventure end on a very happy note.

* * *

Dan would have been willing to help Nancy with the cleaning but Mrs Bates said that wasn't appropriate. This meant he had several hours to fill before Nancy finished work and he could spend more time with her.

He didn't like being idle, certainly wasn't going anywhere near his old home, so decided to return to the Falcon and see if he could occupy himself there. Norman and his wife Jenny were a friendly pair and wouldn't kick him out. He might be lucky and get a bite of lunch to if he mucked in and did a few chores.

In the end, he shifted barrels in the cellar, polished dozens of glasses and pewter pots and even made up his own bed in a room above the bar. He was well fed at midday and left for Harbour House at six o'clock; he wasn't sure when Nancy finished but thought it was around then.

As he pushed open the back gate, she stepped out into the freezing darkness. He knew it was her because she used rosewater and the scent wafted towards him. He shone his torch in her direction and she stepped backwards with a gasp.

'Blimey, I didn't see you there. How did you know I'd be coming out now?'

He stepped in, pulled her close and kissed her before he answered. 'An educated guess, love. There's a nice bit of rabbit pie and some sort of crumble for afters waiting for us at the Falcon.'

'I was going to go home and change into something nicer, have a bit of a tidy; I thought you'd pick me up there.'

'There's no need to go home unless you really want to. The darts match starts at seven and we want to have eaten before then, don't we?'

She snuggled into him. 'Oh, all right then. It's a good thing we live in the country or we wouldn't get so many rabbits for the table. Imagine how hard it must be in the big cities to find anything decent for the family to eat.'

'Percy, my skipper, says round the docks where he goes with his loads, they'd live on fish and chips if they had the coppers to spare.'

As it was only a few yards from Harbour House to the Falcon, they arrived as he finished speaking. He pushed open the bar door, knowing they had to stand in the small gap between the door and the curtain, close the door behind them before opening the curtain.

Nancy crowded into him, not realising the setup, and he was shoved face first into the voluminous blackout curtain. It was a miracle they didn't bring it down. Jenny rescued them.

'You two need locking up; this ain't the place for canoodling,' the landlady said as she untangled the heavy material from both of them. She was laughing as much as they were.

'Sorry, I tripped. Thanks for coming to our rescue,' Dan said as he grabbed Nancy's hand and led her towards the alcove by the fire where he'd laid the table for them himself.

It wasn't a fancy meal but it was tasty and filling and he enjoyed every second he spent with his girl. The bar began to fill up with eager darts players as Jenny cleared the last of the things from their table.

Norman was busy behind the bar serving half pints of mild, bitter, or bottles of pale ale. Dan wasn't a big drinker and usually stuck to half a shandy. His Nancy was the same: usually had a lemonade. Beer wasn't rationed but it did run out.

'I haven't got my own darts, love, so I'd better go and find some before they all go,' he said to her as they stood up, brushing the crumbs from their clothes.

Norman yelled from the bar. 'If your girl will be our scorer then you can borrow me best darts and have your first drink on me.'

Nancy nodded and happily shouted back, unbothered by the heads that turned when she did so. 'I'll be glad to do it, Norman, and mine's a large lemonade and Dan's will be a pint of bitter shandy.'

There weren't many women in the bar, just a sprinkling: probably too cold for the wives to come out. Nancy nodded towards her friend Doreen and another girl Dan thought was called Patsy, who'd just come in with a couple of blokes he didn't recognise.

'I thought Doreen got her papers yesterday. What's she doing here and with those strangers?' Nancy said.

'Why ask me? Go and ask the horse's mouth,' he replied.

Playfully, she punched his arm and her smile was better than any drink he'd ever had.

'I'll tell her you called her a horse; I expect she'll be over to speak to you later.'

He watched her move smoothly through the press of customers, ready to intervene if any of them even looked at her in a way he didn't like. She seemed to know most of them and they greeted her politely and moved aside to let her reach her friends.

Arthur, someone he'd known since he was at school, tapped his shoulder. 'Crikey, Dan, you've put the fear of God in them blokes. None of them would dare upset your girl when you're around.'

Dan hadn't realised how tense he was or that his hands were

clenched. He forced himself to relax. 'We've only just got engaged; I'm a bit overprotective at the moment. I'm not here much now I'm working as mate on a barge down Brightlingsea. I want to be sure no one tries anything when I'm not here.'

'Fair enough. But I reckon your girl can take care of herself. Do you know the two blokes with Doreen and Patsy?'

Dan stared at them and then nodded. 'I thought they looked a bit familiar; I think that they work over the river at the Rowhedge Ironworks. I might be wrong, but I could have seen them when we moored that side the river. There aren't any ferries at night so they must be stopping somewhere.'

There was something about these two that bothered him. Why would they want to come over to Wivenhoe in this weather, have to fork out to stay somewhere, when there were a couple of decent pubs in Rowhedge they could go to easy enough?

He shouldered his way across to join Nancy and the girls, who'd stepped aside from the two blokes, who didn't look too pleased about this. Dan deliberately stood between these men and the girls.

'Not seen you in here before. Do you live across the river?'

The men exchanged a glance. The taller of the two must have thought he was a ringer for Cary Grant from the way he'd got his dark hair slicked back with Brylcreem, and a fancy white shirt and tie and blazer on. The bloke pasted on a smile but his eyes were anything but friendly.

The other one was heavier built, nice enough looking but his eyes were set too close together. He looked as if he could handle himself in a bust-up. Now he was up close, Dan realised they weren't who he'd thought they were and this put him on edge. Tough-looking strangers just didn't come to Wivenhoe and certainly not to the Falcon Hotel. Hardly normal for a Wednesday night at a darts match in a village local.

'I'm Tommy Smith, me mate's Chalky White, we're down from the Smoke on a bit of business. We're staying at the Grosvenor. We met these two ladies on their way here and they kindly invited us to join them,' the taller man said. He leaned in a bit closer and spoke softly, with menace in his voice. 'You got a problem with that, mate? We don't want no trouble.'

Dan straightened. 'You won't get any from me as long as you bugger off right now and leave the girls behind.' He too spoke quietly so in the hubbub, nobody would hear what he said. There were two dozen locals in the pub and only two of them – they weren't stupid even if they were from London.

For a second, the matter hung in the balance. It was obvious neither of these Londoners were used to being given their marching orders. Then, without answering, they turned and left.

Dan received a shove in his back that sent him stumbling forward into a group of dart players from the Black Boy. They weren't too happy about this.

'Sorry, someone pushed me. I'll refill your glasses if you lost any beer.'

He turned to see Doreen glaring at him from a couple of feet away. 'It weren't any of your damn business to interfere. We liked those two and we'd have had free drinks all evening.'

'They wouldn't have been free, Doreen, and you know it. They'd have wanted payment and not the sort you'd want to give. Anyway, why are you still here?' He thought a rapid change of subject might defuse the situation. He was right.

'Suppose so, can't think what the two of them were doing in a place like this. I doubt they were up to much good.' Doreen turned her back on him and went to join Nancy, who was collecting their drinks from Jenny behind the bar.

Patsy had overheard the exchange. 'I told her, but she wouldn't listen. Doreen's that upset that they don't want us in the ATS for another couple of weeks. She's left the sewing factory and won't have any money to give her family until she does go.' The girl sniffed. 'I can still work at the canning factory so it ain't so bad for me.'

'You won't have any money for the first couple of weeks anyway. Soldiers only get paid twice a month and it's not in advance neither.' Then he understood what Doreen had intended. 'Bloody hell – are you saying she was going to charge them for her favours in order to help out her family?'

Patsy nodded, her cheeks scarlet, and he felt sorry for the girl. Their families lived down the Folly, a nasty row of ancient cottages that flooded regularly and were occupied by the poorest of the down-streeters.

The girl had been going to do the wrong thing for the right reason. He had a bit put by at the post office and he'd get it out and give it to Doreen before he went back to work on Friday. Nancy had taken the blame for Doreen's actions and now the girl had left the factory too. He frowned, then smiled. Better Nancy was working at Harbour House than the factory.

8

Nancy enjoyed keeping score for the home team and was able to write on the blackboard almost as soon as the third dart landed on the board. She wished she could have had a go but ladies weren't encouraged to participate – at least not in Wivenhoe; probably in other places not so old-fashioned, they might be allowed to play.

There was scarcely any time to talk to her friends and she and Dan had barely exchanged a word since the match began. At least there'd been time for him to tell her why her friends had been with those strangers. She knew Doreen was free with her favours but hadn't realised she was so desperate she'd sell herself to feed her family. Nancy knew how lucky she was to have a loving family and a good job.

Dan was an expert darts player and it was a foregone conclusion that the Falcon team would win with him on their side – no wonder Norman had been so keen to have him there.

Last orders were called and the pub emptied. Finally, she had a moment to talk to her friends and immediately made her feelings clear about what Doreen and Patsy had been planning to do.

'Don't ever think of doing that again, either of you, I've got a bit put by and won't let your families go hungry.'

'That's ever so kind of you, Nancy, as with what your fella's going to give us, I reckon me mum will be able to manage,' Doreen said with a happy smile.

'What about you, Patsy? Do you give me your word you'll not even think about earning money like that however desperate things are?'

Patsy shrugged. 'I ain't so fussy as you, Nancy; I'll do what I have to do to keep food on the table. Mind you, I'm glad it weren't tonight I had to start. Too bleeding cold out there.'

Nancy hugged Doreen but just touched Patsy's arm – they weren't that close. There were dozens of glasses on the tables, the ashtrays were full, the place reeked of cigarette smoke and she decided to offer to help clear up. Jenny didn't look too well tonight.

She turned to Dan, who was deliberately standing out of earshot to allow her to talk to her friends privately. 'I'm going to help Jenny so why don't you walk Doreen and Patsy down to the Folly? I should be done by the time you're back and then you can walk me home.'

His smile made her pulse skip. 'Norman says we can make ourselves a cuppa and chat for a bit. Will Bert be waiting up for you if you're late?'

'No, he knows I'm with you. Don't be long.'

* * *

Jenny left her to it, pleased that Nancy had volunteered to help, and the place was sparkling in no time. She glanced at the clock, surprised that Dan had been gone for so long.

'I'm locking up everywhere but the front door. Your Dan'll be back in a bit. Don't fret; he's a big lad and can take care of himself,' Norman said as he began his round of checking doors and windows. Not that any window would be open because of the blackout.

Until Norman had said that Dan could take care of himself, it hadn't occurred to her that Dan might be in some sort of trouble. What if those two men had waited for him? He might be big, but he couldn't take on two and his mates wouldn't be there to back him up.

Nancy busied herself by making a pot of tea and helping herself to a couple of generous slices of fruit cake. Jenny had said they could eat anything they found so Nancy didn't feel guilty about taking this. She did wonder where Jenny had found the dried fruit as it couldn't be had for love or money in any of the local shops.

She was just beginning to panic when the front door opened and closed and Dan stepped from behind the curtain. He was a bit dishevelled, his woolly hat was missing, but apart from that seemed unharmed.

'What happened? Did those Londoners attack you?'

He grinned sheepishly. 'Nothing so exciting, love; I met my stepfather staggering home from the Rose and Crown and we had a few words. Luckily for him, I was in a good mood.'

'Where's your hat?' Nancy wasn't sure why she'd asked this when she should have been showing more sympathy.

He touched his head. 'God knows, somewhere out there. It fell off when we had a bit of argy-bargy. We both ended up on our arses because of the ice. I helped him up and we parted on better terms. Silly old sod.'

He draped his donkey jacket over the back of the chair by the fire. 'A cuppa and a piece of cake – just what the doctor ordered.'

They sat and chatted for an hour or more and it was he that called a halt to the evening. 'I'd better get you home, love; it's nearly midnight. You have to be at work at seven and I can have lie-in.'

'Crikey, I didn't realise it was so late. I'll just get my things on. You don't need to walk me home – you'd have to leave the front door open if you did. I'll cut through the churchyard and be back in minutes.'

He scowled and was about to argue.

'No, what would you do if someone broke in whilst you were out? I'll be tickety-boo, don't look so fierce. I tell you what, come across the churchyard with me and I'll just run home the last few yards from there. You'll still be able to hear if anybody goes near the Falcon.'

'All right, we'll do that. I'm not happy about not seeing you right to your back door and I doubt that Bert will be impressed.'

'Dad won't know; he'll be fast asleep. Come on, get your coat on; I'm ready to leave.'

They ran hand in hand through the creepy churchyard and he pulled her close and kissed her passionately before he let her go.

'I'll be round after the kiddies have gone to school. Then it's high tide and I want to catch up with me mates down the hard. They'll have unloaded their catch by then and I'll buy them a beer at the Station.'

'Goodnight, Dan. See you in the morning.'

Neither of them had said they loved each other and he was usually the soppy one. Too late to worry about that, she needed to get home. Nancy shone the meagre beam of her torch in front of her, but she reckoned she could have got home with her eyes shut as Alma Street was so familiar to her. She crept in and locked the back door after her. She topped up the range and then snuggled into her dad's old wooden rocking chair and covered herself with the two blankets Mum had left out for her.

It wouldn't be fair for Nancy to go upstairs when she was home so late as she'd then wake up her three brothers with whom she shared the back bedroom. She'd slept in this chair a few times, and usually, she fell asleep without much trouble. Tonight was different. She was restless as thinking about what her friend Doreen had been prepared to do for her family was quite shocking. She thought that probably most girls ended up on the streets because they had to – none of them would be doing it from choice.

As she was finally drifting off, it occurred to her that there were the empty rooms in the attic at Harbour House – would they let her live in one of them if she asked? She'd gone up there only recently with the children when they were playing hide and seek. It hadn't occurred to her that it might be possible for her to live in the attics – they were all crammed with old things – but tonight had convinced her she needed her own room, even if it was somewhere that had previously been used for a live-in servant.

The following morning she spoke to Mr Roby and he was delighted with her suggestion that she move into the attics.

* * *

Dan decided that as his brothers would be at school, or playing truant somewhere, and his stepfather would be at work, he would likely find his mother at home. She took in laundry, didn't make much from it, but without that and the money he'd been giving her, they'd often have gone hungry.

He'd spent an enjoyable hour at Harbour House with Nancy, wandered down to the hard and caught up with the blokes he used to fish with and bought them a beer and now had a few hours to kill before he picked Nancy up. This time, he was going to collect her from her home in Alma Street. There was an away match at the Black Boy and he was playing darts for the Falcon again.

It seemed odd walking down the covered passageway that divided his old house from that of his neighbour's and it didn't seem possible he'd only left a couple of weeks ago.

That morning, both he and Nancy had withdrawn thirty bob each from the post office on the corner of Queen's Road and he'd taken out a further two pounds to give to his mother. Nancy had promised to divide the money between her friends as soon as she saw them.

Dan had seen Patsy sloshing about in the cannery gutting fish and getting them ready to be put in the cans. He wasn't sure why Doreen couldn't go back to the sewing factory – but that was none of his business.

The copper, where his mum boiled up the clothes, wrung them out and hung them to dry, was in a lean-to next to the bog. He could hear her banging about in there. For some reason, he didn't want to speak to her, he wasn't sure why, so quietly opened the back door and tucked the money into her battered handbag. It occurred to him that if she didn't return to the kitchen before his stepfather came home then he'd likely have the money instead of her.

He was making his way back to the Falcon when he bumped into Mr Roby, who was home early for some reason. 'Good evening, sir, there was something I wanted to ask you if you've got a moment.'

'Fire away, Dan, and you don't need to call me sir. What's bothering you?'

'Last night, a couple of chancers from London turned up at the Falcon. They said they were here to do a bit of business. I was wondering if you knew what they might have been doing. I can't imagine it's anything legal.'

'I'm sure it isn't. Smuggling, I expect. Not that much will be coming in from France nowadays but there might still be the odd barrel of brandy getting through the U-boats in the channel. Some of your ex-colleagues, I'm pretty sure, are involved.' Mr Roby didn't seem particularly bothered about this.

'Ta, I should have thought of that myself. It'll stop if Hitler has his way and conquers the whole of Europe.'

'Absolutely. Always a silver lining.'

Dan thought Mr Roby was serious for a moment but then he chuckled. 'I don't know if Nancy told you but she's going to live in, makes sense for all of us, and if you happen to be at a loose end, could you lend a hand sorting out an attic for her so she can move in?'

Dan grinned. 'She never mentioned it, but she said she'd got some exciting news to tell me this evening. I'd be happy to help as I've got nothing to do until after tea.'

Mr Roby slapped him on the back. 'Good man. If you're going to help then I can go back to work. Elizabeth rang the office and asked me to return to help lift a few heavy items. God knows why she didn't think of you. Cheerio, no doubt we'll see each other again fairly soon if your young lady's going to be residing with us.'

* * *

Nancy opened the door for him and her squeal of delight when he told her why he was there echoed around the kitchen.

'I don't know why we didn't think of you this morning as you're lazing about doing nothing.' She pulled his head down and kissed him, making it clear her words weren't meant to be taken seriously.

Her mum didn't object this time. 'You have to take your boots off, son; you can't clump about in them upstairs. Have you arranged to have your tea with Norman and Jenny?'

He shook his head.

'Then I'll lay a place for you here just this once. I'd have thought Jenny would be happy for the extra pennies making you tea would give her.'

'Ta for the offer; I'd be happy to stop. Jenny's not too well. It's a good thing there's a darts match at the Black Boy as the bar at the Falcon will be closed tonight.'

Mrs Bates looked concerned. 'There's a lot of it about; I've heard of three families who've gone down with it. The weather's to blame, everyone being cooped up inside for the past two weeks. Now it's getting a bit more seasonable, I reckon there'll be less of it about.'

She didn't call whatever this illness was by name as, like everybody else apart from the doctor, she didn't know it. Every winter, hundreds of people got sick and sadly a lot of them died and no one ever knew what it was that had killed them.

'Should I poke my head round the door and say good afternoon to Mrs Roby?'

Nancy shook her head. 'The baby's sleeping; I'm sure she'll be doing the same. Mr Roby's been in the spare room the past few nights because of Grace crying. If this other bloke from the

Admiralty turns up in a couple of weeks then that'll have to stop.'

Fortunately, he was wearing thick socks with no holes so padding through the house without his heavy boots wasn't a problem. The stairs to the attic were on the left-hand side of the passageway outside the bedrooms and had been propped open with half a dozen old books. Dan had to walk around a substantial pile of useless wooden furniture.

'There's no electricity up here, I'll have to use an oil lamp and candles, but I don't mind. It'll be heaven to have my own space for the first time in my life.'

He stepped close behind her, put his arms round her waist and pulled her gently backwards against his chest. 'Once we wed, you'll be sharing with me unless I'm at sea so make the most of it,' he said softly and for a few seconds, she relaxed against him.

'That's enough of that, Mr Brooks; no shenanigans in this house. You know that's the rule.'

It wasn't as cold as he'd expected at the top of this old house and this was because the two massive chimney breasts went up through the attics and took the worst of the chill off. There were three rooms running into each other and Nancy had selected the nearest to the stairs. That made sense – why have to walk through an empty room if you didn't need to? Also, the other two were rammed full of trunks, chests, usable furniture and stuff that was beyond repair.

'You've already scrubbed the floor and cleaned the windows. Why don't we stick a bit of whitewash on the walls before you start bringing in any furniture and that?'

She frowned and looked around at the flaking lime and wattle which the walls were made of. 'If we do that then I'll not be able to move in today.'

'Crikey, you could be living up here for eighteen months; surely it makes sense to make it as nice as you can before you move in. It won't delay you more than a day.'

She looked at him as if he was an imbecile. 'I'm not asking Mr Roby to heave things about for me – that's what a fiancé's for. You won't be here tomorrow and you're here today. Goodness knows when you'll be back again. It could be two weeks or even more.'

'Fair point. I don't see why you couldn't do it once the furniture's in place. Is there anything for the floor?'

'I've not had time to look in the other two attics; I've just concentrated on clearing the junk from here. Mr Roby told me to dump the broken furniture in the hall outside their bedrooms for now and then take it down to be chopped up for firewood.'

Nancy had to abandon him when the boys came home as she was in charge of their tea and overseeing homework if they had any. Dan found a couple of old rugs, a chest of drawers with only one drawer missing, and hammered in half a dozen nails for her to hang things on. All she needed was a bed and she'd be all set.

* * *

Emily couldn't wait for the bell to ring so she could dash off to the station and start the half-term break. Claire wasn't at school today so she didn't have to escort her home. With any luck, she'd get out really quickly and if she ran, she'd be able to catch the earlier train. Her brothers had a half-day so they'd already be at home.

Helen, who was sitting next to her, nudged her just in time as Miss Overy – a name that always made Emily smile – their science mistress was approaching her desk. She'd have got a rap over the knuckles with a metal ruler if she hadn't been paying attention.

'Excellent work, Emily Roby, as always. I just wish everyone else was as industrious and dedicated to their lessons as you are,' the elderly teacher said as she walked past.

Ten minutes later, their books were packed in their satchels and they were lining up. It seemed that even Miss Overy was eager to leave tonight as she didn't usually let them wait at the door for the bell.

Emily flew out, broke all the rules by running along the corridor and reached her form's row of pegs and shoeboxes before the rest of her class. She had her outdoor shoes and clothes on before the other classes were even out of their doors. Not waiting to say goodbye to her friends, she hurtled out onto the pavement and ran across the road, almost being knocked over by a gentleman on a bicycle.

She hadn't been looking forward to this half term because three noisy land girls had started at the farm and she wasn't really needed to look after the children any more. Mrs Patterson had said she was welcome to come any time but as Jimmy was now more interested in the land girls than her, Emily thought she might as well stay at home and get to know her new sister. Not that a tiny baby did anything interesting and she couldn't really see the fascination herself.

Emily was desperate to get home because Nancy had told her this morning that she would be moving into the attics and living with them in future. Nancy was her favourite person and having her available all the time almost made up for not going to the farm and being able to bring back treats for everybody.

Today, she was lucky as the train was still at the platform and the friendly guard, who knew her well by now, held open the door so she could scramble in. Emily glanced down the train but couldn't see any other High School girls. She grinned and found a seat, knowing that there wouldn't be many people getting on at Hythe station because the whistle didn't go at the factories until much later. She settled in for the journey back home.

9

Nancy had enjoyed having Dan help set up what was now to be her very own room. He was so kind and helpful and this visit had been different. He was different and she rather thought she had actually fallen in love with him.

He'd even gone round to her house and fetched her bed from the room she'd been sharing with her three brothers. It had taken him three trips but he'd done it with a smile and no complaints. Mum and Dad had been happy for him to take it. The boys had more room and her moving out meant one less mouth to feed, which was always a good thing.

She heard the front door bang and smiled. 'Right, boys, Emily's home much earlier than usual so I'll take all three of you up to see my room. It wouldn't have been fair if you'd gone first without her.'

They'd been sitting at the kitchen table drinking tea and munching freshly baked ginger nuts but had been asking every five minutes when they could go to inspect the attic.

George dropped his biscuit on his plate and was at the door before Sammy even reacted. 'Okay, let's do it. We're both really happy you're going to be living here with us, Nancy; you're like one of the family already.'

Sammy was now beside him, hopping from one foot to the other. 'Please, please, can we go now? We want to see how you've made a nasty old attic into a nice bedroom.'

Emily had already taken off her outdoor shoes and was wriggling her feet into her slippers as she rushed past to hang her coat and gas mask up with the others.

'I ran all the way from school and then all the way from the station because I'm so excited to have you here.' She stopped and her cheeks flushed. She looked at Dan. 'I'm very sorry for being so impolite, Mr Brooks; I should have said good afternoon to you first.'

Dan laughed and gave her a casual hug. 'Don't be daft, love, and you can call me Dan.'

'I don't think my mummy would like me to be so informal. Perhaps I should call you Uncle Dan.'

George pushed his sister in the back, not something he did very often any more as she was now so much taller than him. 'We don't call Nancy Auntie Nancy, do we? Sammy and I are going to call him Dan as that's what he's asked us to do.'

Emily didn't retaliate. She smiled in a superior way at her brother and patted him on the head. 'Then I'm sure our parents will be perfectly happy for us to be so impolite to someone who isn't a member of the family and doesn't work here.'

Nancy hastily stepped in before things became heated. George had obviously not enjoyed being patronised and she didn't blame him. 'Come on, no arguing or nobody will go upstairs at all.'

Emily tossed her head, nodded at Dan and Nancy laughed when he winked at her. The girl was a bit disconcerted and stared at him.

'I've never winked at anybody; isn't it a bit rude to do that, Mr Dan?'

Mr Roby emerged from the sitting room, obviously having overheard this exchange. 'For heaven's sake, children, what a silly thing to be arguing about. Emily, don't be ridiculous and George, behave yourself.'

The children exchanged a glance and immediately, the atmosphere changed. When their father told them to do something – or in this case, not to do something – they listened.

Nancy led the way up the narrow staircase and with due ceremony flung open the door to her new domain. Even though she said so herself, she thought the transformation was astonishing.

She stepped aside, allowing the children to crowd through the narrow door and see for themselves. Dan put his arm round her waist and she leaned against him. Yesterday, this had been a dump for broken furniture and other odds and ends and between them, they'd transformed it into a bedroom.

She glanced up at him. 'This is how it will be when we set up our own home, Dan, and I can't wait to do that.'

His eyes flashed and his smile was blinding. 'I'll show you the cottage when the weather's better and I've had a chance to do a bit to it.'

The three children were wandering about touching everything and exclaiming.

'It's so pretty, Nancy, I can't believe you managed to get this done in a day. Where did all the furniture come from?' Emily asked as she walked about, admiring the highly polished surfaces of the chest of drawers and bookcase.

'Everything apart from the bed was up here already. That's the one I was sleeping in at home. Dan did all the heavy lifting and I just added the finishing touches.'

George lifted the blue candlewick bedspread and peered underneath. 'Look, Sammy, she's got a china pot like the one we've got but she hasn't got the little cupboard for it.'

Dan snorted and Emily wisely changed the subject.

'Where did you find these pretty pictures, Nancy? I'd like something similar for my room.'

Dan answered this question as he'd been the one who'd found an old trunk full of watercolours of country scenes, flowers and cottage gardens.

'There must be at least another dozen – why don't you come and choose some and then you can ask your dad if it's all right for me to knock in a few nails so we can hang a couple of them up.'

Emily followed him through the door on the left-hand side of the room, but the boys remained with Nancy. 'We don't want any girly pictures in our room, do we, Sammy?'

Sammy nodded. He always agreed with George. 'I'd like a picture of a Spitfire or a Hurricane – do you think there might be any of those?'

Nancy thought for a moment. 'I've seen a couple of photographs in my dad's newspaper of fighter planes. I reckon if I ironed them and then you stuck them on a piece of cardboard, they'd look a treat on your wall.'

Her suggestion was greeted with squeals of delight and a demand that she go at once to fetch the newspapers.

'I know that Mrs Bates uses newspapers to light the fires; do you think she might have used your father's newspaper already?' George asked anxiously.

'Why don't you go and ask but do it very politely. She might even let you go back with her and collect the pages you need. Now I'm here, she's finishing earlier – in fact, in the next twenty minutes.'

This was enough for the boys to scoot downstairs and she spent the few minutes while she was waiting for Dan and Emily to return from the room next door to straighten the things that had been moved. She liked things where she put them. She hadn't asked Dan how he felt about this sort of thing but was pretty sure he was easy-going when it came to things in the house and would leave it to her.

Emily came out clutching three of the framed watercolours, her eyes wide and obviously really pleased with them. 'I'm going to ask my daddy immediately if Dan can put these up before he goes.'

'He won't be leaving until I do, Emily, as he's staying for tea tonight.'

'Goody, he deserves a nice meal after helping you like this.' She frowned. 'There won't be room round the kitchen table for all of us, though.'

Dan was just pulling the door closed behind him. 'Good heavens, love, Nancy and I won't be sitting down with you. We'll eat when you've finished.'

Emily looked a bit unsure. 'We could have used the dining room but that would be a waste of coal. Mrs Bates and Nancy always eat with us; I don't like the idea of you having to wait. Why don't my mummy and daddy eat in the sitting room on a tray? I'll take it through to them.'

'No, love, I wouldn't be comfortable knowing me being here had caused an upset in the family,' Dan said immediately.

'Never mind then, I suppose it doesn't matter just this once,' Emily said and with her precious paintings under her arm followed her brothers downstairs.

'Dan, you shouldn't have said that. You should have left it to me; I work here and live here now and you're a visitor.'

His lips tightened and she waited for him to snap at her but his face relaxed and he smiled and was her old Dan again. 'Jumped in with both big feet: something I do a lot. Sorry, love, for speaking out of turn.'

* * *

Dan thought it wrong that Nancy and her mum acted as if they were family members when they were actually servants. Calling Mrs Bates a housekeeper didn't change that. Now Nancy was living in, she was just a maid, at the Robys' beck and call whenever they fancied. Maybe working at a sewing factory might have been better after all, even if she did get more in her wage packet at the end of the week.

He kept out of the way whilst the family were served and helped clear the table afterwards. 'Nancy, love, do you get a weekly wage or paid yearly like the maids at Wivenhoe House do?'

She didn't take kindly to his question. 'It's none of your business, Dan Brooks. Do I ask you how you get paid or how much? When we're married, you can ask me that.'

'When we're married, you won't be working; you'll be at home. I don't hold with married women working.'

'Oh, don't you? So my mum shouldn't be here? There's a war on, in case you've forgotten, and we all have to pitch in.'

He'd touched a nerve and she wouldn't let it go.

'I'll be working until I have children so you'd better adjust your notions before we're wed or there'll be no wedding at all.'

He should have nodded, smiled, apologised, but he wanted to make his position clear.

'When the war's over, things will go back to normal: men will provide and women will run the house and bring up the kiddies. I'll have to lump how things are now, but no wife of mine will work if she doesn't have to.'

Instead of yelling at him, she nodded, her expression cold. 'Good. I'm glad we've got that clear. Off you go, Dan, or you'll be late for your darts match.'

She turned her back on him and he regretted every stupid word he'd said. Nancy wasn't like other girls, she was independent, and if he wanted to keep her, he'd have to be the one to change.

Sadly, he collected his things and was obliged to leave without any further words being said by either of them. He lingered outside the back door, trying to think of an excuse to return and put things right. He could hear her talking to the boys about sticking the newspaper pictures onto some cardboard from a cereal box.

Nancy didn't sound upset and that bothered him even more than the argument. He was unhappy that they'd parted on such bad terms and especially because he knew it was his fault. He'd been looking forward to taking her to the darts match and then to having a cosy half an hour in the kitchen with her drinking tea before he had to go to the Falcon to sleep.

In the beginning, when she'd first agreed to walk out with him, he'd suggested that they take things further but she'd firmly rebuffed him, saying she wasn't that kind of girl and he loved her too much to mention it again. Her friend Doreen wasn't so fussy and he'd thought Nancy was like her until she'd put him straight.

He could hear a crowd of blokes heading for the Black Boy and from the light of his torch, he could just about make out their shapes. There was nothing he could do tonight, and he had to catch the eight thirty train to Brightlingsea in the morning. Nancy was bound to be up before then as it was her responsibility to get the children off to school.

He muttered a curse under his breath. One of the boys had said it was half term and nobody went to school tomorrow; they were off until next Tuesday. He'd write her a note of apology and push it through the door if he couldn't speak to her in person.

The pub was heaving, the bar too busy to wait just for a shandy, and he forced his way through the press of men – none of whom were on his team – until he found Norman and the others at the far side of the long room.

'There you are, thought you'd forgotten. I brung your darts for you,' Norman said as he held them out.

'Ta, I guessed you'd bring them. There's a lot in here tonight. Didn't know that darts matches were so popular.'

'If we win this match then we'll be playing the Station Hotel team next time. It's cutthroat stuff, son. The winning team at the end of the season gets a pin of ale.'

Dan hadn't known there was a season for darts but then he didn't spend a lot of time drinking and tended to drift from one establishment to another so couldn't really call himself a regular anywhere. Normally, it was just the regulars who played in a darts team. He guessed being a resident made him acceptable.

The landlord rang the last order bell and a sort of hush fell. 'Right, you miserable lot, let's get this match underway.'

* * *

Despite his row with Nancy, Dan played well and although it was a nail-biting finish, the Falcon team came out on top. Norman slapped him on the back.

'We need you back next weekend – do you reckon you can

come? We'll not win without you. Free board and lodging, son, if you make it.'

This was generous and there must be more to this than just winning a small barrel of ale.

'I don't know where I'm going to be going. If it's a short run, like to Ipswich and back like we just did, then I'll be here. But if it's to Yarmouth or Kent, then I won't.'

'Fair enough, them Thames barges have to wait for the wind and the tide. Must be hard for you after being a mate on a fishing boat with an engine.'

Now this was a question Dan could answer. 'I love being on a barge, just using sails and relying entirely on the skill of the skipper. I've learned a lot. I'll not be taking over the *Lady Beth* for a year or two; Percy's not going to take a chance, especially not with so many U-boats and mines in the way.'

'I'm surprised Wivenhoe hasn't lost any fishing boats – I've heard that there's already been several blown out of the water, but not round here, thank God.' Norman dipped into his pocket and handed over a large key. 'Here, you get off, son. Leave the door on the latch; I don't reckon anyone will break in tonight.'

'You need a guard dog, Norman; they've got one at the Station and the Greyhound.'

'My Jenny don't hold with pets.'

Dan said his goodbyes and with the key to the front door of the Falcon in his pocket, he left the smoky fug of the pub with considerable relief. He was tempted to walk back via Harbour House but everybody would be in bed by now. Instead, he went the other way and took the cut between two houses that led into the churchyard at the rear of the church itself.

If his mind hadn't been on Nancy, he might have heard the men approaching before they attacked him. He was sent sprawling onto his face and instinctively curled into a ball to protect his vitals, intending to roll over, then surge to his feet and fight back. He yelled out his defiance. 'I know who you bastards are; you'll not get away with this.'

The overpowering smell of cologne and expensive tobacco had given it away. It was the two men from London. As his world went black, his last thought was that he should have realised they'd want their revenge and he shouldn't have identified them.

Emily was disappointed that Dan didn't stay long enough to put up her pictures. Daddy had said Dan could do that so why had he left so suddenly? Also, Nancy was supposed to be going out with him that evening but she'd remained in the house. When she asked Nancy why she hadn't gone, she'd been told it was none of her business and this upset Emily. She didn't like to be at odds with anyone and especially someone she considered almost a big sister. Grown-ups were hard to understand and she wasn't looking forward to becoming one.

She'd been in bed reading an adventure story by Enid Blyton that was too good to put down – Daddy had poked his head in the door and told her to turn the light out but she'd ignored him. She hadn't heard Nancy go past to spend her first night at Harbour House. She wanted to stay awake so she could hop out of bed and apologise to Nancy before she went up to the attic. She'd read somewhere that you should never let the sun set on an argument. It hadn't been her that had had an argument, but she had asked an impertinent question and that was wrong of her.

After a while, she decided to go down and make herself a second mug of cocoa. Horribly extravagant but it would give her an excuse to be downstairs and find Nancy and put things right.

She daren't keep a light on much longer as Daddy would be able to see it under her door and would be very cross with her for disobeying.

Another thing that was different tonight was the fact that Ginger, who now considered her bed his personal possession, hadn't come up to join her. If Nancy wasn't pleased to see her then she'd say she'd come down to look for the cat.

The grandfather clock ticking noisily in the hall said it was after ten o'clock – she couldn't remember ever being up so late in her whole life. The kitchen door was closed – that was probably why the cat was missing – it must mean that Nancy was in there too.

She pushed open the door and Nancy, who was sitting at the table looking really fed up, looked up in surprise.

'You shouldn't be down here, Emily; are you feeling poorly?'

'No, I'm looking for Ginger. I can't go to sleep until he's snuggled on my feet. Have you seen him?'

'No, I thought he was already upstairs with you. If you stay here in the warm, I'll grab my coat and put my boots on and see if I can find him.'

'Don't forget your torch, Nancy,' Emily called out.

'Don't worry, I've got one in my coat pocket. Why don't you put on a saucepan of milk and we'll have another mug of cocoa before we go up?'

Emily smiled; things were fine between them and she'd been worrying unnecessarily. There was no point in answering as the back door had already closed.

Minutes ticked by and the milk was already hot. If it boiled, it would be nasty and have skin on it; the mugs were ready with the cocoa powder and sugar stirred into a paste, and there was still no sign of Nancy. She'd been gone for ages and she should only have been outside for a moment.

There was a sick feeling inside her. Nancy being missing brought back memories of the afternoon when Sammy's older brother, Pete, had tried to strangle her. She didn't know what to do. Then Daddy came in. He took one look at her, held out his arms and she fled into them.

'Nancy went out to look for Ginger ages ago and she's not come back. I'm so scared someone has hurt her.'

10

Nancy couldn't see the cat so called his name quietly, hoping if he was in the vicinity he'd come in. She walked out into The Cut – this bit of Alma Street – not calling loudly in case she woke up the doctor and his family who were only a few steps from her in their house, Little Wick.

It was cold, not nearly as bad as it had been, just a bit of a nip in the air. She was about to abandon her search when she heard someone call out and recognised the voice. Dan was in trouble.

Without thinking, she was running towards the churchyard where she thought the shout had come from. She hit her knee hard on something as she hurtled through the gate but didn't stop. She could hear the unmistakable sound of someone being hurt. She ripped the tape off the glass on the front of her torch and shone it full beam towards the noise.

'I can see you. I know who you are. Leave him alone,' she screamed, her voice echoing round the empty churchyard and the light on their faces and her racket was enough to stop the pummelling. The two of them vanished into East Street and she dropped to her knees beside Dan. He was unconscious, blood dripping down his face. It looked as though they'd stamped on his hands. How could he sail a barge if his hands were broken?

'Dan, dearest, I'm going to find someone to help.' She stripped off her coat and was just draping it over him when the sound of pounding feet approached from East Street and from the main gate of the churchyard. Her screams had been heard.

Mr Roby was beside her. 'Run back and wake the doctor; ask him to ring for an ambulance and then to come here at once,' he said as he gently pulled her to her feet.

Having something to do stopped her from breaking down and sobbing. Dan needed her to be strong. He was surrounded by men who'd probably come from the pub after hearing her screams. They'd take care of him.

The ARP warden would have a field day with so many torches, including hers, being flashed about the place. Nancy hammered on the front door of Little Wick and Dr Cousins called from behind the door.

'I'm on my way. I've called for an ambulance. Stay where you are and I'll give you a couple of blankets and a cushion to make the man who's been attacked more comfortable. I've also called the police. They'll be coming from Colchester too.'

She stood to one side. She leaned against one of the stone columns outside the door. Her heart was hammering in her throat; her knees were wobbly. She only had to wait a couple of minutes, although it seemed like a lifetime, before the door opened and a shadowy figure emerged. The doctor shone his torch in her face.

'Here, young lady, take these. I'm right behind you.'

'I'm Nancy Bates, Dr Cousins, it's my Dan that's been beaten up by those two villains from London. I saw them clearly.'

'Good show, that will make it even easier to catch them. I've seen them skulking about the village for the past two days, up to no good. They're staying at the Grosvenor Hotel. I told the constabulary who they were and where they were living.'

Nancy had to run to keep up with his long strides and carrying an armful of blankets made this difficult. 'How did you know it was them?'

'I got up to use the WC and heard you scream and then saw you shine your torch on them from the window. Dan was obviously seriously hurt.'

'Out of the way, Dr Cousins here,' he said and the crowd surrounding Dan moved aside. Mr Roby was sitting with Dan's head in his lap. Her lovely man was scarcely recognisable as his face had been so badly damaged.

A cushion was put under Dan's head so Mr Roby could stand up, the blankets were wrapped around him, and her coat was handed back to her.

'You stay here, Nancy; you'll want to go in the ambulance with him. I've got to get back as I left Emily in the kitchen worried sick about you.' Mr Roby hugged her briefly and then vanished into the darkness.

The men were directing the light of their torches so the doctor could work. They were silent and then, to her surprise, she caught a glimpse of Mr Hatch, one of the ARP wardens. He wasn't shouting about turning off the lights but shining his own torch on her injured fiancé like the others.

After pulling on her coat, she dropped down again beside Dan, terrified those horrible men had caused fatal injuries. Why hadn't he opened his eyes? Did he have anything else broken apart from his hands and his face?

'Is he going to die, Dr Cousins?'

He looked up from expertly wrapping a bandage around Dan's head. 'His vital signs are reasonable; he's badly injured but I don't think critically. However, until they get him into hospital, and he's been X-rayed and properly examined, I can't really give a definitive answer.'

She swallowed, unable to reply. The doctor moved on to the damaged hands and they too were bandaged. By the time he'd completed this, everybody heard the screech of several cars arriving outside the Grosvenor. There were no trains stopping at Wivenhoe during the night so at least those men couldn't have escaped on one of those.

Then the ambulance turned up and she stood to let them transfer Dan onto the stretcher. 'I'm coming with him; he's my fiancé,' she told them and they didn't argue.

The men were dispersing, muttering and swearing, and she caught a few snatches of conversation. They were going in search of the Londoners themselves. If the police didn't find those two quickly then she doubted they'd be found at all. Dan was popular, a local boy through and through, and people stuck together when one of their own was hurt.

Without a shadow of a doubt the men that had so brutally attacked Dan would be much safer with the police than they would be roaming about Wivenhoe. It would be high tide in a couple of hours and if a lone fishing boat left the hard unexpect-edly, it would be to dispose of two bodies out to sea.

She wasn't a violent girl but after what she'd seen them do to her beloved man, she wouldn't shed any tears if they did meet a grisly death.

* * *

Dan didn't regain consciousness on the bumpy journey to the Essex County Hospital in Lexden Road. Although Dr Cousins had been moderately hopeful about the outcome, the longer Dan remained the way he was, the more fearful she became.

On arrival at the rear of the hospital, two orderlies were waiting with a trolley and a flock of white-coated doctors immediately surrounded Dan. He was taken away at speed and she was left standing outside the entrance to the emergency department with no clear idea what to do next.

'Miss Bates, are you feeling up to giving a statement as to what you saw tonight?'

She was jolted from her misery by this question, which came from a grey-haired plainclothes policeman.

'Yes, I'd be happy to. I'm hoping the two men who did this have already been arrested.'

'I should have introduced myself. I'm Detective Inspector Jolly, and yes, the two men have been apprehended. Therefore, taking your statement is just a formality. When Mr Brooks recovers, no doubt he'll be able to identify them as well.'

Hearing him talk so confidently about Dan getting better steadied her and she was ready to follow him into the hospital. She'd never been inside this place, in fact none of her family had; the local doctor kept them healthy. It was clean, the lino so polished, it was almost dangerous. There was an overpowering smell of carbolic and boiled cabbage in the corridor which for some strange reason she found reassuring.

* * *

Emily was paralysed with fear. Now her daddy had disappeared. There was something really bad happening out there. The scullery window banged and her cat stalked in. Seeing him was a good sign.

'Ginger, darling boy, where have you been all this time? I've been so worried about you. I'm glad that you're home even though Nancy and Daddy are still out there.'

The cat jumped onto the table so she could hug him and he purred and pressed himself against her, sensing she was upset.

'I'm going to make the cocoa for all of us as in church they're always telling us we have to have faith – I have faith that Nancy and Daddy will be back in a minute and nothing dreadful has happened.'

'Emily, what on earth's going on?' Mummy had come down to look for Daddy and this was the first time she'd left the baby on her own.

She quickly explained what she knew, which wasn't very much really, and her mummy nodded and smiled.

'Now I'm sure they'll be back in a minute. He came down to look for you and what a good thing he did. I see you've found your precious cat.'

Mummy reached out and scratched Ginger's head and he purred even louder. She wouldn't have done that a few months ago but now Emily thought she loved the cat as much as everyone else in the family.

'I was going to make cocoa. I've only put three mugs out – I haven't put enough milk in to make four drinks,' Emily said.

They both looked round as they heard the back door open and shut and her daddy walked in. Nancy wasn't with him, and he looked very serious.

'Darling, I didn't expect to see you up but I'm glad that you are. I'm not sure Emily should hear this but as you're here, sweetheart, I'll tell you what's happened. If that's cocoa, then it's exactly what I need.'

Emily made the cocoa and put it on the table whilst listening to the awful things that had happened to Dan. She couldn't stop the tears by the time he'd finished. He put his arm out and pulled her close and kissed the top of her head.

'Don't cry, sweetheart; he'll be fine. Nancy will stay with him and will let us know what's going on as soon as she does. Dr Cousins thinks he will make a full recovery.'

'Can he stay here in the spare room until he's better? He doesn't have anywhere else to go when they let him out of hospital,' Emily asked hopefully.

Daddy didn't answer but looked at Mummy, who smiled and nodded. 'To be honest, I'd much prefer to have Dan here even if he is an invalid than a strange gentleman from London.'

Emily knew this man was to work for Daddy in the shipyards, she'd heard her daddy telling Mummy that whoever this was, he should have come months ago.

Daddy picked up her mummy's hand and kissed the knuckles and they smiled at each other in that special way they had.

'Then that's settled. Dan will come here and Nancy can look after him. This will mean extra work for you, sweetheart, as your mother will be occupied with your sister.'

'She's a good baby and doesn't take up too much time. I'm going to take my cocoa up with me, Jonathan, just in case she wakes up whilst we're down here.' She turned to Emily. 'Now I don't have to stay upstairs that means I'll always be downstairs with the baby and more than able to take on some of Nancy's duties.'

'Mummy, you can't possibly do the cleaning; that just wouldn't be right. I can do that for you when I'm home.'

'Thank you, my dear, your offer's much appreciated but you do more than enough for this family already. Are you going to spend time at the farm over the half-term break as the extras that Mrs Peterson sends down are very helpful?'

'I wasn't planning to go and really think that I'll be needed here. Mrs Bates can't do everything.'

Her parents laughed. Daddy pointed to her mug of cocoa. 'You sound like your mother, sweetheart. You're not even twelve; please stay a little girl for a bit longer.'

They sat together finishing their cocoa and then she took the empty mugs into the scullery and rinsed them under the tap. Ginger followed her upstairs and this time, when she snuggled under the blankets and eiderdown, his familiar weight was across her feet and she was able to drift off to sleep.

When Emily opened her eyes the following morning, for a second she thought everything was tickety-boo then she recalled what had happened last night and a heavy lump settled in her tummy.

Ginger was never on her feet when she woke up – cats always hunted at dawn and dusk. She didn't understand why her cat still wanted to hunt when he was so well fed indoors.

She'd now got bigger vests which were lovely and comfortable and was glad she didn't have to wear a brassiere but her mummy had said when her bosoms got bigger, she'd have to. There were two girls who had a bigger top than her and they didn't wear a bra – she felt very grown-up even thinking that word – so if she didn't mention it again then with any luck, she could avoid that peculiar garment for ages yet.

Her breath steamed in front of her, but there wasn't any ice on the inside of the windows this morning. In her specially made slacks, warm flannelette blouse and thick woolly jumper, she wouldn't feel the cold.

Mrs Bates was in the kitchen but nobody else seemed to be

up. Her brothers didn't get up early as a rule. Nancy said that was usual for boys and that her three brothers lay in bed as long as they could at weekends and holidays in the cold weather.

Downstairs, the sitting-room fire was lit. She hoped it would be warm enough for the baby if she came down today. It seemed like months since Grace had arrived at Harbour House but it was only two weeks.

'I've come to help you, Mrs Bates, as Nancy's at the hospital.'

Mrs Bates dropped the metal ladle she was holding with a clatter and porridge splattered on the tiles. Emily realised nobody had told her about Dan.

'No, Nancy's fine, Mrs Bates; she's with Dan. He got badly hurt by the two men from London but they're in prison now. Nancy went in the ambulance.'

Mrs Bates fanned her face with her apron. 'My word, that was a shock. You'll not do any cleaning, young lady; I'm not having that. But if you'll help in the kitchen, doing the veg, washing up and that, I'd be ever so grateful.'

The telephone in the hall jangled noisily and she wasn't sure if this was the ring for them or next door. Emily glanced at the clock on the dresser and saw it was still only just after seven. As it was a party line, with Dr Cousins next door, it was usually for him.

Emily tensed, hoping it was Nancy with good news. She heard Daddy coming down and he called out. 'I'll get it, sweetheart. I'm up now. I've got to go to work in an hour.'

He picked up the receiver and she and Mrs Bates watched the door, waiting. Daddy came in smiling and the knot in Emily's stomach undid.

'I'm so sorry, Molly; I should have come round to you last night. Has Emily told you what happened?'

'She has, Mr Roby. From your smile, I'm guessing it's good news.'

'It certainly is. Nancy just rang. Dan's not nearly as badly hurt as we feared. No internal injuries, a lot of stitches in his head and face, but no broken bones at all. He's going to be kept in for observation for another day in case of any hidden head injuries.'

'Thank God for that. Evil pair of buggers. They need stringing up; prison's too good for them,' Mrs Bates said fiercely. She blushed. 'Beg your pardon for my bad language.'

'Nancy's going to stay at the hospital until Dan's discharged. He'll not be well enough to travel by public transport so the hospital will send him back by ambulance. The spare room's ready as we were expecting my assistant from London. Which reminds me, I mustn't forget to ring the Admiralty and postpone his arrival.'

'It's very good of you to let him come here and for my Nancy to be able to look after him,' Mrs Bates said. 'Someone will have to tell the skipper of his barge. He'll be expecting him first thing.'

Emily thought the housekeeper's voice sounded strange, as if she was getting a head cold. She hoped not as they couldn't manage without her, especially now.

* * *

Dan regained consciousness slowly. Everything hurt, especially his face, hands and torso, but his first rational thought was that he hadn't expected to wake up at all. He didn't move. Allowed his brain to react to his surroundings. He was in hospital – it had a distinctive smell. He breathed in more deeply and his eyes flew open. Nancy was here.

'Darling Dan, I can't tell you how happy I am to see you awake. Keep still and I'll find a nurse.'

He tried to speak but only an incoherent mumble emerged. His face was too sore, his lips felt huge, and even his tongue hurt.

'The consultant who saw you just now said the swelling will go down by tomorrow and you should be able to talk normally. You won't be able to eat either but I've got an invalid cup filled with water. I'm going to hold it to your lips. See if you can swallow some.'

He tried to nod but doing so was too painful. He did want a drink but wasn't sure he'd be able to swallow it without choking. He must have bandages around his neck for some reason – he certainly had them around his head and from the pull he felt when he tried to move his mouth, there must be several stitches in his face.

Nancy held the spout against his swollen lips and gently tipped a few drops in. He let it trickle down his throat and with some difficulty managed to empty the container.

His eyes swivelled as a middle-aged nurse, crisply dressed in navy blue, with an impressive starched cap, came into view.

'Excellent, Miss Bates. Mr Brooks needs to drink if he can. The saline drip in his arm is a poor substitute for the real thing.' The nurse, a ward sister he thought, checked his pulse and nodded. 'You're making a satisfactory recovery, Mr Brooks. I'm sending two nurses to see to your personal needs as I can see that you're in some discomfort.'

Nancy understood immediately, smiled at him and went away whilst the sister briskly pulled the curtain around his bed, giving him a degree of privacy.

Being a sailor, he was used to peeing in peculiar positions and unusual circumstances so using the china bottle was no problem. The fact that it was held in place by a girl younger than him didn't bother him either. This was their job, and they did it with calm efficiency and professionalism.

'I'm afraid you can't have anything to eat tonight, Mr Brooks, but try and drink as much water as you can.'

He managed to gesture with his chin at his bandaged hands. They bloody hurt, and he thought one of the men had stamped on them. 'No bones broken at all, thankfully, Mr Brooks, so you should be fully functioning and able to return to your barge in a couple of weeks.'

He managed a sort of smile. One of them had already taken the filled receptacle away to empty and sterilise and the other one rattled the curtains back. Nancy returned and resumed her place on the chair next to him. She looked knackered, dark circles under her eyes and not a smudge of lipstick visible.

If he could hold a pencil then he'd write what he wanted to say but he couldn't move his hands any more than he could his face. He wanted to tell her to go home and get some sleep. That he was fine, more worried about her welfare than he was his own.

Then a young doctor with a pronounced limp arrived at the bedside. He took one look at Nancy and said exactly what Dan had been thinking.

'There's no need for you to keep vigil, Miss Bates; your fiancé will recover quicker if he's not worrying about your wellbeing. Go home and get some sleep. Mr Brooks will be returned to you in due course.'

Nobody argued with a doctor, even one as young as him. Nancy nodded. 'If you're sure, then I will go.' She leaned over and kissed him lightly on his forehead – about the only place on his face that didn't have stitches in it. 'I love you. You're coming to Harbour House when they let you out and I'm going to look after you until you're able to go back on your barge. Mr Roby will have told the owner what's happened so don't worry about that.'

He managed a lopsided smile. She touched his cheek lightly and then was gone, leaving him to thank God – if there was one – that he was still alive. Maybe the fact that he'd been attacked outside the church had saved him, but he doubted it.

Percy would be okay; he wouldn't sack him for something that wasn't his fault. The fact that his hands weren't broken, that nothing was, was certainly a miracle. With any luck, he'd be out of here in a day or two and then be able to spend the next two or three weeks seeing Nancy every day. That was almost worth getting beaten to a pulp for as he didn't think they'd spent more than a few hours together in the two years that they'd been walking out.

He closed his eyes and let the sedative and pain relief work its magic.

11

Nancy was ravenous; two tepid cups of tea and a couple of stale rich tea biscuits was all she'd had since yesterday's tea. If she could find a café somewhere that still had something hot on the menu then that's what she'd do before she caught the bus to Wivenhoe.

She walked briskly down Lexden Road, into Crouch Street then headed for the High Street where she knew there were a couple of decent restaurants and a café or two – at least they'd been there before the war. She hadn't been into Colchester since then so didn't know whether they were still trading.

She was briefly tempted to go in search of Uncle Stan's new property in Head Street but was too tired today. She walked down the other bit of Crouch Street and through a passage into the main road, the High Street.

There was a nice café right next to the bus stop she'd be using. This was probably why it was so popular with housewives and shoppers.

The little bell over the door rang as she walked in and her stomach gurgled loudly as the delicious aromas of something meaty drifted towards her. There were two empty tables and she took one. The walk from the hospital wasn't that far but she was done in. A night without sleep plus all the worry made her feel like a very old woman, not a young girl of not quite eighteen. Mum had made her a nice cake and her aunt and uncle had given her five whole pounds. She'd never told Dan when her birthday was but now they were engaged, she thought they ought to exchange these details.

'Afternoon, miss. I'll bring you a nice pot of tea, shall I? You don't look too clever,' the waitress said with a sympathetic smile.

'Thank you. I've been up all night at the hospital. Do you have anything left from lunch that I can eat? As long as it's hot and filling, I don't care what it is.'

'Bless your soul, love, we've got some lovely shepherd's pie, with greens and carrots. That'll do you a treat, I reckon.'

The food was exactly what Nancy needed and by the time she'd drunk an entire pot of tea, demolished the pie and eaten a portion of spotted dick and custard, she was feeling much better.

The bill wasn't too bad considering what she'd eaten and she left a generous tip. The world was smiling on her, she thought, because as she exited the café the Wivenhoe bus rattled to a halt right beside her.

She didn't think her legs would carry her up the stairs so was glad she found a seat on the lower floor. She collapsed into it, not realising who she was sitting next to at first.

'Well, if it ain't Nancy Bates looking as if you've been dragged through a hedge backwards. I'm going to be your ma-in-law next year, but you ain't been round to see me since you got engaged.'

Nancy almost brought back her substantial lunch. The very last person she wanted to talk to was Dan's mum. She swallowed furiously then managed to force a weak smile. 'I'm not sure if you know, Mrs Reynolds, but Dan was attacked last night by two blokes from London. It was touch and go for a bit but he's making a good recovery now. I've been with him all night at the hospital.'

She waited for the woman to exclaim in horror, to ask for more details, to react as if it mattered to her that her oldest son had nearly died. Instead, Mrs Reynolds just shrugged.

'I heard about it; I reckon everyone in the village heard about it. Tell him he can't come home to be looked after so he'll have to make other arrangements.' The horrible woman shifted about in her seat and pulled her tatty shawl closer around her shoulders. 'If he ain't working, he won't have no money to pay and I ain't got the money to feed him.'

If there'd been an empty seat anywhere else, Nancy would have moved so she wouldn't have to sit next to this woman until the bus arrived at Wivenhoe.

'Actually, he's coming to Harbour House; Mr and Mrs Roby are very happy to have him stay until he's well enough to go back to work. I'll be looking after him.'

'Fares, please,' the bus conductor said as he stood beside her.

Paying for her ticket was a welcome distraction and after doing this, she turned slightly on the seat so her back was almost towards the unpleasant woman, making it abundantly clear she'd no wish to continue the conversation.

Poor Dan to have such an uncaring mother. If it had been her in the hospital, Mum would have been beside herself and so would Dad. Small wonder Dan had left home when he did.

The bus stopped and started many times before she was able to hop off outside the Greyhound pub. Mrs Reynolds would get off at the station as it was closer to her house. It took her ten minutes to walk the hundred yards to Harbour House because every person she passed stopped to ask her how Dan was doing.

Even just giving the briefest details brought back the horror of last night. She could hear two women approaching along The Cut and she'd have to talk to them if she went in through the back door which was the one she ought to use. Instead, she dodged through the front gate and almost ran up the path.

The door was opened before she reached it and by Mrs Roby of all people. 'My dear girl, you look absolutely shattered. Molly has put a hot water bottle in your bed. You're to go straight up and get some sleep. You can tell us everything when you wake up and feel better.'

'Thank you, Mrs Roby. I'll just speak to my mum and then turn in. Dan's doing well and the consultant said he will probably be sent home the day after tomorrow. I just need a few hours and then I'll be back to work.'

Mum had heard them speaking and tore down the passageway and pulled Nancy into a hug. 'What a dreadful thing to happen, love, I thank the good lord that it wasn't any worse and that your Dan will be here with us very soon.'

'I'll just have a quick wash down here before I go to bed. Is Emily all right?'

'Yes, she decided to spend the afternoon at the farm. She's a good girl; she helped me out a treat in the kitchen all morning and the boys have kept out of the way.' Mum nodded at the dining room. 'Mr Roby said we could have a fire in there and use the wood that came from the broken furniture in the attics. The boys are doing something clever with Meccano in there. The baby's downstairs in the sitting room in the crib and I've not heard a peep.'

Whilst she was washing, she told her mum about Mrs Reynolds and her callous attitude.

'Never thought much of that woman; anyone who'd be stupid enough to marry that man doesn't deserve any sympathy. I know I used to say that Dan isn't the man for you, but I've changed my mind and so has your dad.'

Nancy popped her head in the dining room but the boys barely acknowledged her and she left them to their game and hurried up the two flights of stairs and into her own room. Imagine having so much space just for herself, even if it was in the attics.

It wasn't exactly warm but certainly better than either Emily's or the boys' rooms as they had no heat at all and she had the warmth of the chimney breast. Despite being so weary she could barely lift her arms and legs without enormous effort, she still folded her underwear onto the chair for when she got up later and hung her frock and cardigan on the pegs that Dan had put in for her.

This room would remain tidy whatever the circumstances. She was lucky to be here and valued her position and wasn't going to jeopardise it in any way. There was a small gable window high up on the wall but it didn't let in much light, sufficient to dress and undress but not to read if that's what she wanted to do.

She tumbled into bed, revelling in the luxury of having a hot water bottle to hug. It was one of those lovely rubber ones, not the old-fashioned china things that she was used to at home.

Nancy didn't often pray; she was a believer, but not as devout as her mum. But before she fell asleep, she thanked whoever was listening up there for what had to have been a miracle last night. If Ginger hadn't been outside, then she wouldn't have gone out and heard the attack and her beloved Dan would prob-ably be dead.

Emily wished that she had her own friends in Wivenhoe, that the girls she liked from school didn't live scattered about in the villages around Colchester. George had Sammy so he never got bored. She decided after she'd helped Mrs Bates that she'd go up to the farm; after all, it didn't really matter if she wasn't needed because she enjoyed playing with Gwen, Jenny and Neil and wasn't bored when she was there.

Nanny, who had looked after them when they'd lived in the grand house in London, had said that no one should ever be bored as there was always something to do. She'd also said that the Devil liked idle hands. Emily hadn't really understood what this meant then but now she did, and it was true. If you were busy then you didn't have time to be miserable, get into trouble or think bad thoughts.

She didn't need to be walked home – she was almost a woman, so Nancy had told her. Emily thought there was more to it than just getting taller but didn't like to ask. She no longer skipped when she was out, not because she thought people would think her childish but because she didn't want to.

She stopped in Anglesea Road to look down to the river which was at high tide and there was a row of fishing boats approaching, followed by the huge, red sails of the barges. There were also two tugs waiting to tow the barges up to Hythe port as the river was too narrow for them to sail and they didn't have engines. She hadn't known anything about these old-fash-ioned boats, but when Dan had gone off to work on one two weeks ago, she'd asked her daddy and he'd taken her down to the quay so she could see one close up for herself.

Her torch was in her pocket, she had on her boots and her slippers were in her satchel along with some sweets that she'd saved from her ration for the children. She was almost at the farm when she stopped, horrified, looked over her shoulder as if expecting to be arrested at any moment. It was illegal to go out without your gas mask and she'd forgotten to bring it.

'What's up, Emily, you changed your mind about visiting us or something?' Jimmy's voice came from the barn and she looked over and waved.

'I've forgotten my gas mask. I've never done that before. I hope I don't see Mr Hatch on the way home.'

He grinned. 'Don't worry about it; no one here bothers. Hitler's not going to drop gas on us, is he?' He clambered onto the tractor – a new arrival which could do far more work than the two big Shire horses they had already.

Emily would be sorry to see them go as they were friendly giants, and she always took them a carrot or a bit of apple if they were in their stables when she was there.

Her attention was drawn to the kitchen window where Mrs Peterson was waving to her. She waved back and hurried over and Neil, the second oldest of the family, opened the door with a broad smile.

'We're getting on Mum's nerves and she says we're for the high jump if we don't behave,' he said. 'Not sure what that means but I reckon she's fed up with us.'

Emily leaned down and hugged him, something he wouldn't have let her do when she first started coming here last year. 'Then I've come to save the day. I'll just speak to your mum and then we'll find something exciting to do.'

He ran off, calling for his sisters whilst she went into the kitchen to see Mrs Peterson.

'I hope it's all right to come this afternoon when I'd said I wouldn't, Mrs P.'

The farmer's wife was up to elbows in a bowl of dough making bread for the family and the extra girls that now lived with them.

'You're an absolute godsend, love; the blighters are driving me crackers. Having the girls to feed as well as my own family means a lot of extra work. You wouldn't believe how much those land girls eat. The more time you can spend entertaining my little horrors, the better.'

'I'll come after lunch until I go back to school on Tuesday if I can.' She quickly explained what had happened at home and Mrs P was shocked.

'Poor lad, what a dreadful thing to happen to such a nice boy. Family first, Emily love, so you come when you're not needed at home.'

'I'll do that. Is it all right to play hide and seek all over the house? They love that and it will tire them out.'

'Whatever you like, love, just not in my room or the office.'

* * *

Emily enjoyed the afternoon and so did the children. When they were exhausted, Mrs P gave them all orange squash and bread and jam. After that, Emily read to them and then got them to act out *The Three Little Pigs* and they laughed so much that Gwen wet her knickers.

It was full dark when she was ready to leave. She promised the children she'd be back the following day if she could and kissed them each in turn and said goodnight.

'Here, Emily love, I've packed a few bits and pieces for the family. I can't send my Jimmy with you as I don't know where he is.'

'Thank you so much, Mrs P; I don't expect to be given something every time I come. I love being here and enjoy it as much as the children do. I'm quite capable of walking home in the dark now; I don't need an escort.'

Jimmy spoke from the boot room behind her. 'That's a shame; I've come back specially to see you home.'

* * *

Dan hated being confined to bed but the slightest movement sent shafts of agony through his hands and chest. The young doctor who'd just examined him had said it was a miracle nothing was broken.

'I'm afraid we're going to have to keep you in another night, Mr Brooks, as the consultant has said we must do another set of X-rays just in case we missed something. If everything's clear, then we'll arrange for hospital transport to take you to Wivenhoe to recuperate.'

'At the moment, I doubt I could even get up, let alone walk up the garden path at Harbour House. How long, assuming nothing's broken, before I can go back to work?'

'I see from your notes that you're mate on a Thames barge. That's hard physical work and I don't think you should even attempt to return to such a strenuous job for a month at least.'

'Bloody hell! I'll be skint before then. Also, I doubt that I'll still have my position if I'm off so long.'

'Well, once you're discharged from here, it's entirely up to you when you go back to your job.'

'Right, then I'll make my own mind up.' Even though

moving was excruciating, if he wanted to get fit so he could rejoin his vessel, he'd better grit his teeth and start moving right now.

Ignoring the raised eyebrows of the medic, he pushed himself upright and moved the covers aside. His head spun and for a moment, he thought he was going to be sick, then his stomach settled, the pain subsided to bearable, and he was ready to give it a go.

The doctor shook his head and left him to it. Dan knew he wouldn't get any sympathy if he ended up flat on his face and unable to get back into bed. It took him several minutes to slowly swivel in the bed and then lower first one foot and then the other to the shiny linoleum.

There was a chair at the end of his bed and he needed that to lean on. A bloke on the opposite side of the ward had been watching his struggle.

'Hang on a minute, lad; I'll get the chair. I reckon you're going to need it.' The old man nipped across the ward and moved the chair. He winked at Dan. 'Don't tell them nurses I can walk about; they'll send me home and I tell you, it's a real blessing being in here away from my nagging wife.'

Dan nodded his thanks, needing all his concentration and his breath to transfer his damaged hands to the back of the chair. He wasn't sure he could put any weight on them but his legs were like jelly and he didn't reckon he'd be able to stand without the chair.

He leaned forward and was about to try it when two nurses burst in. 'Good heavens, Mr Brooks, we didn't believe Dr Brownlee when he said you were going to get up,' one of them said.

'I have to; I've got to go back to work next week or I'll lose my job.'

She nodded as if she understood that sort of problem. 'Right, then the last thing you want to do is put weight on those damaged hands. Nurse Phillips and I will support your elbows so you can stand up.' She moved the chair and took a position on his left side and the other girl on his right.

'One, two, three, up we come.'

With them holding his arms, he pushed down and to his surprise found himself upright. In fact, being on his feet was far less painful than being flat in the bed.

'Can you take me to the WC?'

'We certainly can. Are you sure you don't want a wheelchair?'

He didn't shake his head because to do so would be painful. After the first few tentative steps, he felt more secure and although his face hurt, his hands and chest as well, it wasn't as bad as he'd feared.

However, by the time he returned to bed, he was knackered. 'Well done, Mr Brooks. I'm sure you'll be able to leave tomorrow as long as those X-rays are clear,' Nurse Phillips said.

* * *

He slept better that night and was taken to the X-ray department in a wheelchair instead of on a trolley. He managed to stand in front of the machine without support.

'How soon will the consultant get the results?'

'We'll take the plates to him immediately. If everything is as it should be, sir, we'll start your discharge. The stitches will have to come out in a week, or maybe a day or two less, but by then, you should be feeling tickety-boo,' the nurse told him.

He wasn't sure if she was a student nurse or qualified, but she certainly seemed to know what she was talking about. She was right and half an hour later, the young doctor, not the consultant, came back to give him the good news.

'I've asked the almoner to ring Harbour House and let them know that you'll be coming by ambulance sometime today.'

'Ta. I need my clothes; I'm not going home in these borrowed pyjamas,' Dan said.

'The matter's in hand, Mr Brooks; they needed laundering and will be returned to you before you leave. You will need assistance to get dressed so I'll make sure a nurse of some sort arrives with your garments.'

This time, Dan didn't get into bed but reclined on it. He noticed that the bed opposite was now unoccupied and waiting for the next patient. The old gent must have been sent home because he'd moved the chair. Nurse Phillips would have known the chair could only have been where it was if someone else had done it for him. He felt a bit guilty that the old man had lost his cushy billet because of helping him.

12

———

Nancy was hovering at the window in the sitting room of Harbour House watching for the ambulance to turn up. She'd not been in to see Dan again as she felt bad about missing the whole day when Mr and Mrs Roby were being so good to them.

'Don't look so bothered, Nancy love; if he's well enough to leave hospital then he's on the mend. I'm here to help you get him up the stairs to bed – we'll be able to see how steady he is when he walks up the path.'

'Goodness, Mum, he'll not be walking up alone. Why do you think I'm waiting here?'

'No need to wait; it's just pulling up. If you're going out, you need your coat and shoes on. It's parky out there.'

By the time the ambulance doors were open, Nancy was running down the path. Quite a crowd had gathered to see Dan's return – she hadn't realised just how well liked he was until this had happened.

Dan was standing in the road, stitched and bandaged, but upright and smiling. 'It's good to see you, love. I look a sight but I'm getting stronger all the time.'

Ignoring the interested crowd of spectators, she stepped close and put her arms around him, not tight as she knew his ribs were bruised. He couldn't do the same with his damaged hands but he leaned into her embrace.

'I love you, Dan Brooks, and I can't tell you how happy I am to see you on your feet.'

'Not near as happy as I am, love. I'd give you a kiss but my mouth's too sore at the moment.'

It took a few minutes more to get him inside as so many of his friends wanted to wish him well. The ambulance driver slammed the doors of the vehicle and was back inside as she closed the front gate behind them.

'I see I've got a welcoming committee,' he said.

The three children were waiting at the front door and when she glanced at the sitting room, she saw that Mrs Roby was also watching with the baby in her arms.

'The lady who telephoned earlier said you need bedrest but can get up for an hour or so at a time.'

'I'll go up to my room but I won't go to bed. I don't suppose anybody thought to get my ditty bag from the Falcon.'

Emily answered him. 'Someone brought it round for you yesterday; it's in your room. Daddy said you can have a fire until you're well enough to be downstairs all the time.'

'Blimey, it'll be like living in a palace being here. Ta for coming to greet me.'

Nancy walked behind him, just in case he felt dizzy and needed her assistance. He was overwhelmed by the comfort and size of his temporary home.

The fire, mostly the wood from the broken furniture fetched down from the attics, was crackling in the grate but didn't give a lot of heat. Sammy had persuaded George to go down to the gasworks off Brook Street and buy a bucket of coke with their pocket money.

'I'm not sure how that will burn on here but the boys paid for it with their own money.'

'It'll do a treat, pongs a bit, but I've done the same a few times as a lad. I'll thank them properly later. Is the tray of tea and that for me?'

'Of course it is, dafty; Mum brought it up when the ambulance arrived. I'll sit with you and drink a cup but then I have to get back to work. There's a commode behind that screen if you need it or you can wait until you come downstairs and use the real one.'

'I'll wait. No one's emptying a po for me, that's for sure.'

As the room had been made ready for a paying guest, it had an armchair in front of the fire, a table and chair in the corner, a chest of drawers as well as the commode and screen. There was a walk-in cupboard to hang clothes – not that Dan had many. Nancy thought it very grand, more like a hotel than a home. She couldn't wait for Dan to be in this room so she could take care of him.

Dan was now stretched out on the bed and was fast asleep. He'd refused to get into his pyjamas so was on top of the covers and Nancy had put the eiderdown over him.

Emily was in the dining room doing something with the boys who were going stir-crazy because they'd wanted to go and play football in the recreation ground but it was raining so they had to stay indoors. From the laughter coming from the three of them, they were obviously enjoying themselves.

Emily was going up to the farm after lunch, even if it was raining. She was a good girl, because she'd told the three Peterson children that she'd come and she wasn't going to let them down.

Nancy had popped upstairs a couple of times to check on Dan but he was sleeping peacefully and his colour was good. The swelling around his mouth and face had almost gone but been replaced by dramatic blue, purple and black bruises.

She'd finished all the cleaning for the day, just had a pile of ironing to do. This afternoon, she'd spend with the boys as Emily was going out. She was employed to take care of the children as well as to do domestic chores. Betty had been only too happy to take Enid's old job as working every morning had been too much for her.

'Nancy, would you keep an eye on Grace for me,' Mrs Roby asked an hour before lunch. 'I've not had any fresh air for what seems like weeks and I thought I'd go across to Mr Moore's lovely emporium.'

'Of course. I helped out with my brothers when they were little, so tiny babies don't scare me.'

'That's good. I think my children are terrified of her because she's so small. She was just over seven pounds which is a good weight and has gained eight ounces in just over two weeks.'

'She's doing well then, Mrs Roby. Do you just want me to rock the crib if she cries or pick her up?'

'I've just fed her so I don't think she will stir for hours and I'm not going to be gone very long. Mrs Cousins said to call in for a quick cup of coffee when I was up and I think I might do that as well. You can always send one of the children to fetch me if I'm needed.'

The baby was good as gold and her mum returned all smiles and happy. Getting out of the house was a good idea; nobody wanted to be cooped up when they didn't have to be.

* * *

The boys were back to their Meccano and didn't need her interference so Nancy was happily reading a nice magazine that Mrs Roby said she could borrow. Then the most horrible scream echoed through the house. The boys jumped to their feet, eyes wide and mouths open. She was out of the door in seconds and up the stairs, closely followed by her mum.

The door to Dan's room was open and he was thrashing about, moaning and screaming in turn. Was he just having a nightmare or was something horribly wrong?

* * *

Emily was a bit damp when she reached the farm and Mrs P tutted and fussed.

'You didn't have to come up in the rain, love; the children would have understood. Here, give us your coat and I'll get it dry before you go home. Don't leave it too late; it's going to get even wetter tonight.'

'How do you know that, Mrs P?'

'Experience, love. I seem to have the knack of knowing what's coming. Helps my old man no end with getting the dairy herd in and out.'

Neil burst into the hall and flung himself at Emily. 'We never thought you'd come today. We've been fed up on our own.' He grinned. 'The girls are fine. They're playing dollies.'

'What do you want to do? What about hunt the thimble?'

'I ain't got one of those.'

Mrs P immediately corrected him. 'I haven't got, not I ain't got, Neil.'

'Sorry, Mum. Anyway, Emily, there still isn't one of those.'

'It's just a name for hiding something. We can hide anything we want; something small's best.'

They'd walked through to the smaller sitting room, the one the children used to play in. The little girls immediately abandoned their toys, two rag dolls, a teddy bear and a wooden dog, and rushed over for a hug.

'We want to play with you too, Emily. Can we play, can we play?' Jenny danced around her, chanting.

'Of course, the more the merrier. Now, shall we play hotter and colder?'

The remainder of her time at the farm was spent searching for various toys whilst she told them if they were getting closer or further away. After a few goes, even little Gwen was taking a turn hiding things.

'I must go now, children. Thank you for being so good. I'm back to school tomorrow so won't see you until next Saturday.'

There were no extras today, but Mrs P thanked her for coming. There was also no sign of Jimmy, so she hurried home in the drizzle on her own. She was getting braver at being out in the dark but didn't really feel safe until she was in sight of her home.

As she was passing the sewing factory at the top of Hamilton Road, she saw Dr Cousins come out of the side door that led to his surgery and hurry across the road and into her house through the back door.

She ran the remaining distance and burst in to hear the most awful screaming coming from upstairs. It had to be Dan. Something must be dreadfully wrong. She kicked off her boots, dropped her coat on the floor and, still in her socks, rushed into the kitchen.

Mrs Bates was standing gripping the edge of the table and staring at the door.

'What's wrong with Dan? Will he have to go back into hospital?'

The housekeeper looked at her blankly and then her face relaxed. 'It's some sort of nightmare, I think, but Nancy can't wake him up.'

'I'm going in with the boys; they'll be terrified,' Emily said and skidded down the passageway, but the dining room was empty. They must be in the sitting room. She opened the door and found Mummy sitting with the boys, the baby on her lap, and they appeared to be fascinated by Grace. She was the girl and it should be her that found their sister interesting – maybe when the little scrap started to smile and look at her properly and not with her crossed eyes, it might be different for her.

Emily was about to speak when the screaming stopped abruptly. The boys jumped up and rushed over to her.

'Dan's not well. The doctor's upstairs. Ginger's gone under the sideboard in the dining room because he was terrified of the noise,' George said.

'Right, let's see if we can entice him out. I'm sure Dan will be fine and he's just having bad dreams because of what happened to him. Remember after... after I was attacked last year, the same thing happened to me. I don't think we need to worry about it. Dr Cousins will help him to sleep better.'

She smiled at Mummy, who was looking at her thoughtfully but gave her a lovely smile anyway. 'We'll be in the dining room if you want us; we need to find the cat.'

The dining-room furniture had been inherited; it was very old, very ugly and very big. The table was always covered with a tablecloth so it didn't matter but the massive sideboard that almost filled one side of the room was another matter.

'We'll have to lie on our tummies and look under it. I don't think even I can reach to the back so if Ginger doesn't want to come, there's nothing we can do about it,' she said.

'He's a big cat, Emmy, and he might be stuck.' Sammy had

started calling her Emmy a few months ago and she didn't like to correct him even though she didn't really like her name being shortened. But if it made him feel more comfortable then it would be unkind to object.

The three of them stretched out on their tummies and peered into the narrow gap beneath the sideboard. This was where the silver cutlery, the best dinner service and the crystal glasses were kept. They were rarely used as mostly they ate in the kitchen now.

They couldn't hear the cat and they certainly couldn't see him. George jumped up and went to the nasty elephant's foot in the corner that held half a dozen walking sticks and canes.

'I'll poke about with one of these – we can't see him but I should be able to feel him.'

Emily sat up. 'I don't think that's a good idea, George; Ginger isn't the sort of cat who will take kindly to being poked with a long stick. He might retaliate and he's got very sharp claws and teeth.'

George laughed but Sammy looked concerned. 'He won't do that to me. I'm not stupid, Emily, I'm only going to do it gently so if I do touch him, it won't hurt him and he'll barely feel it.'

She rolled to her knees and stood up. 'Then I wish you luck. Sammy and I are going to stand at the far side of the room just in case.'

* * *

Nancy looked down at Dan, now quiet, as the doctor had given him an injection of something. His thrashing about had opened a couple of the cuts on his face and the doctor was gently re-stitching them.

'Is he going to have those nightmares every time he closes

his eyes, Dr Cousins? Why couldn't I wake him up? I was really scared for him.'

'If you're thinking it might mean there's something sinister going on, Nancy, then I can assure you there isn't. He won't have slept properly since he was attacked. Naturally, he's exhausted and when he was beset by nightmares, a combination of this fatigue and the trauma of his attack prevented him from waking despite your best efforts.'

'But you've just sent him to sleep again? Surely that's going to make things worse, not better?'

'Would you have preferred me to leave him as he was?'

She shook her head. 'I'd have preferred him not to be in this position at all. Mrs Roby must be very upset by all this kerfuffle and might not want him to stay. The boys will have been terrified. I can't be up here with him all the time; I've got to work.'

'Well, you don't have to be with him at all until tomorrow. He'll sleep for twenty-four hours and when he wakes, I'm sure he'll feel much better and his head will be clearer. I'm absolutely certain that Mrs Roby won't ask him to leave so don't look so worried, my dear.'

How he could possibly know this Nancy wasn't sure, but she wanted to believe him.

'I hope you're right, Dr Cousins, as if he goes then so will I.'

He chuckled as he shoved everything back in his old leather bag. 'Ah, young love, how admirable! He's a lucky young man to have you on his side.'

He left her alone with Dan. Twice in as many days, she'd thought she was going to lose him. She didn't want to go through anything like this again. She thanked God her man wasn't in France with the army, flying in a fighter or bomber and was only sailing in a slow old Thames barge up and down the rivers and coast of Essex. His boat could sink but unlike many sailors, he was a strong swimmer and would most likely be able to get safely ashore.

Dan would have to sleep in his clothes; she wasn't going to undress him, and he wouldn't want her to. On her way out, she shook a few more lumps of coke on the fire and added some wood then left him to sleep.

Mum was making a pot of tea, a hot cuppa always helped any situation, and the smell of toasted cheese filled the kitchen. This was a rare treat as all dairy produce was strictly rationed; four ounces a week per adult didn't go far.

'He's asleep, Mum, the doc knocked him out, and he'll not wake until tomorrow.' She sniffed appreciatively. 'That smells good. I'm suddenly starving; I haven't eaten much since it happened.'

'Nothing like a lovely bit of cheese on toast and a mug of tea to improve the mood. Here, take this in to Mrs Roby and fetch the children, then we can tuck in. Emily bought a nice big wedge the other day from the farm.'

Nancy carried the tray into the sitting room and Mrs Roby beamed. 'How delicious, exactly what we need after all the excitement.'

Leaving her happily munching, Nancy opened the dining-room door. 'Good lord, whatever are you doing, George?'

The boy was on his front poking a long walking stick under the hideous sideboard.

Emily giggled from the other side of the room, where she was standing with Sammy. 'He's cat mining. Ginger's under there and we want to get him out.'

Nancy laughed. 'No, he's not; he's been in the kitchen for ages cadging bits of toast from my mum. Come on, you three, cheese on toast and a slice of sponge cake is ready and waiting for you.'

13

Dan hadn't felt well enough to be properly up until yesterday, three days after turning up more or less uninvited at Harbour House. Today was his first day downstairs. He couldn't shave because of the stitches in his face and the children said he looked like a pirate with his beard. As soon as he was able, he'd shave and have a strip wash. He no longer had nightmares, he could move his fingers and the doctor was coming to take off the bandages and remove his stitches that morning.

He hadn't seen much of Nancy during the day as she was busy but she'd spent the evenings with him. She was now acting as nursemaid to the baby as well as her other duties so that Mrs Roby was able to go to her meetings. He was sitting with her – he'd been told to act as one of the family whilst he was there – in the sitting room enjoying the light music on the wireless.

'Did you know it's 1 March today, Dan?'

'No, but I do know it's Friday and it's a week since I was beaten up.'

'Apart from the stitches and the bruising, your face looks more or less as it did,' she said.

'I'll look even better when the stitches come out. Do you get a day off? You've not had one since I've been here.'

'Tomorrow, I'm hoping we could go somewhere if you're feeling up to it. I told you about my auntie and uncle inheriting a shop in Colchester, didn't I? Mum's asked me to go in and see what sort of place it is.'

'Why haven't the new owners gone themselves?'

'My Uncle Stan's not up to it; he's got some sort of tummy trouble and rarely leaves the house and my auntie stays with him.'

'I need to go down to Brightlingsea and speak to Percy. I was hoping you'd come with me then I can show you the cottage I've leased.'

'That sounds even better. Do you think we could do both? How do you know that your skipper will be at home? Mightn't he have found a temporary mate and be off somewhere?'

'Possible but unlikely. The blokes that want to sail in a barge are mostly to be found at Hythe port; I don't reckon there'll be anyone looking for a berth at Brightlingsea – at least I hope not.'

He didn't like sitting down for long and annoyed Nancy by marching around the room. She said it made her dizzy but she understood he had to get fit if he wanted to go back to work next week.

'The doc's on his way. I'll go in the dining room – save him coming upstairs and there's more light in there.'

Dan called out to Mrs Bates that he was opening the door as he didn't like to presume. 'Morning, Dr Cousins, I'm more than ready to get this lot off.'

'I'm sure you are, Mr Brooks. I'll do your hands first – you might not realise that there are several stitches to be taken out from them as well. Then the ones in your face can come out too.'

The bandages were grubby, his hands itched but they seemed to work well enough.

'What about your ribs? Any problems with those?' the doctor asked as he expertly unwound the bandages from his left hand.

'Not now. I can breathe in and out without any pain at all and the bruising's fading fast. I still don't understand how nothing was broken.'

'A medical miracle, my boy, as we don't either. I think you must have strong bones – you certainly have an excellent constitution. You've recovered far more quickly than I'd expected.'

Dan looked down at his hand, flexed his fingers, and nodded. 'All tickety-boo, once the stitches are out, I'll be ready to work again.'

'Good God, not yet. Sailing a barge is strenuous physical work; I'd strongly advise you to give it another week at least before returning.'

Dan bit back his sharp answer. Folks like Dr Cousins didn't understand how things were for working men. If you didn't work, you didn't get paid. Mr Roby had refused his offer to pay his keep and if it wasn't for that, his savings would be almost gone. He didn't regret helping Nancy's friends out, but it had left him a bit short.

The stitches came out painlessly on both hands and the scars were almost invisible – just faint pink lines. Then the ones in his face were removed and the doctor stood back and smiled.

'They did a good job; you've healed well. However, be careful when you're shaving as you might catch a scar and reopen it. If I was you, I'd keep the beard for another week to make sure that doesn't happen.'

Dan ran his fingers over his face. 'The children like it but Nancy isn't keen. It'll have to come off before I return to work but I'll leave it until then. Ta, Dr Cousins. How much do I owe you?'

The doctor shook his head as he was dropping his instruments back into his bag. 'Nothing at all, your friends had a whip round and settled the bill. Good luck. I don't envy any man at sea at the moment – far too dangerous.'

'We stick to the coast and the rivers. It was far more hazardous being in the fishing fleet. Wivenhoe hasn't had any boats blown out of the water so far, but I know they've lost a lot in Kent.'

'Sadly, I agree with you. Crossing on the river Colne on the ferry to Fingringhoe three times a week for my surgery outside the Whalebone pub is more than enough time on the water for me.'

Dan went immediately to the WC where there was a mirror over the sink. He wasn't a vain man, but rather liked being thought of as the best-looking bloke in Wivenhoe. He leaned forward and examined his face closely and wasn't disappointed. Once the multicoloured bruising had faded and he'd removed his beard, which he hated, he'd be as good as new.

He was well aware that initially, Nancy had only walked out with him because of his looks. It was different now, but he didn't want to give her an excuse to break it off.

'Mrs Bates, can I get some hot water and take it into the WC and have a good wash?'

She waggled her eyebrows at him and grinned. 'No need to do that, son; there's a lovely hot bath waiting for you. Nancy fetched down what you needed.' She continued, 'I think we'll all be grateful when you've had a bath.'

For a moment, he thought her serious then she laughed and he joined in. He couldn't remember the last time he'd been able to fully submerge himself into hot water. There was certainly more than five inches in that bath but as the door was closed, it was only his business and hers.

Nancy had even given him her lemon soap to use but he had a bit of carbolic in his wash bag and he used that instead. Not because he wouldn't like to smell of lemons but it was hers and she probably wouldn't be able to replace it when it ran out.

Feeling renewed and refreshed, he stepped out onto the rag rug used as a bath mat and dried himself vigorously, wincing a little when he pulled the towel too hard. He'd lost weight this past week but he'd soon put that back on – his muscles didn't seem to have shrunk at all and that's what mattered.

He was half-dressed when Nancy knocked on the door. 'Lunch is on the table. Hurry up; we thought you'd fallen asleep in the bath.'

'I nearly did, absolute luxury. I'll be out in a jiff.'

Emily was gazing out of the window in the art room on the top floor of Greyfriars House, uninterested in the task she was supposed to be absorbed in. The art mistress had set up a still life which consisted of a bowl of apples, a bugle and a bunch of daffodils – hardly inspiring.

She'd sketched it out, she was good at art so that had been easy, but it wouldn't take her more than fifteen minutes to complete the drawing and there was another hour to go. Normally, she loved her time up here, got on well with the art mistress Mrs Brown, but today, she just wasn't motivated.

Then something attracted her attention. It wasn't in the street below but in the sky. Forgetting where she was, she jumped to her feet and pressed her nose against the window. 'Look, it's a squadron of fighter planes. Aren't they magnificent?'

With any other teacher, this would have meant an immediate order mark or, even worse, a conduct mark, but Mrs Brown was different.

'Come along, girls, we can't miss this.'

There was a rush to the four windows that ran along the side of the art room and they stood for several minutes watching the sun glint on the silver sides of the planes as they flew in a V-shaped formation across the sky and out of sight.

Her friend Ellen, whose older brother was a fighter pilot based at Hornchurch, clapped her hands. 'It was Neville; he said he'd try and persuade the squadron leader to fly them over Colchester today. I didn't dare hope he'd actually do that.'

She was immediately the centre of attention and Emily listened as eagerly as the other girls. The planes were Spitfires, not Hurricanes, but she wasn't exactly sure how she'd tell the difference in future as she'd never seen one of the others. Until today, she hadn't even seen an actual fighter of any sort.

After that, nobody was interested in the still life but Mrs Brown asked them to quickly complete their drawings while she went in search of a picture of an aeroplane they could use to help them recapture what they'd seen.

Even though Emily only had pencils – paint and pastels were no longer available – seeing the brave pilots and knowing that one of them was actually the brother of her good friend Ellen, inspired her. Her finished drawing was the best thing she'd ever done and Mrs Brown, who was somewhat stingy with her praise, held it up to the rest of the girls as an example of how to produce an exciting picture.

'Can I please take this home, ma'am? My brothers are absolutely mad for anything to do with the RAF. I just hope the war's long over before they're old enough to enlist as at the moment, all they can talk about is being a fighter pilot.'

'Yes, Emily, I shall allow you to take it. It's so good, I'd much prefer to put it in a display but who am I to deprive your little brothers from having such a treat?'

Ellen pointed to the discarded still life. 'This is top notch too, don't you think, Mrs Brown?'

Emily blushed as all the girls crowded round to look.

'Yes, it's excellent. You're really a very talented artist. I'll put this up instead as it's a fine example of penmanship. Come along, girls, put everything away as the bell will be ringing soon and I know some of you have trains or buses to catch.'

With her drawing carefully rolled and put into her satchel, Emily flew down the stairs, weaving in and out of the other girls and risking a serious ticking off by one of the prefects who stood on duty at each corner. Since the incident when Claire Cousins had hidden, she didn't like to be even minutes late in case the child vanished a second time.

She delivered her charge to her front gate and remained to check that she went into the house before dashing across Alma Street and up her own front path. The door was never locked during the day. The evenings were light and it wasn't dark yet so there was no need to worry about letting the light from inside out into the street.

Not only was it Friday and she had the weekend to look forward to, but she also had a truly splendid gift for her brothers. She hoped that everybody else would be impressed with her artistic skills as well.

The boys were playing marbles in the hall as it didn't have as many items of furniture for the marbles to roll under and be lost forever.

'Dan's all better now,' Sammy said. 'He can't shave his beard off for another week and we're glad because we think he looks like a jolly pirate.'

'He's going to Brightlingsea tomorrow with Nancy and he says he'll take us with him. You won't be able to come because you're going to the farm as usual,' George said. 'You don't spend any time with us now 'cos you like those children better.'

'That's not true; I love you. I've got a gift for you both – do you want to see it?'

A few months ago, she'd have reacted to his remarks but she thought she was more grown-up now and he couldn't help being silly because he was three years younger than her.

This got their attention, and they crowded round her, demanding to know if it was sweets or biscuits or chocolate.

She shook her head, laughing. 'No, much better than that. Just give me a minute whilst I change my shoes, hang up my coat and gas mask and put my satchel on the table in the dining room.'

Whilst she was at the other end of the house doing this, she heard the boys telling Mummy about the gift and Emily smiled, pleased she could now show it to her as well as to her brothers.

Sometimes, Nancy would be looking after Grace but it seemed she'd gone for a walk with Dan this afternoon. One of Emily's friends had a new brother and that baby cried all the time so at least even if her sister didn't do anything worth looking at, she didn't cry unless she was hungry or needed her nappy changing.

When the three of them were gathered at the table, she ceremoniously unbuckled the leather straps on her schoolbag and carefully removed the rolled-up picture. She spread it out on the table, smoothing it flat with her fingers.

'Did you do that, Emmy? It's a spiffing picture. Is it really for us?' Sammy said, his eyes wide.

George hadn't spoken and was looking at it closely. 'Did you see these with your very own eyes? They look so real. They didn't come over our school, worse luck.'

Emily explained why the squadron had flown over Colchester and they were fascinated. Mummy hugged her.

'I didn't know you were so artistic, my dear. Daddy will love it. Boys, I think it's far too good to be hidden away in your bedroom. I'll get it framed and put in the sitting room so we can all see it every day.'

The boys were so disappointed they weren't to have the picture that Emily, for the first time ever, disagreed with her mother over this idea.

'I gave it to them, Mummy; it wouldn't be fair to take it away. I've got some paper in my room; I could do another one for here.'

Her heart was thudding painfully and her hands were clenched. She hated to upset her mother, but she also didn't want to upset the boys either.

'I'm sorry, you're quite right, darling girl. I tell you what, boys: if I have this professionally framed with real glass at the front, could we possibly share it? You have it upstairs with you for a while and then we have it down here with us?'

Emily didn't really hear much of the answer as she was so astonished to be called darling girl. That was the sort of thing that Daddy said; Mummy always called her 'my dear' or by her name. She'd never been so happy.

* * *

Nancy loved having Dan under the same roof as her as it showed her what it would be like to be married to him. She didn't understand why she'd been so hesitant and wondered if it had been her mother's initial disapproval. The oldest of his three half-brothers was now in juvenile detention after attempting to rob Harbour House last year. Dan wasn't like any of them and her mother realised that now; she was as enthusiastic about the forthcoming marriage as Nancy was.

They'd spent a lovely day last Saturday visiting Brightlingsea and she'd seen *Lady Beth*, the barge that he sailed on, and admired the beautifully done out cabins and liked his skipper. The boys hadn't come with them as Mr Roby had said it wasn't the right time.

The cottage wasn't half as bad as she'd feared, was about half a mile from the port on the end of nice terrace. She couldn't wait to be Mrs Brooks and be living there.

They'd never got to Colchester, but she'd promised her family that she'd go on Saturday as Dan would be back at work then. She was playing a game of Monopoly with the children and her mind wasn't on it.

'It's your go; are you going to buy Bond Street?' Emily demanded and Nancy laughed.

'Sorry, you know that I'll buy it even if I have to mortgage some other properties. I'll then have the two best streets on the board.'

Monopoly was a firm favourite with the children but it did tend to go on too long. Dan wasn't here this evening but was out somewhere playing darts. There were over sixteen pubs in the village and he could be at any one of them.

She couldn't have gone with him even if she'd wanted to as tonight, she had charge of the children, including the baby. Officially, she finished work at six o'clock but had been happy to help out. The Robys had gone for supper at Little Wick, which was just next door, so if either of them was needed, Emily could nip across and fetch them.

The noisy game eventually came to an end and tonight, she

triumphed, much to the annoyance of the boys, who thought they should have won.

'Right, you three, get washed and into your night things and by the time you've done that, I'll have your cocoa waiting,' she said firmly and with some grumbling from George and Sammy, they stood up. 'Emily love, could you get them some hot water and take it into the scullery? I'm just going to check on Grace.'

The baby was sleeping peacefully, not due for a feed for another hour. Nancy watched her and smiled. Maybe in a year or so, she'd be the proud mother of a baby herself.

Emily joined her. 'Nancy, I think there's something wrong with me.'

'Oh, are you feeling poorly?'

The girl looked away, fiddled with her plaits before finding the courage to explain.

'No, nothing like that. It's much worse. I don't like my sister very much. I think that's unnatural, don't you? I've tried to love her, to take an interest, but I don't even like the smell of her.'

Nancy wasn't sure what to say as this was a shock. Even the boys were happy to hold the baby for a bit when she was awake and until Emily had dropped this bombshell, Nancy hadn't realised how little contact the girl had with Grace.

'I know that my mum didn't bond with one of the boys, I can't remember which one, but she loves them all now. Babies aren't everybody's cup of tea, and once Grace is smiling, taking an interest in things, I'm sure you'll change your mind.'

'I hope so. I was so looking forward to being a big sister to a girl, and it's all a dreadful disappointment. Do you think that my mummy and daddy know how I feel?'

'I'm sure they don't, love, as I didn't know until you just told me. I wouldn't worry about it; just carry on like you are and you'll see that I'm right. In a few weeks, you'll feel differently.'

14

Nancy got the children to bed and then sat with the baby, listening to the wireless. This was a real treat as she wouldn't dream of staying in the sitting room when her employers were there in the evening.

Tomorrow, Dan would be returning to work and she was going to miss him. Tonight was the first time he'd gone out and left her alone. She'd loved their evenings sitting in the kitchen talking about their future together, the war, and what was going on in the village.

Doreen and Patsy had finally got their papers, they hadn't had to wait as long as they'd feared and had left on the train to London. They wouldn't be trained there but somewhere else and she couldn't remember exactly where that was.

Mr and Mrs Roby were back by nine o'clock and thanked her for taking care of the children.

'Here, Nancy, put this in the post-office account. I know you and Dan are saving to get married.' Mr Roby handed her a ten-shilling note and Nancy was speechless.

'Thank you, but I can't take it. It's my job to take care of the children. You don't have to give me extra. You've had Dan here nearly two weeks and won't take a penny from him.'

'Apart from the first few days when he couldn't get up, Dan's more than earned his keep. He's chopped a tonne of wood, cleared out one of the attics and repaired a dozen things. I'd have had to pay a handyman to do those things – if I could have found one. No, Nancy, I want you to have it. Think of it as a bonus.'

'I'll take it this time, Mr Roby, thank you, but not again. Now I'll bid you both goodnight.'

* * *

Dan wouldn't stay out late. If his team won, he'd promised to come home rather than join in the drunken celebrations. Just after ten, Nancy heard him outside and went to greet him. She hadn't liked being kissed by him when he'd had all that hair on his face but now he was clean-shaven, it was lovely. His face was cold, his lips hard and she tingled all over. She took his coat from him and hung it up whilst he was pulling off his boots.

'You reek of cigarette smoke and beer.'

He grinned, unapologetic. 'Nothing I can do about that, love; until this blooming war's over and we can have the windows open, it's going to be like that. I told Norman that was my last match as I'm back to work tomorrow.'

'Don't remind me; I've so loved having you here.'

'We're going to Ipswich again to collect barley and then take it to Marriage's mill in Colchester. We rarely know what we're loading next, but the skipper said we'll be doing that run until May. The *Lady Beth* should be able to find her way there and back easy enough after that.'

She smiled. 'I'm glad as that means you're less likely to meet a U-boat or have bombs dropped on you once they start.'

The house was quiet, everybody asleep and they had the kitchen to themselves. Then Ginger banged his way into the scullery and trotted past, ignoring both of them on his way to join his favourite human in her bedroom.

Nancy was tempted to tell him what Emily had said about not liking the baby but decided she'd been told this in confidence and it would be betraying the child's trust to share it, even with Dan.

'We'd better go up; we both have to be up early.' There was something she wanted to tell him and she was certain he'd be delighted, although she wasn't quite sure how she felt about it herself. 'Mum and Dad have been talking about us and have decided that if we want to get married later this year, as I'll be over eighteen, then we can.'

She'd expected him to pick her up, hug her, give her one of those blinding smiles he was so good at but instead he looked horrified.

'We can't; I'll never get the cottage ready by then. I'm not even sure it'll be finished by the following September. I'm not starting our married life sharing with your parents.'

She giggled. 'Fat chance of that, unless you want us to squeeze in with my three brothers.'

Now he smiled, leaned over and kissed her. 'Of course I want to marry you as soon as possible but it has to be done right. We have to have somewhere to live, start our life together properly.'

She was about to tell him that very few couples were lucky enough to have their own place straight away but he shook his head, guessing what she was going to say.

'I know few people have a home at the start. But we're not like them. I'm only just twenty and you're not quite eighteen –

let's get our home ready, save as much as we can from our wages, and do it as planned in September next year.'

Nancy wasn't sure if she was disappointed that he hadn't been overjoyed or relieved that she could stay in her lovely job for another eighteen months.

'I don't know why my parents think we should get married this year. Maybe they think if I don't then I'll be in the family way and they don't want me to have that sort of wedding.'

His eyes blazed and a wave of heat settled somewhere it shouldn't.

'I know you want to wait and I think that's the right thing to do. You've got a room of your own, you're working for good people and getting a good wage. If we did get married this year and you moved to Brightlingsea, it might be hard to find decent employment and you'd be away from your family and friends.'

She punched him playfully on the arm. 'I thought you said no wife of yours was going to work – you soon changed your tune.'

'Fair enough. I was talking out of the back of my hat when I said that. I don't want you to end up doing something you don't like. You've missed out by not going to the grammar school when you could have done. When we have children, I'm going to make damn sure they go if they're clever like you and pass the scholarship exam.'

'Then that's worth saving for. I'm just going to rinse these mugs and check the doors are locked and then I'm finished for the night.'

* * *

Dan dropped his ditty bag on the *Lady Beth* before going in search of his skipper. The grub locker was empty so Percy was probably buying supplies. He found him, not at the grocers, but at home sitting slumped in front of the fire. He didn't look himself.

'What's up, skipper?' Dan asked as he picked up one of the kitchen chairs and put it opposite.

'It ain't me, son; I'm right as ninepence. It's that interfering navy bloke. He says we've been sequestered and we ain't allowed to go to Ipswich. We've got to wait and be told what's what. I'm buggered if I know what sequestered means, but we ain't sailing light, not to nowhere.'

Sailing light meant they had no cargo stowed and the *Lady Beth* would be faster and easier to manoeuvre.

'I'll go and speak to him. What's the bloke's name, the one that told you we belong to the navy now?'

'I ain't no idea, son; he was just a jumped-up little bastard what thinks he knows more than we do. I should have stayed at Hythe; we'd be sailing all right from there,' Percy said sadly.

'Are we ready to go if I can get permission?'

The old man sat up, his eyes a bit brighter and his expression more hopeful. 'I've got the grub for the locker; it's in the pantry. The tide's right to sail in an hour.'

'Then you get things stowed away, but do it quietly, and I'll see if I can find a bloke with a bit more sense. Marriage's needs that grain for the mill.'

The sun was out, a decent breeze blowing in the right direction and Dan was determined to leave Brightlingsea on the tide with or without permission. He'd no intention of asking anyone; that would just draw attention to them. He'd tell Percy everything was tickety-boo and they could slip away quietly. The Royal Navy had better things to do than chase after an old Thames barge – they'd hardly send an armed boat out after them; that would be daft. Earning was more important than taking a small risk like this.

Lying to his employer wasn't something he was eager to do but he'd face the consequences once they were away from the port. He'd take the blame if they were called to account when they were home.

He returned to the barge, taking a roundabout route, keeping his head down, making no eye contact with anyone who looked official. The place was busy, the shipyards working flat out just like in Wivenhoe, and nobody gave him a second glance, even the official-looking blokes.

Putting a couple of stripes on an ordinary bloke's arm gave him the mistaken notion he knew what he was doing. Dan surreptitiously began to loosen the mooring ropes so they would be easy to toss on board. The barge was facing the open water, the wind was picking up, the tide just on the turn, with any luck, they'd be away and clear before anyone noticed they'd gone.

Percy arrived, tossed a sack of food onto the deck and scrambled on board. He didn't ask if they'd got permission, just nodded, and ten minutes later, the mooring ropes were coiled away and the sails were going up. The boy, Fred, wasn't sailing with them today.

Nobody shouted, no one took any notice at all, and whilst Percy was at the tiller, Dan stowed the grub in the locker, lit the cast-iron stove in the fo'c'sle, filled the kettle and put it on the trivet so that could be pushed across to boil when the stove was hot enough.

It was a short run past Harwich to where the Stour and Orwell merged into the estuary that met the sea, then just a run into Ipswich. The weather was clement for the beginning of

March, but Dan knew it could change in an instant and they could find themselves in the middle of a gale-force wind.

'Are we expected in port this evening, or do we anchor somewhere overnight?' Dan asked.

'Loading tonight, then back on the tide. Make us a brew, son; I'm that parched and I could do with a bite to eat.'

The kettle boiled quickly as it was already hot, and he made the tea first as Percy liked it strong. Then he found two fresh meat pasties and a couple of buns. He grinned. These wouldn't keep so they'd eat like kings now and make do with bread and dripping tonight.

Whilst they were happily munching, the old *Lady Beth* gliding over the waves like a swan with red feathers, he told Percy that he hadn't asked for permission.

'Didn't think you had, son; you're not daft. Once I'd been told not to go, it couldn't be me what made the decision. I'll plead ignorance if anyone says aught.'

'We haven't got the stamped papers for this voyage but if any nosy bugger wants to board us then I'll show them those papers you've got stuffed in your locker. They won't know the difference.'

Percy chuckled. 'I knew I'd made the right decision, son, when I took you aboard. Them papers are covered with official-looking stamps and that, just the ticket; I should've thought of that meself.'

'We can't afford to miss a load, we're helping the war effort by ignoring the idiots telling us to stay put; folk need what we bring,' Dan said.

* * *

They had to hang about waiting to be loaded and spent the night moored to a couple of barges also waiting to leave the next morning. He hadn't met the others before but by the end of a noisy evening, he counted them as friends. Sailormen were a different breed from those that sailed on powered boats and, he thought sadly, a dying breed too.

Barges had to wait at Wivenhoe for a tug to come down from the Hythe to tow them up as the river was too narrow to sail. The top mast and the mainmast had to be lowered for the barge to pass under the bridges.

They delivered the barley to the mill, sailed light back to Ipswich and repeated this journey four times. By the end of it, the grub locker was empty, he was filthy, unshaven and knackered, but apart from that, Dan suffered no consequences from his injuries.

His ten-day shift was over and he now had three nights free. He'd booked at the Falcon, but wished he could stay at Harbour House and spend the evenings in comfort with Nancy. They docked late Sunday night and he followed Percy back to his cottage There he was able to wash and shave, change into clean clobber and, after a huge rabbit stew with dumplings, fell into bed and slept like a dead man until he woke with a start, fearing he'd overslept and would miss his train.

Emily was glad that Dan had left as now she had Nancy's full attention in the evenings. They sat in the kitchen while she did her homework and chatted. She loved this time and felt closer to Nancy than to anyone else in the family. George had Sammy, Daddy had Mummy, Grace didn't care, but Emily had no one of her own apart from Nancy.

As it was lent, church on Sundays was solemn and gloomy. She knew that Christ had risen after being murdered on a cross, that he'd died for the sins of the world, but she wasn't sure she really understood what it was all about. If fairies weren't real, if there was no such thing as Father Christmas and grown-ups had told her both of those were real when she was little, how could she know that this wasn't the same?

This wasn't the sort of thing she could ask any grown-up but maybe Nancy could explain it to her. As Dan was coming back tomorrow, Nancy had worked on Saturday and today so she could have Monday and Tuesday morning free.

The vicar went on and on and Emily wasn't the only one glad to escape the freezing church. She could hear the congregation muttering as they left, saying that their Sunday lunch would be ruined. There would be a magnificent lunch waiting for them as Nancy had stayed behind to cook it for them.

This was the first time Mummy had been to church since Grace had been born but the baby had stayed at home with Nancy. On the way back, her parents were talking about the forthcoming baptism and who they were going to invite.

'I don't think that either the doctor or his wife will want to come to the church as they rarely come to any services,' Mummy said.

'I'm sure they'll come to a christening. It's a shame Grace won't have any godparents present, but travel's all but impossible for civilians nowadays. My parents and sister were delighted to be asked even if they couldn't be here,' Daddy replied.

George had been listening. 'Do we have godparents? Aren't they supposed to take an interest in us? I've never met one, have you, Emily?'

'That's a good point, George. Daddy, can you tell us who's supposed to be taking care of our Christian upbringing?'

'I can't honestly remember, but whoever it was they've done a rotten job. Do you know, darling?'

Mummy laughed and shook her head. 'I haven't the foggiest, my love. I don't think anyone takes it seriously. I'm sure we've got a certificate with their names on it in the box with all the other bits and pieces.'

'Then can we look after lunch, please?' Emily didn't hold out much hope they'd be allowed to, but she was given permission.

'I'll find the box, sweetheart, and you and George can rummage through it. It's got your birth certificates and that sort of thing in it as well.'

Her parents didn't seem bothered that the so-called godparents hadn't been taking an interest in them so Emily decided this meant they didn't completely believe all the miracles and stories either. If the doctor and his wife weren't Christians, then did this make them heathens?

It was the boys' job to help on a Sunday so they rushed off to the kitchen to wash their hands and assist Nancy in dishing up. Mummy had gone to collect the baby and taken her upstairs to give her a feed. This was the ideal opportunity to ask her daddy about this difficult question.

'Daddy, Mrs Carly at Sunday school this morning was talking about missionaries going to Africa to teach heathens about God. Does that mean if someone doesn't believe in God that they're heathens? And what exactly is one anyway – from the way Mrs Carly talked about them, they're very bad people.'

'A heathen is a rather unpleasant word that's applied to anyone who isn't a Christian. Millions of people in different parts of the world believe in a god, or gods, but call him, or them, by different names and worship differently to us. As far as

I'm concerned, if there is a God, and I'm not absolutely certain about that, then there has to only be one. Wouldn't make any sense for there to be dozens hanging about somewhere. Therefore, sweetheart, I don't like the term heathen and hope you won't use it.'

She nodded. 'I'm not sure that I absolutely believe it either, but I'm going to give God the benefit of the doubt for now. It was a dreadful shock discovering there's no such thing as Father Christmas – imagine my disappointment if I find out that God doesn't exist either.'

He laughed and put his arm around her shoulders. 'That's my girl, but if I was you, I wouldn't mention any of this to your schoolmistresses. People can be very narrowminded about some things.'

'I think our religious education teacher said that somebody who can't make up their mind is called an agnostic. I think I might be one of those.' Emily frowned. 'She made it sound as if being an agnostic was a dreadful thing. Am I a dreadful person, Daddy?'

'Absolutely not, sweetheart, you're the kindest, delightful, most helpful daughter anyone could wish for.' He tugged gently at one of her plaits before continuing. 'I'm an agnostic too so you're in good company. Come on, we'd better get our hands washed as I just saw a dish of roast potatoes and Yorkshire puddings go into the dining room.'

15

Nancy hadn't been able to tell Dan that she had Monday and Tuesday morning free and prayed that the barge had actually docked in Brightlingsea last night and that he would come to Wivenhoe on the first train today.

She'd got their time together carefully planned. They'd go into Colchester and visit the shop that her aunt and uncle now owned. Her aunt had given her the key to the back door in case it was shut. Nobody actually knew what the shop sold, and Nancy was eager to find out.

Then they'd catch the train to Brightlingsea and spend the rest of the day working on their future home before returning to Wivenhoe. They'd spend the evening together in the kitchen of Harbour House as she had permission to entertain him as long as he didn't go upstairs.

The children understood she wasn't working today so they couldn't ask her to help with anything. She'd laid out their school clothes, checked that Emily had everything she needed in her satchel, and finished the ironing and put all the clothes away. She'd worked well past her official hours, but it was more like being part of the family than a job really.

The first train from Brightlingsea arrived at Wivenhoe station around six o'clock. Dan wouldn't be on that one, but she'd be down there for the next which was at eight o'clock. The early train was for the businessmen who had to go to London to work. She wondered if they'd still be going in their smart suits and bowler hats when bombs started to drop.

At seven forty-five, she put on her best hat – actually, her only real hat as the other one was a beret – checked her hair was neatly pinned into the pleat at the back of her head, that her stocking seams were straight and there were no holes in the fingers of her gloves. Then she was ready to meet the train. It was a shame she had to carry the wretched gas mask as well as her handbag, but it couldn't be helped.

'Cor, Nancy, you look a treat,' Sammy said as she walked past the open door of the bedroom he shared with George.

'Thank you. I need to look my best as I'm going into Colchester with Dan.'

'Bring us back some sweets,' George yelled from behind the door and she laughed.

'I don't have any coupons; the only way I'll be bringing you back sweets is if by some good fortune, the shop I'm going to visit was a tobacconist and confectioners. I hope you're both ready to leave; your sister is at the door.'

'We are, we're just coming down,' George said and the boys emerged looking smart in their purple blazers and caps.

Emily was just about to leave to collect the little girl next door and all of them had to catch the eight o'clock train.

'I'll walk down with you all, as I'm meeting Dan.'

Nancy liked March as it was the beginning of spring, the daffs were out and there were still a few snowdrops around. If you looked closely, there were little green buds on the hawthorn trees and hedgerows and the promise of those always cheered her up.

At the station, Emily, clutching Claire's hand, waited for a train to rock to a halt. The boys stood quietly beside their big sister. The guard opened a door for them and they scrambled inside. Nancy looked up and down the platform, hoping to see Dan jump out, but as the steam cleared, she realised he hadn't been on this train. Disappointed, she turned to go and collided with him.

'I never expected you to meet me, love; I only just made the train so was travelling in the guard's van.' Dan hugged her and she flung her arms around his neck and they kissed.

'Here, you two, none of that on my station platform if you don't mind. You might be engaged but it ain't seemly, even if you are,' the stationmaster said sternly.

'Sorry, but we've not seen each other for ten days,' Dan said, trying to look apologetic but failing as he was laughing. 'Come on, love, let's get rid of my bag at the Falcon.' He stopped and shook his head. 'Why aren't you at work? Have you got an hour free or something?'

'No, silly, I changed my days off so I'm all yours until tomorrow lunchtime. We can spend every moment of it together.'

He smiled and his eyes glinted dangerously. 'Not every moment, love, unfortunately.'

She nudged him and giggled. 'Get on with you, Dan Brooks, none of that talk if you please.'

He slung his bag over his right shoulder and put his left arm around her waist as they walked back down Station Road. As they walked, she explained what she'd planned and he was only too happy to fall in with her suggestions.

* * *

Jenny, the landlady at the Falcon, invited them into the kitchen and made them a pot of tea. 'I've just been across to the bakers and got some lovely sticky buns. My Norman loves a sticky bun with his morning tea. There's plenty, so help yourself.'

'Ta, that's kind of you. We're in Colchester this morning – is there anything we can get you?'

'I don't reckon you'd be able to buy anything even if I wanted it. Gladys Fisher, she's landlady at the Station, said you can't get a saucepan for love nor money even if you don't need coupons.'

'The government asked housewives to give in any spare saucepans to go towards making Spitfires and Hurricanes, same as the railings they've taken,' Dan said. 'Stands to reason there wouldn't be any new ones as everything's for the war effort now.'

'Even the sewing factory's making clothes for soldiers and not for posh folk like they were,' Nancy said.

Jenny still had things to do in the bar and Norman was out somewhere, so they were left alone in the kitchen.

'Have you heard from Doreen or Patsy since they left to train for the ATS?'

'I haven't, but Doreen's not one for writing letters. I doubt I'll hear from her and probably won't see her again unless she gets a few days' leave and comes back to see her mum. We'd better get off, Dan, or we'll miss the train.'

'Right, are you excited to see what your aunt's been left?'

'I am. She's promised to share what she's been left with us so of course I'm excited.'

* * *

It was a short walk from St Botolph's station to Head Street and Nancy enjoyed walking arm in arm with her handsome fiancé. They didn't have the name of the shop they were looking for, but they had the number – 47 Head Street – therefore Nancy was confident that they'd find it. There were plenty of shops in this busy street. She could see that there was a confectioners, tobacconist, boot manufacturers, a fish and game merchant as well as a wine shop and grocers.

'It's a shame it's not one of those big, bustling places; it would be worth a fortune then,' Nancy said as they viewed the street from the top of North Hill. 'At least we know it's on the left-hand side as the even numbers are on the right. We just have to walk along until we find it. There're lots of small shops and it has to be one of those.'

'What was the name of the people who owned it, the one that died and left it to your folks?' Dan asked.

'Mortimer, so we can look for the number or the name, or we can ask one of the shopkeepers in a place that's open.'

Eventually, they discovered Mortimer's had been a haberdasher. The blinds were down and it was locked up. They made their way round the back and into the yard. Nancy was impressed. The building was in good repair, stood four storeys high and there was no rubbish in the yard. This wasn't a poky, dark space but big enough to have a washing line and sit out in the sun if you had the mind and the time to do it.

'I know it's in a row with lots of other buildings, Dan, but it must have six or more rooms as well as the shop. I'm surprised there aren't people living above it. I can't wait to explore.'

'Several outbuildings and shed, seems like a well-kept place to me,' Dan said.

* * *

Dan watched his future wife unlock the back door as if she'd been doing this sort of thing all her life. He knew he wasn't good enough for her, not really; he was just an ordinary bloke with an ordinary job, they'd never be rich and she deserved better. Bargemen did it because they loved being afloat and he wondered if he'd would have been better staying with the fishing fleet or signing up for the actual navy. He'd have better prospects then, but he wasn't one for following rules and was happier where he was.

He grinned and followed her. It didn't matter what she deserved; she'd chosen him, and he wasn't giving her up.

'Look at this, Dan, everything's immaculate. Dust every-where, that's only to be expected as it's been unoccupied for months, but it's as if whoever lived here knew they were dying and made sure to leave it tidy.'

'Where do you want to look first? In the shop itself or the rooms upstairs?'

Nancy's eyes were shining; he'd never seen her look so excited or so desirable. 'Dan, what if we run this shop for them? I know all about haberdashery, having worked in the sewing factory for years. I'm good with numbers; I'd have no trouble keeping the books straight.'

Without waiting for his answer, she dashed into the shop and he could hear her exclaiming and laughing as she exam-ined the stock. Dan had a nasty feeling his life was about to change and not in a way he wanted.

The idea of being cooped up all day selling bits and bobs to housewives horrified him. He was a seaman to the core, couldn't imagine doing anything else. It didn't matter how bad the weather, how cold and wet he was; he loved being at sea doing the job he was good at. His father, God rest his soul, had been a fisherman too. What was he going to do if Nancy wanted him to abandon his life at sea and become a landlubber?

'Dan, Dan, come and see this. You won't believe what's in here. I can't understand why nobody has tried to rob the place – they could have come in through the back door at night and nobody would have known. The shelves look as though they've been recently stocked, as if the place is ready and waiting to be opened again.'

Reluctantly, he joined her and even with the blinds down, there was just enough light filtering through to look around. The place was immaculate, like the kitchen was, there was a long, polished counter down the right side of the shop and mahogany shelving from floor to ceiling with little drawers starting from waist high and each had the name of the contents embossed in gold leaf.

'Looks just the ticket. I reckon your folks will get a fortune for this.'

'I hope they don't want to sell it, that they'll let us run it for them...'

'Hang on, you've only just taken a full-time job at Harbour House. I can't believe that you'd abandon the family that's been so good to you. Anybody could run this shop – why does it have to be you?' He warmed to his theme. 'You'll not be eighteen for a month; I reckon you're not old enough to deal with all the financial stuff and that. You'd best forget about it, love, until you're over twenty-one.'

Her expression changed, the light in her eyes faded, and she nodded. 'I suppose it doesn't have to be me, but I wish it could be. But don't you see, Dan, I can do much better for myself than being a cleaner and nursemaid, even if it is for a lovely family.'

'Anyway, let's look at the rest of the place so you've got all the details to take back.'

She wasn't listening to him but had dropped to her knees and was pulling out the longer drawers behind the counter and exclaiming at the contents. Even he was forced to admit that this little shop was a treasure trove, that for the right person, it could make them a decent living – but that wasn't his Nancy, and it certainly wasn't him.

'You carry on here, love; I'll have a quick look everywhere else.'

On the ground floor was the kitchen, a decent size with a big table on the left of the back door and an old-fashioned range on the right. There was a freshly painted dresser with everything you could possibly need hanging from hooks or stacked on the shelves.

He opened a door and saw it led to a small laundry room, a coal shed and an outside privy. This was a flush WC, but it wasn't inside – maybe that would put her off.

The cottage at Brightlingsea had a big garden, room for chickens – even a porker if they wanted one – and flowerbeds, fruit trees and a large, overgrown vegetable patch. Would this be enough to convince her that they'd be better off in Brightlingsea in the fresh air, growing their own veg, collecting fresh eggs and with him doing the job he loved? Until the babies started to arrive, he wouldn't object to her catching the train every day to Wivenhoe and carrying on with her job.

The property was one room wide and two rooms deep, all of them about fifteen feet one way and maybe as much as twenty the other, he reckoned. This meant there was no sitting room on the ground floor. There was a small hallway between the kitchen and the shop and behind a door were the stairs to the upper floors.

'I'm going upstairs, Nancy; are you coming?'

Her reply was muffled but he thought she'd said no. There

were two larger rooms on the first floor plus a smaller one, and these had been used as a sitting room and bedrooms. There were two more floors, plus the attics, but these rooms were empty – in good repair, dry and quite spacious. He was surprised that they weren't already occupied by evacuees and that. Probably because Mr Mortimer had died before the war started so the billeting officers couldn't access them. When the bombing started in London, he was sure there'd be East Enders desperate for safe accommodation.

He met her looking around the sitting room. 'The other two floors are empty, but there's quite a lot of trunks and things in the attics. It's all in good nick; I'm impressed.'

'So am I. I suppose Mr Mortimer must be a distant relative of mine. I don't know why but I feel really connected to this place. It's as if I was meant to be here.'

Dan hoped he looked enthusiastic and somehow smiled convincingly – she was so pleased at the possibility of running this shop that even if he'd scowled, he didn't think she'd have noticed.

Then he remembered they were going to the cottage after they'd had a bit of lunch somewhere; there was a British restaurant where you could get decent grub at a decent price down the High Street. He just had to pray that she'd see the potential of their future home and, if he made a point of telling her how much they could provide for themselves, what a healthy environment it would be for any children, how convenient for him to come home after each trip, then maybe she'd change her mind.

They were on the train to Brightlingsea when something else occurred to him, made him think that maybe he was worrying unnecessarily. 'Nancy love, I shouldn't get your hopes up; I'd think that your Uncle Stan and Auntie Ethel will want to sell the place. They can't run it themselves with his health being so poor, but with the money this would bring in, they could buy themselves a lovely house in Bellevue Road and get someone in to do the hard work.'

'I know that, but it doesn't hurt to have a dream, does it? I'm really lucky because I've got a job I like, a smashing room all to myself, and the best fiancé in the world. I'll go round and see Auntie Ethel and Uncle Stan this evening. You never know, they might be happy for me to run the shop for them. I know they love their little cottage and have lived there all their lives.'

He thought it best if they didn't talk about it, as the more she said, the more worried he was. He'd sing the praises of the little cottage, point out how much there was to do in Brightlingsea, and hope that would be enough.

If she was given the opportunity to take over the shop, maybe it wouldn't be so bad; he could still stay as mate on the barge and visit her in Colchester instead. The weight that had settled in his gut began to shift. He couldn't stay in the same house as her without tongues wagging unless they were married. Once they were wed, he would be in charge, that's how things were, and if he didn't want to live in Colchester then she'd have to abide by his wishes.

16

Emily arrived at her front gate at the same time as a tall gentleman wearing an overcoat just like her daddy's and carrying a large leather suitcase. He had on what she thought was called a trilby hat, not something that her daddy wore, so she couldn't see what colour his hair was. He must be Daddy's new assistant who was due to arrive today. He'd not been coming from the station or the bus stop but from the river – had he arrived by ferry?

'Good evening, sir. I'm Miss Emily Roby, welcome to Harbour House.' She spoke from behind him as it would have been rude to push past.

Immediately, he turned and put his suitcase down on the path.

'Good evening, Miss Roby. I am Mr Richard Stoneleigh. I'm delighted to meet you.' He held out his hand and she shook it, feeling very grown-up.

'Daddy will be at work and Mummy will be upstairs with the baby. I can show you your room and everything else.'

He stepped aside so she could walk in front of him which

she thought was very polite, and she opened the front door with a flourish.

'Welcome to Harbour House, Mr Stoneleigh. Please come in.' She'd already kicked off her outdoor shoes and saw that he was about to walk on the polished boards without removing his.

'I'm sorry, outdoor shoes aren't allowed indoors. Do you have slippers in your case?'

He looked a bit startled by this – perhaps where he came from, people didn't bother to change their shoes when they came in.

George appeared in the dining-room door. 'Do you have socks on then?'

Mr Stoneleigh laughed. 'I take it that you're George Roby. I'm pleased to meet you.' Again, he offered his hand and after a moment's hesitation, George shook it vigorously. 'I do have socks on – is that also required here?'

'If you haven't got slippers and you've got no holes in your socks then you can walk about in those. I thought as a grown-up, you'd work those sort of things out,' George said with a cheeky grin and then vanished back into the dining room and closed the door.

Emily had her coat over her arm and her gas mask and outdoor shoes in her hand and was ready to go to the boot room. She turned back and her eyes widened. He'd taken off his hat and she now knew why he wore one. He had very bright hair, not ginger like the cat but like the colour of the sky when the sun set.

'I love your hair; I've never seen anybody with hair the same colour as yours.' She then flushed scarlet, knowing she shouldn't have made a personal remark – it was very rude.

He nodded and continued to remove his coat and slip his feet from his highly polished shoes. 'Thank you, Miss Roby, it's not to everybody's taste. I'm sure you now understand why I wear such a ridiculous hat.'

She giggled. 'I do, but I don't think you should. Nancy, she's not here today as it's her day off, once said to me when I was worried about something that everybody's unique and we should be proud of who we are. Be proud and loud – that's what she said, I remember now.'

'I can't wait to meet this young lady as she speaks excellent sense. Now, am I allowed in as I've removed my shoes?'

'I'm sorry, of course you are, this is your home now. Why don't you put your coat and so on over the banisters and I'll show you to your room?'

He followed her upstairs and seemed pleased with his accommodation. 'As you're a paying guest you will have a fire up here – us children don't have them in the bedrooms.'

'Right, understood. Is there anything else that paying guests have to do in order to be acceptable?'

She closed her eyes for a second – this always helped her to think – and was about to answer him seriously but when she looked at him, he was smiling down at her. She realised he was teasing. This was something that Jimmy Peterson did and she always enjoyed it but this was different. Mr Stoneleigh was patronising her and Jimmy treated her as an equal.

She smiled brightly. 'As we have all female staff, Mr Stoneleigh, you will have to take care of your own bodily wastes.'

She heard his sharp intake of breath at her outrageous reply and dashed downstairs before he could reprimand her. He was only a lodger, even if he was a very tall man and obviously something quite important at the Admiralty. She frowned. He couldn't be that important because he wasn't as old as Daddy, just a few years older than Dan, she thought.

Mrs Bates looked up as Emily burst into the kitchen. 'I heard you taking the new arrival to his room – what's he like?'

'He's taller than Dan, a bit older than him, not quite as good looking but has the most spectacular-coloured hair. I don't know if I like him or not but then it doesn't matter as he won't be mixing with us much, will he?'

'No, his room's been set out as a sitting room and your dad's found him a wireless of his own. He'll spend his evenings up there unless he's invited down.'

'Who's he going to eat with?'

'He'll eat with your parents, love, in the dining room. I don't know how your dad wangled it, but we got a load of coal yesterday and the shed's full to the brim.'

'That's good. I suppose as George and Sammy will now have to play in their bedroom, and I'll have to do my homework up there, we'll need a fire.'

If Nancy was here, Emily would tell her the dreadful thing she'd said to their new guest – she hoped he didn't mention it when he met her mummy later.

* * *

Nancy was tired, grubby and happy when she flopped onto the seat in the train that would take them back to Wivenhoe. Dan seemed in a better mood after spending the afternoon clearing the cottage with her.

'I can't believe we got so much done in just a few hours, Dan. If we spend the morning there tomorrow and you put those slates back, it'll soon dry out.'

'Percy's got a set of chimney brushes I can borrow; I'll do that as well, then we can light a fire. I reckon those pots and pans, cutlery and crockery we found in the cupboard under the stairs will set us up a treat.'

She nodded and smiled. 'The only drawback for me is that it's an earth closet, not a flush. Maybe when running water and sewage is available, we can get connected.'

'I know it's just an old-fashioned pump to bring the water up from the well, but at least it's in the scullery. Imagine having all that space to ourselves; neither of us grew up with spare rooms.'

'That's true. And I can't wait to have chickens, grow my own vegetables and even have a few marigolds and daffs along the edges. I've never had a garden; I don't know anything about growing things but I'll soon learn.'

He stretched out his booted feet and grinned. 'I'll go back to the Falcon and get cleaned up, love, and I expect you want to do the same. What time shall I come round for tea?'

'We had fish and chips for lunch so we don't need much. I made a big pot of soup yesterday and there should be some of that left over and we can have that with toast.'

'Sounds good enough to me.'

Nancy hadn't thought about the shop in Colchester all afternoon. Had Dan been right to say someone her age wasn't old enough to run a shop, to have that sort of responsibility? Working with the man she was going to marry, the man she loved, clearing the cottage that would be their home had pushed that dream aside.

* * *

It didn't take her long to wash and change into something clean – she'd made herself a pair of smart slacks like the ones that Emily and Mrs Roby wore – this would be the first time she'd gone out in them.

Her mum would be in the kitchen ready to serve the children's tea. As she emerged from the attic stairs, a young man with red hair emerged from the spare room. His smile was charming and she liked him immediately.

'Good evening. You must be the elusive Nancy Bates. I am Richard Stoneleigh. Delighted to meet you.'

He offered his hand and she shook it. His grip was strong, but the skin was softer and less calloused than her Dan's. Only to be expected as he didn't have a physical job; he worked in an office like Mr Roby doing something clever with the blueprints for ships.

'If you need anything, Mr Stoneleigh, I'm usually around but won't be back at work until after lunch tomorrow. Excuse me, I have an errand to run before my fiancé comes round for tea.'

She wasn't sure why she'd mentioned that she was engaged but there was something about this man that made her wary. One thing she knew with absolute certainty was that Dan wouldn't be happy a young, attractive, professional gentleman was living under the same roof as her.

The cottage in Anglesea Road was only a few minutes from Alma Street; she had her torch in her pocket but didn't need it as it was still light enough to see. The chickens were clucking and fussing in their coop, already shut up for the night with a handful of grain. There wasn't a lot growing in the garden right now, but there were still leeks, cabbages and sprouts waiting to be picked. In the summer, there wasn't an inch of this long, narrow back garden that wasn't packed full with vegetables.

Like most houses in Wivenhoe, doors were only locked at night or when there was nobody in the house. She knocked and went in. 'Uncle Stan, Auntie Ethel, it's me, Nancy, come to tell you all about your new shop.'

Her uncle wasn't always bedridden and this evening was one

of those times he was downstairs looking cheerful and rosy cheeked. 'You been there, then? Come on, sit yourself down, girl, and tell us all about it.'

When she'd finished the description and added that she'd really like to run it for them one day, the two of them were nodding and chuckling.

'Now your Uncle Stan's on the mend, I don't have to be with him every day. I've always fancied running a little shop myself. Will you come in with me tomorrow so I can see for myself if it's worth the trouble?'

Nancy hesitated for a moment, knowing that she'd agreed to go to Brightlingsea and work on the cottage with Dan, but family first is what she'd been brought up to abide by. These were her blood relations, her godparents; he was her fiancé. If they were married, it would be different.

'I'd love to, Auntie. I don't have to start work until after lunch. Have you got all the books from the solicitor yet so you can see if Uncle Mortimer was doing well?'

'I need to pick them up. I'll have to go to the bank as there's some money in it for us as well. Imagine us being well off after all these years.'

'Dan suggested you sell it as it must be worth a lot of money, then you could buy yourself a nice house in Bellevue Road, go up in the world. Why would you want to take on more responsibilities when you could live the life of Riley?'

Uncle Stan shook his head. 'No, that's the last thing we want. I'm not leaving this little cottage nor my nice garden. Mind you, I'd like to get the freehold if that was possible and know it was my own place.'

'Then perhaps that's another reason to think about selling,' Nancy said, hoping that they'd decide to sell so she didn't have to make a difficult choice.

'I'm up bright and early, love, so shall we get the eight o'clock train? You need to be at work by one, don't you?'

'I do, so the early train suits me fine. I'd better go now as Dan's coming round for tea.'

She kissed them both on the cheek and then left them talking and planning and it made her warm inside knowing they were so happy, that this unexpected bequest had changed their lives – maybe hers too.

* * *

Dan turned up at Harbour House to discover that Nancy was round at her aunt and uncle's in Anglesea Road. Mrs Bates greeted him with her usual friendly smile.

'Come in, Dan, why don't you? Nancy won't be long. I've still got to serve supper in the dining room but you're welcome to sit at the table if you keep out of my way.'

'Dining room?'

'Yes, the young gentleman from London has arrived, a Mr Stoneleigh, he seems a very nice sort of man. He's going to be working with Mr Roby, sometimes in Wivenhoe and sometimes in Brightlingsea. In future, the adults will be eating in the dining room, but the children will stop in here.'

'Right, Nancy did say someone was expected. I'll keep out of your way. I'll fill up the coal scuttles and that, shall I?'

'Yes, ta, that'll be a great help. Another thing, because the dining room's out of bounds for the children, they have to play and do homework in their own rooms.' While she was talking, she was busy tipping the soup he thought Nancy had made for them into a tureen.

'This means they've got fires up there – such luxury, but

that's because of the new lodger. The Admiralty arranged for a large delivery of coal yesterday.'

Mrs Bates dashed off with the tray and he nipped over to the old range and peered into the large cast-iron pot. He grinned; there was plenty left for him and Nancy later. It took him half an hour to fill every scuttle, top up the range, and take fresh coal to the bedrooms and the sitting room. He owed it to the family to help out whenever he could and was happy to do this.

Afters, some sort of fruit pie and custard, had gone through before the back door banged and Nancy arrived.

'Sorry I'm late, they wouldn't let me go without explaining every last detail.'

'I'm that hungry, I was worried when your mum dished it up for them in the dining room.' He nodded at the pan. 'There's plenty left for us but I reckon we'll have to wait a bit as they're only eating their afters.'

'We don't have to wait; we're not getting in Mum's way on this side of the table. All she's got to do is make them some coffee – some of that arrived from London too. I'll make the toast under the grill if you get out the bowls and plates.'

Mrs Bates was back as he was ladling soup into the bowls. 'Finish that up, Dan; there's not enough for tomorrow anyway. I've really taken to this Mr Stoneleigh. He's a nice young man, such good manners and ever so friendly. It's just his hair that's put me off a bit.'

Dan, surprised by this comment, inadvertently slopped some soup onto the top of the range and it hissed and bubbled. 'What's wrong with his hair, Mrs Bates?'

Nancy answered first. 'It's the colour of a sunset, Dan; I've never seen the like. He's got sea-green eyes and a lovely smile.'

Dan stared at her. He'd never heard her describe anybody

like that. He wasn't happy about her being here with an unattached professional gent. He could turn her head, make her realise Dan wasn't good enough for her, and then he'd lose her.

'Mrs Bates, has Nancy told you she wants to leave here and run this haberdasher shop in Head Street?' From being dead set against this plan, he was now all for it as it would mean she would be away from this possible danger.

'She never told me nothing about that. Surely you don't want to leave Mr and Mrs Roby and the children in the lurch, Nancy? They've been ever so good to you; they took Dan in as well. It wouldn't be right for you to swan off like that.'

'It's only a pipe dream, Mum, so don't look so worried. Auntie Ethel has asked me to go to Colchester with her tomorrow morning, Dan; she wants to see for herself and then collect the books from the solicitors before going onto the bank. I said I'd go with her. I'm sorry, as I did say I'd come to the cottage.'

'No, love, it doesn't matter. I'll come with you; we can have a bite to eat before we come back, make a bit of a treat of it.'

Her smile was worth the sacrifice. 'I thought you'd be put out, love. I'm really pleased you're coming with us as we don't get that much time together.'

Mrs Bates left after she'd cleared away and finished the washing up, leaving him to sit in the kitchen with Nancy. They'd drunk every mouthful of the soup, toasted half a loaf of bread, and were now finishing up the fruit pie and custard.

'Mum's right, isn't she? I shouldn't even think about leaving this job; I've only been here a few months. I love those children; I'd miss them if I wasn't seeing them every day.'

Dan was torn. He wanted her here waiting for him, not moving to Colchester and finding she liked being independent, that she wasn't ready to get married after all. On the other hand, he wanted her away from this new lodger and didn't know which option would be worse for him.

17

Emily had been reading under the blankets, using up the precious battery in her torch, waiting to hear Nancy come up. She'd be in trouble if anyone found out. She'd been unable to eat her tea tonight because she was so worried that Mr Stoneleigh would tell her parents what she'd said.

Daddy never smacked them, although he'd threatened to once or twice, but she hated it when he was cross with her. She sat up and shone the torch on the clock on top of her bookcase. It was just after ten, her parents were upstairs, so where was Nancy?

The back door had banged a while ago, which meant that Dan had gone home. Her friend must be downstairs tidying up even though Nancy wasn't supposed to be doing any work until tomorrow afternoon.

Emily thought that if she pretended she needed the WC then she wouldn't get into trouble if she was seen leaving her bedroom. There was sufficient light from the embers of the fire for her to find her slippers and dressing gown. With her torch in her hand, she ventured out, knowing there'd be no lights anywhere after Daddy was in bed.

She'd just reached the bottom stair when she froze. Nancy was talking to someone and it couldn't be Dan. The light was on in the kitchen. She sat down and peered around the newel post, thinking that if anybody looked in her direction, they wouldn't see her at floor level.

Mr Stoneleigh, fully dressed but in his socks, was leaning against the kitchen door frame chatting happily to Nancy. She couldn't hear what they were saying but she did hear Nancy laugh several times.

He was telling her what she'd said and Nancy was laughing at her. She scampered up the stairs into her bedroom and only just managed not to slam the door. How could her friend have laughed at her? Why had this new man told Nancy? She hated them both and jumped into bed wishing she'd not been so rude. Her parents would know tomorrow morning and then she'd be in terrible trouble.

* * *

Emily intended to leave the house before Nancy or the lodger came down. She'd tell Mrs Bates that she wasn't feeling too well and didn't want any breakfast.

'Have you got any pennies?' Mrs Bates asked.

Emily nodded.

'Then buy yourself a bun at the bakers and eat it on the way to school,' Mrs Bates suggested kindly.

'I wouldn't dare do that; we're not allowed to eat in public when we're wearing our school uniform. When I bought that bag of cakes ages ago, we didn't touch them until we were safely in the guard's room.'

'Your train doesn't leave for another half an hour, does it? I don't think your parents would want you to go so early.'

'I don't usually have the chance to get into the art room before school because of taking Claire, but I can do so today. The boys can look after themselves now.'

Claire had the mumps so wouldn't be coming to school again until after the Easter holidays, which would be in two weeks. If she wanted to, she could catch the earlier train every day until the Easter break.

She was just going into the station when someone called her name. She looked round and saw Nancy and her Aunt Ethel hurrying down the pavement towards her. She wanted to run, didn't want to speak to either of them, but that would be almost as rude as what she'd said to Mr Stoneleigh.

'Emily, love, what are you doing here so early?' Nancy said.

'As I don't have to bring Claire, I thought I'd try and catch this earlier train. I'm allowed to go up to the art room before school if I want to.'

'I see. Auntie and I were going to get the eight o'clock train but as I was up early, I persuaded her to catch this one. Don't you want to know where we're going?' Nancy asked and Emily was so curious, she quite forgot she was cross and wasn't speaking to Nancy.

'I do, please tell me at once before I burst.'

'I'm going with my auntie to look at a shop that she and my uncle have unexpectedly inherited. Isn't that exciting?'

'What sort of shop? I wish I could come with you as that sounds much better than boring old school.'

On the way to St Botolph's station, Emily heard all about the shop in Head Street. School didn't start for almost an hour; she was sure she had time to come with them and still be there for registration and not get a late mark.

The three of them hurried up St Botolph's Street, turned into Short Wyre Street which was the third turning on the left up the hill. The streets weren't yet busy with pedestrians and shoppers, but the shopkeepers were putting out their awnings, opening the blinds and getting ready for business. Emily wasn't sure of the names of the streets they passed through on the way, but it wasn't far and they arrived at Head Street in no time. Immediately, Nancy pointed across the road.

'Look, Auntie, it's the shop just over there a few doors down from the post office and next to the wine merchants.'

'And the solicitors I'm seeing are opposite in that little courtyard,' Auntie Ethel said happily. 'Come on, Emily, we'd better hurry if you want to have a look before you have to run to school.'

* * *

Nancy said nothing to Emily about the possibility that she would be moving here one day and made sure the girl dashed off in good time to get to school before the bell went. Her aunt was as impressed with the property, and especially the shop part, as she'd been.

'I must say, Nancy love, that if anything, you undersold this place. Such a shame it doesn't have a garden or I might have persuaded Stan to move here.'

'I know, it's perfect, isn't it? What do you think about running this yourself with me helping you? I'd live on the premises and make sure everything's kept safe.'

'I don't know about that; it's a bit of a trek from home to here. I don't think my old legs could do that every day as well as be on my feet serving in the shop. I reckon it'll be better to sell, then Stan can buy the freehold of our cottage. He'll be as happy as a pig in clover if I did that. What do I want with all the bother of this big place?'

'I understand, Auntie Ethel, but it's a shame as this would be my dream job. Although Dan's not keen on me being here, especially if I were to take in lodgers for the empty rooms.'

Her aunt smiled. 'You've already got this planned out, haven't you, Nancy love? We'd do anything for you and the boys, you know that, but being able to give you all a lump sum must be better than keeping the shop, don't you think?'

'Yes, if you put it like that, of course it is. Shall we collect the books from the solicitors...' She clapped her hand to her face in horror. 'Oh my God, I forgot that Dan was supposed to be coming with us. He'll have turned up at Harbour House expecting to find me. He's going to be ever so cross.'

'Don't worry about it, love; he's a big boy, he'll find his way here. I tell you what, you stay put and I'll get the books. I reckon he'll be here by the time I get back.'

Her aunt went off, leaving Nancy to examine the stock neatly contained in the little drawers that the customers would see, as well as in the long drawers that they couldn't. There was everything you could need for sewing from ribbons to buttons, embroidery thread and knitting yarns.

The back door banged and she looked round to see Dan walking towards her. He didn't look best pleased.

'I'm so sorry, I forgot you were coming with us and we got an early train. I'm glad you came as I thought you might decide not to.'

He stopped, leaned against the wall and folded his arms across his chest. For some reason, this reminded her of Mr Stoneleigh, which wasn't good at all.

'Forgot about me? I thought it must be an emergency – God knows what it could be as you don't know anyone in Colchester.

I nearly didn't come.' Then he grinned. 'I didn't have anywhere better to go, love, so here I am. Give us a kiss to show me how sorry you are.'

She didn't need asking twice and she was still in his arms when her aunt returned.

'That's enough of that canoodling, you two. Let's go to the bank then find ourselves somewhere we can have a pot of tea whilst we look at the books.' Auntie nodded. 'The solicitor explained that Uncle Mortimer left everything just to me as he fell out with our mum before Molly was born.'

'That's a bit unfair, but it was his money so he could do what he liked with it.'

'Also, I was named after his wife, Ethel, so that must have helped.'

The three of them left the shop in high spirits. Dan had the books under his arm as well as two or three manila envelopes – they all looked important.

'Did you make an appointment to speak to the bank manager, Auntie Ethel?'

'I didn't, Nancy, but as it was the bank that asked me to come in, somebody will see me.'

'I wouldn't be too sure of that, Auntie; it's Uncle Stan they'll want to speak to,' Nancy said.

'Bless you, love, all this was left to me, not Stan. Mr Mortimer was my uncle on my mother's side – that would make him your great-uncle.'

'Uncle Stan carried on as if it was his inheritance – I'm glad it's you that will make the decisions, not him.'

The bank was quiet, the people waiting to go to the counter as solemn as any sitting in a church pew. The bank tellers were, naturally, all men in black suits and most of them elderly. Nancy supposed that the young men had been conscripted.

A fussy, grey-haired man with gold-rimmed spectacles, in a suit like the businessmen who travelled to London, approached them.

'Can I be of assistance, sir? Perhaps your family would like to wait in the seating area for you?'

Dan ignored the question and winked at Nancy and she tried not to laugh. Auntie Ethel wasn't going to be patronised by anybody.

'I'm Mrs Ethel Frost. I received a letter from the manager. Kindly conduct me to him.'

The man smirked, probably thinking the letter had been about an overdue bill or something of that sort.

'Don't just stand there. Go and speak to him. I don't have all day.'

Nancy wanted to cheer. Auntie's voice carried across the bank and every head turned to gape at them. The men behind the counter looked disapproving but several of the customers grinned and nodded.

The man who'd spoken down to them stalked off but was back moments later and couldn't have been more different.

'I do apologise, madam. Mr Potter will see you now. Would you care to follow me?'

He looked up as if he was going to tell Dan and Nancy to remain where they were but they stepped up, one on either side of Auntie, making it perfectly clear they'd no intention of going anywhere but to see this Mr Potter.

If the bank manager was put out by having three visitors, he certainly didn't show it. He was on his feet and came over and shook hands with each of them.

'Welcome. I do apologise for the slight misunderstanding, madam. I'm so glad you came so promptly. Now, where shall I start?'

* * *

Auntie had gone into the bank the owner of a haberdasher's shop in Head Street and come out with more than a thousand pounds to her name. They were all stunned.

'I don't have to sell the shop, love; I've got more than enough to buy our cottage. What was it that man said: that he'd be happy to deal with you on a daily basis as long as I was still involved.'

'I can't believe it. Now it's a possibility, I'm not sure if I want to up sticks and start again in Colchester where I don't know anyone. We need to talk about this and I need to give it more thought.'

'Let's go to the Red Lion,' Auntie said as they stepped out onto the busy pavement. 'I could do with something a bit stronger than a cup of tea after that. Always easier to talk about difficult things with a nice glass of sherry in your hand.'

Nancy agreed and Dan nodded. 'They do a decent lunch, usually some sort of pie and mash. I know it's early, but they might have something ready.'

'I've got to catch the train at twelve thirty if I'm going to be at work by one,' Nancy said. 'It's just after eleven so plenty of time for an early lunch if they've got any. Maybe they can make us a sandwich if they haven't got anything hot.'

Why were they talking about food? This was a momentous occasion – she was being given the opportunity of a lifetime, so why was she hesitating?

* * *

The Red Lion wasn't busy and they were seated at a window table to encourage passersby to drop in for a bite or hot drink.

Pies were just coming from the oven, the waiter told them; their meal would be ready in ten minutes. Dan relaxed with the ladies, sipping his half of mild. Nancy had a shandy and her aunt had a large, sweet sherry.

Dan listened to them talking enthusiastically about the shop, about the possibility of keeping it, and he was conflicted. When he'd called for her first thing, he'd met the new bloke from London and had taken an immediate dislike to him. This Stoneleigh was, in his opinion, a smarmy bugger, all smiles and flashing eyes, overconfident and over interested in his Nancy. He'd certainly got his feet under the table sharpish at Harbour House.

'Dan, what do you think? You've been very quiet,' Nancy said.

'I'm enjoying my pie, love; I wasn't really listening. Tell me again.'

'I don't have to decide today, but I do in the next week or so. Should I leave Harbour House and run the shop for my aunt?'

He realised he'd missed several crucial points whilst he'd been lost in thought. 'You can't do it on your own, love; you need someone there with you.'

'Are you saying I'm not capable of doing it?' Her tone was sharp and he raised a hand, hoping she'd allow him to explain.

'Of course you can do it; you can do anything you turn your hand to. I was just thinking that if you're on your own, you'd have to shut the shop every time there was a call of nature, you had to go to the bank and that. You need an assistant; there must be a girl just out of school who'd be happy to work there.'

'You're right; if I do decide to take on this responsibility, there's going to be more to it than I realised.' Nancy turned to her aunt, who'd been listening closely. 'What do you think, Auntie?'

'Like what your Dan just said, we can't make rash decisions. I reckon after we've both had a look through the books, we'll know if my Uncle Mortimer was making ends meet. Another thing, love, there's plenty of stock in the shop but I don't reckon it'll be possible to get anything more. It's all going to the war effort now, nothing for domestic use.'

Dan chipped in. 'Then why don't you leave it as it is for now? Doesn't seem much point in opening it for a couple of months only to close it again. Nancy would have given up a good job for nothing.'

'I've got a better idea,' Nancy said. 'I could run it as a bed-and-breakfast or guesthouse; it's criminal to leave those rooms empty, don't you think?'

The matter was still undecided when they returned to Wivenhoe. Nancy dashed into work and he returned to the Falcon. He'd got the books from the shop under his arm as he'd offered to give them once-over first. He was collecting Nancy when she finished work at six o'clock and they were going to have a meal with her aunt and uncle in Anglesea Road.

Dan found himself a quiet corner in the bar, under a window so he'd plenty of light, and began to read the columns of figures. He wasn't a bookkeeper by any means, but he'd been good at numbers and understood immediately what he was reading.

Mr Mortimer had immaculate accounts; every penny he'd spent, where he'd spent it was recorded. Also, every penny he'd taken in over the counter was there. By the end of the afternoon, he'd looked at all the books and at the bills and that in the manila envelopes.

He'd plenty of information to share with them this evening. If it wasn't his Nancy involved then his suggestion would be to reopen the shop for as long as possible as it was making excellent profits. Then to close it again until the war was over and it could be restocked.

What he didn't want was for his future wife to be running a lodging house – he reckoned that would be even worse than her remaining at Harbour House with their new lodger. If that Stoneleigh tried anything on, he'd swing for him. Nancy was his; he wasn't going to lose her to some jumped-up posh bloke from the Admiralty. He was pretty sure this man wouldn't be looking for a wife but just a pretty girl to flirt with whilst he was there. He scowled as he put the books and envelopes under his arm and went to fetch Nancy.

18

Nancy was just coming out from the back gate as Dan walked around the corner of Alma Street. Although it was pitch dark, she'd recognise his outline anywhere, even in the dim shadow thrown from his torch.

'I'm here, Dan. I was going to walk round and meet you this time. I hope you're hungry. Auntie Ethel won't care that we had a big lunch; she'll expect us to eat enough to feed an army.'

He laughed and pulled her close with his free arm and kissed her. 'I'm back at work tomorrow and we often only get one meal a day, especially if there's a storm.'

'Do you want to tell me what you found in the books or are you going to wait until we get there?'

'No point in saying it twice, love, but I don't think they should sell, not now; it'll be worth a small fortune when this lot's over.'

She snuggled against him, not sure if this was what she wanted to hear. The Robys would be devastated if she handed in her notice – she didn't reckon her mum would be too happy either. Girls of eighteen only left home for two reasons: for work or to get wed.

Nancy knew she'd have to make up her mind before Dan returned to Wivenhoe the next time. She thought it'd be easier coming to this decision when he wasn't around as just being with him made her so happy that the very thought of upsetting him appalled her.

'You're quiet. That's not like you, Nancy; you're always full of chat.'

'I'm not sure I should tell you this, but that Mr Stoneleigh makes me nervous. He's not said or done anything but a girl can tell when someone's thinking things they shouldn't.'

As soon as she spoke, she regretted it. Dan stiffened and almost stopped walking. If she hadn't continued forward, she thought he might have turned back.

'I'll call in and speak to him before I go to the Falcon. I don't want my girl made to feel uncomfortable in her own home.'

'No, please don't. I'm probably imagining it as I'm just not used to men like him even looking in my direction. I'm an ordinary Wivenhoe girl, nothing special. Someone like him wouldn't be interested in me – not like that.'

This time, he did stop and brought her closer. 'You undersell yourself, love; you're a looker but even more important, you're as beautiful inside as out. Don't you think I spend most of my time worrying if you'll meet somebody better than me and I'll lose you to them?'

Nancy glowed inside. She'd never find anyone who loved her as much as he did. She was lucky to have him.

'Then you won't mind if I decide to move to Colchester? I know I'll be on my own apart from whoever I have helping out, but I still think I'll be better there. If my aunt and uncle have decided to keep the shop and let me run it for them then I'll suggest that I only take in ladies and children as paying guests, no men at all.'

He laughed, the sound booming down the gravel road. 'I'd never thought of that, but it's the perfect solution. I can come to Colchester as easy as I can to Wivenhoe and if you've got a gaggle of women under the same roof then I can stay there with no eyebrows being raised.'

'What about the cottage? I really love it and I'm so torn; I want to live there with you but also taking on that shop is my dream job.'

'Don't worry about our cottage, love; it won't be ready until next summer at the earliest. Do you still want to be married this year?'

'Sometimes I do, sometimes I don't. Let's not think about it until this business with the shop has been decided.'

They turned into Paget Road, made their way through the long, narrow garden and up to the back door of her aunt and uncle's cottage. She knocked on the door and opened it. After negotiating the blackout curtain, which involved a lot of giggling and silliness from both of them, they emerged into the light of the kitchen.

'There you are. Your uncle's been complaining this past ten minutes that I'm starving him,' Auntie Ethel said with a smiling nod in the direction of the middle room.

'I'll go and talk to him, Mrs Frost, and leave you girls to dish up. I'll only be in the way. I'll put the books somewhere in the other room, shall I?'

'Do that, Dan. We'll talk about it after supper.'

The middle room, supposedly a dining room, was also their living room as nobody used the front parlour unless the vicar or someone equally important was coming round.

* * *

Dan and her uncle were the best of friends by the end of the meal. Nancy was so full she was sure she wouldn't be able to eat any breakfast in the morning. As soon as the table was cleared, the books were put there and the discussion began.

Her aunt and uncle listened carefully, looked at the pages he showed them, exchanged glances occasionally, but neither gave any indication what they'd decided. Dan sat back and closed the last ledger.

'There, I think you've got the gist of it. I reckon a proper bookkeeper could tell you more, but I know enough about figures to be sure that what I've told you is pretty accurate.'

'I'll just make the tea, then we'll tell you what we think is the best thing to do,' Auntie said.

Nancy made a move to follow but her uncle shook his head. 'I've spoken to Mr Worsp today, and he's happy to sell me this cottage. Imagine me owning my own home – who'd have thought it? I never knew I was marrying an heiress all them years ago.'

'I wonder why the Mortimers didn't contact Auntie whilst they were still alive. They obviously have no children or other relatives or she wouldn't have got everything – it seems strange to me that they didn't want to have her in their lives.'

'Don't matter to me; if she'd known, she'd never have looked in my direction. I'm that pleased that if I go sudden, and the doc says that could happen, then she's taken care of.'

'I can't imagine a person ignoring the rest of the family like that. I suppose him having fallen out with Nana was why he was never mentioned and my mum wasn't included in the will.'

The rattle of teacups stopped the conversation. Auntie didn't like to talk about the possibility that Uncle Stan might die young. They were only in their fifties and should have another twenty happy years together, God willing.

'We've decided that if you really want to give it a go, Nancy love, then you can. No rush, mind you, we need to be clear how this will work,' Auntie said. 'I've got a lovely Singer treadle I don't use; you can take that with you. I reckon you'd do well offering alterations and such.'

'That's a good idea. I should have thought of that myself. I can do that in the evenings after the shop's shut.'

Uncle Stan beamed. 'That would be your own money, not a part of the shop. You could put a nice bit away for your wedding next year.'

'There's no rush, is there, as the place has been empty since last August; another few weeks won't matter,' Nancy said.

Dan shook his head. 'Don't leave it too long, Mrs Frost; the best time for selling haberdashery is in the spring and summer.'

Nancy stared at him. 'How can you know that, Dan? I bet you've never bought even a yard of elastic yourself.'

This made them laugh. No man in his right mind would go in a shop like this and if they did, it wouldn't be to buy elastic as that was mainly used for holding up a pair of knickers.

'I've just spent the afternoon studying those ledgers. It shows the most money taken is in spring and summer.'

* * *

They left at ten and walked back hand in hand, not talking much. Nancy was thinking about how things had changed for them. She was to visit the shop again and make a list of what she needed in the living quarters for herself and for potential house guests. Auntie Ethel would accompany her and was going to speak to the solicitors and also the bank manager again.

This would be the easy part; the hard part was going to be handing in her notice next month.

They stopped in the small garden at the back of Harbour House.

'I'm going to try and find someone to replace me, Dan, then I'll not feel so bad. I can think of a couple of girls who work at the factory who might be thrilled to have a job like mine.'

'That's a good idea, love. I'd also look for a youngster to live in with you; there must be several girls just about to leave school that would be happy to move.'

'Yes, having someone I already know would be ideal.'

They kissed and then he strode off, leaving her to go in alone. She loved him and whatever he believed, it wasn't going to be as easy for him to come to Colchester as it was for him to come to Wivenhoe. Was following her dream going to eventually cause them to part company?

Leaving her lovely job and the children she'd come to love was going to be so hard. She hoped her new life was going to be worth the loss of what she already had.

* * *

Emily wasn't sure if she liked the man who'd moved into the spare bedroom three weeks ago. He was always smiling and pleasant and got on very well with Mrs Bates and with her parents. Nancy was definitely not keen, and the boys seemed to be avoiding him too. She wished Daddy didn't need someone to help him with his important work for the Admiralty. She wasn't sure why Mr Stoneleigh didn't quite fit in; she thought perhaps it was because his mouth smiled a lot, but his eyes didn't.

She was walking with George and Sammy from St Botolph's

station to where they caught the bus on the Thursday before they broke up for the Easter holidays when George stopped.

'Emily, I think Nancy's leaving at the end of the month. I overheard our mummy and daddy talking about it last night when I went down to the loo.'

'Are you sure? I hope you're wrong; she's like a big sister to us and I know that Mrs Bates will be upset. Is she marrying Dan?' She blinked unwanted tears away. Nancy was her best friend: someone she could talk to when Mummy was too busy and Daddy was at work. Harbour House just wouldn't be as nice with Nancy gone.

'I didn't hear that bit; I just heard them say that they were sorry she was going but that Annie was a good replacement.'

'I've never heard of her; why didn't they tell us? More to the point, why hasn't Nancy said something? I thought she loved living with us,' Emily said sadly. 'It's 21 March today, so that means she'll be gone in ten days. That's awful.'

Sammy tugged at her sleeve. 'We've got to go; the bus has just come in.'

'Right, I'll wait for you this afternoon. We've got a lot to talk about.'

* * *

Emily got her first order mark for not paying sufficient attention in her geography lesson and was annoyed with herself. She was in Plantagenet House and order marks were added up and then balanced against the credits. The house that had the biggest credit balance was given an extra hour of recreation time.

At least she'd won ten credits this term so they still had nine to add to their balance. Some of the older girls from North Hill, the prefects and house captains and so on, attended the end-of-term meeting and she'd been hoping to get a certificate for having done so well.

At lunchtime, it was drizzling so they were allowed to have an indoor break and with the five other scholarship girls in her class, Emily headed for their own special corner to talk about their plans for the holiday. Tomorrow was Good Friday, then they had the following two weeks off and went back to school in the middle of April.

She'd been so looking forward to the holiday but now she knew Nancy was leaving, the time off no longer seemed important.

'You look really fed up, Emily,' Portia said as they settled in the assembly hall.

Emily told them why and only Cynthia was really sympathetic as the others didn't have any sort of staff as they were scholarship girls.

'Oh, you poor thing, your live-in maid is leaving and has been replaced by someone else,' Marianne said sarcastically, and the others sniggered.

'She's not a maid, I've told you that before; she's a friend and like part of the family.'

'Well, she's obviously neither of those things, Emily, or she wouldn't be leaving without having spoken to you.' Marianne rudely turned her back and all of the other girls except Cynthia did the same.

'I'm going to the form room; it's a bit chilly here,' Emily said and stood up; to her relief, Cynthia did the same.

Although she'd never mentioned that her brothers had transferred to the Royal Grammar School, she was quite sure someone must have seen her walking with the boys in their distinctive purple blazers. Since then, the others had been less friendly and Cynthia, who came from a similar background to her, was now her only real friend.

'Don't worry about them; they are just jealous because we're not only more intelligent than them but we're also much better off,' Cynthia said and slipped her arm through Emily's.

'It worries me that I've got to remain here for years and years and I can't see that I'm ever going to really be accepted or enjoy being here. It would have been so much easier if my daddy had just paid the fees like he did at my previous school.'

'I know, but my papa said he'd no intention of paying if he didn't have to. My older brothers are both away at Eton and that's very expensive. We might be well off, but I don't think there's any spare money to send me anywhere like that.'

'Golly, I didn't know that. So, during term time, you're an only child; that must be good having your parents to yourself. I have to share mine with three others. That's why Nancy has become so important to me.'

The form room was where the fee-paying girls congregated which was why Emily and her friends rarely went there when it was wet break. Nowadays, she wasn't intimidated by them. The six scholarship girls were always top in every test, contributed the most credits to their houses, and this made them very popular with the older pupils.

There was a narrow wooden seat that ran under the windows from one end of the classroom to the other and at the moment, it was empty. The dozen girls occupying the room had divided into two groups: one was playing some sort of card game and the other doing cats' cradle.

This was something Emily enjoyed. She often entertained the boys on the train ride home by changing from one complicated arrangement to another.

'Shall we do that? I've got my string in my pocket.' Cats' cradle was a simple game; all it needed was two feet of string knotted into a loop. It required two players, one to hold the cradle and the other to lift it off into a different arrangement. She and Cynthia had become experts as they spent more time together than with the others.

When Marianne returned a few minutes before the bell, they were the ones excluded as everybody was gathered around watching Emily and Cynthia work their magic with their string loop.

* * *

The house meetings took place on the last afternoon of every term and Plantagenet was the winner by six points – Emily glowed with pride, knowing that without her effort, they wouldn't have won. She was called up to receive the much-coveted certificate for being the best in her house. After all the applause and congratulations, she thought that maybe being at the school wasn't quite as bad as she'd thought.

* * *

Dan had agreed to forego his time off and work continuously until Easter. The reason he'd done this wasn't for the extra money but so he could help Nancy move to Colchester at the end of the month.

He was astonished at how resilient Percy was for an old bloke; barge masters seemed tougher than fishermen. The fishing fleet was rarely away more than a couple of nights, whereas the Thames barges could be away from home for weeks. The barges stayed put until they had work before moving on – whether it was to their home berth or somewhere miles away.

Most seamen tried to be at home at Easter and Christmas even if they weren't there any other time. The *Lady Beth* would be docked in Brightlingsea for the week he'd spend in Colchester. The first three days of his break would be Good Friday, Easter Saturday and Easter Sunday and there'd be little work to be had during this religious time. Their next cargo was from the Hythe port, Colchester, where they'd be collecting a load of bricks and taking them to Great Yarmouth.

'Right, son, I'll see you on the twenty-eighth; tell yer young lady you'll be gone three weeks again,' Percy told Dan as the collected his ditty bag from the cabin in the fo'c'sle.

'I don't suppose I'll get a week off again, but it'd be good if I did.'

The skipper grinned. 'That nosy naval bloke didn't take kindly to us buggering off last month and we've got no choice but to work full time for the Admiralty after this Great Yarmouth job.'

'Do we still get paid?'

'I should bleeding well think so. Better pay, in fact, but I'm not a man to be at anyone's beck and call. I don't take kindly to being given orders; I like to make me own mind up.'

Dan frowned. This wasn't good news at all. 'Do you know why they want us so urgently? Will we be working for the navy permanently or can we go back to our own trade?'

Percy shrugged. 'God knows, I certainly don't, and I don't reckon the Admiralty do either.'

'Not much we can do about it. We could be in France waiting for the Germans to arrive. I don't envy those poor buggers; I'd rather be afloat than on the land,' Dan said as he stepped off onto the hard. 'See you in a week, Percy. Ta for everything.'

* * *

Dan didn't get off the train at Wivenhoe but continued to Colchester. The last time he'd seen Nancy, she'd talked of nothing but her new job – how excited she was, how lucky she was – until he was sick of hearing about it. She'd had her birthday whilst he was away so was now eighteen.

She'd stopped mentioning the possibility of getting married this year, or about the cottage, about how this was going to put a strain on their relationship – the only good thing about her change of circumstances was that she wouldn't be under the same roof as the smarmy lodger. If it hadn't been for this bloke moving into Harbour House, he'd not have wanted her to give up her good job and run the shop for her auntie.

Nancy wouldn't be at the shop until Monday when she moved in. The girl, Daphne, a cousin of hers, could be there during the day to help sort things out but he'd be on his own at night. He would save a pretty penny because he didn't have to pay for his lodgings whilst he was in Colchester.

He'd not spoken to Nancy for over three weeks: the longest they'd been without seeing each other. He'd sent her three postcards, one for her birthday, but because he didn't have a permanent address when he was afloat, there'd been no point in her replying.

Monday couldn't come soon enough for him.

19

Nancy was already regretting her decision to leave Harbour House. It had become her home in the past few months, she loved her spacious attic room and being treated as one of the family by her employers.

The young woman she'd found to replace her was somebody she'd worked with at the sewing factory – two years older than her – but Nancy believed she'd fit in well at Harbour House.

Annie Thomas was quiet, another scholarship girl who'd not been able to take up her place and had been recently widowed when her husband had been killed at work a few months ago. She'd been desperate to get away from her in-laws who didn't like her and she'd nowhere else to go. Nancy liked her, was sorry for her, but couldn't help feeling a bit put out that the children and the Robys were so pleased with her replacement that they seemed almost eager for Nancy to leave.

'Mum, I know I'm not supposed to go until Monday, but I might as well leave today. I don't suppose the regular trains will run tomorrow as it's Good Friday. Therefore, if I want to leave here, it has to be today or Saturday.'

'Annie's that keen to move in, Nancy love, I think you'd be doing her a favour. Since her Norm died, she's wanted to get away but there's just no rooms to rent since the evacuees came last year.'

'I'm going to miss the children but they've promised to come and visit me after school once a week. Mrs Roby's happy for them to do so. I'll give them a bit of tea and then get Daphne to walk them to the train.'

'That's the only reason they've not been too miserable about you leaving.'

Nancy smiled. 'Oh, I thought they didn't really care. I feel so much better now. I'm not sure I can do this; I'm going to be ever so lonely until I've got some lodgers. It's going to be scary being alone in such a big house, in a strange place on my own.'

'You won't be on your own, love; Daphne will be living in. Don't forget that your dad and I are coming to see you next Saturday and bringing the boys, you'll have your Dan there for a few days, and your Aunt Ethel will be coming every week to do the banking and all that. You'll be too busy to miss us much.'

Mum dabbed her eyes on the end of her apron and they hugged.

'I love you, Mum. I do hope I haven't made a dreadful mistake.'

'Go on with you. We're both that proud of you. Who'd have thought that a daughter of mine would be doing something like this and her just eighteen years of age?'

'I need to tell Mrs Roby that I'm going to leave this morning. I don't have much to take as most of it went with the carter last week.'

'Run along then, and it's probably best that you don't have to say goodbye to the children again. No need to upset them.'

Nancy thanked Mrs Roby for everything she'd done for her and they shook hands.

'Thank you, Nancy, we're so sorry to see you go but are happy that you've got such a wonderful opportunity. Thank you so much for finding Annie to replace you. You don't have to worry that the children will be too upset as you'll be seeing them every week during term time.'

There was something that Emily had mentioned to her just last night and Nancy knew she had to tell Mrs Roby before she left. It might be several weeks before the girl felt able to confide in Annie the way she did with her.

'Mrs Roby, I think Emily is about to start her monthlies. She asked me why she was getting tummy aches, why her top was getting bigger. I explained to her what was happening, but it's not really my place, is it?'

'Goodness, thank you so much for telling me. I'll speak to her tonight. She'd started to come to me with her worries and problems but then the baby came, and as she's been talking to you about these personal things, I didn't interfere.'

'I wouldn't have said anything, Mrs Roby, but she won't want to talk to Annie in the same way at first.'

Nancy smiled, raised a hand in farewell, grabbed her suitcase and left through the front door. Mum had asked Betty to pop down to the sewing factory and tell Annie that she could move in immediately. She wouldn't have to give any notice as she was on piecework.

Nancy was blinking back tears as she clambered onto the

train a few minutes later. Her two close friends had disappeared into the clutches of the ATS, and she hadn't heard from them again. She hadn't wanted a big fuss made about her departure. However, the fact that there'd been no one at the station to wish her well, no invitations for a final drink from anyone at the sewing factory where she'd worked for over three years, made her realise that her ties to Wivenhoe weren't as strong as she'd thought.

She'd caught the Clacton train, the one that went into St Botolph's and then on to the main Colchester station for passengers to connect with a train to London. This one had the individual compartments and narrow corridor all along the carriage. She went into the first one she passed and was just settling into a window seat when she looked up to see Dan standing in front of her. Instead of looking delighted, he looked worried.

'Nancy love, are you moving in today? Had you forgotten I'm going to be there?'

She stared at him blankly then realised. 'Sit down, love; you're too tall to be looming over me.' She waited until he was beside her, his ditty bag between his legs, before speaking again. They'd attracted more than enough attention already.

'I had forgotten but it doesn't matter. You can find a room somewhere; there are plenty of hotels and guest houses in Colchester.'

'That's the thing: I've not budgeted for paying lodgings; I don't have enough cash on me.'

'Well, you can't stay with me until Daphne moves in on Monday.' She should have stopped there as he already looked cross. 'There's a post office a few doors down; it'll still be open when we get there so you can draw some out, can't you?'

His lips tightened and his knuckles were white. Didn't he

have anything in the post office; had he left his book on the barge for some reason?

'Don't worry, Dan, I can give you what you need. Auntie Edith has already arranged for me to collect a float from the bank tomorrow and she's giving me a hundred pounds from her inheritance so I can buy anything I need for myself.'

To her surprise, he didn't answer but stood up and, with his bag under one arm, walked away.

The train was rocking and shuddering but not as much as she was. She'd not seen him for weeks, had been counting the hours until they could be together and now she'd upset him and didn't know why.

She sniffed and rummaged in her handbag for her hanky. Everything was going wrong and it was her fault. She should have kept to her original plan and not moved until Monday when Daphne would be moving in with her.

She sighed and sat up to find, to her embarrassment, that a young army officer was sitting opposite. She'd not noticed him when she'd gone in.

The officer was smiling in a patronising sort of way.

'It was offering to pay for him that upset him, ma'am. We men are overly sensitive about such things. We like to consider ourselves to be in charge, especially financially.'

'I'm not the queen, sir, so don't address me as ma'am. And what I said to my fiancé is absolutely none of your business.' Nancy was on her feet as she spoke and exited the compartment, fizzing with fury. Not at Dan, but at the man who thought he'd the right to offer an opinion. He was right, she'd upset Dan. Their conversation shouldn't have been conducted in front of that patronising officer either.

* * *

Dan regretted stomping off like a child but didn't have the guts to go back and apologise. He tucked himself around the corner by the exit doors, feeling stupid. Then Nancy appeared and stepped into his arms.

'I'm so sorry, Dan, I don't know what I was thinking. Of course you can stay at the shop; it doesn't matter if it's going to upset people.'

'I'm sorry too, stupid pride. I can't get used to the fact that you're now a woman of means.'

She didn't answer but stood on tiptoes and kissed him. When eventually they recovered their breath, she told him what had happened in the compartment.

'I'm proud of you, love; you told him where to get off and no mistake. I expect you're wondering what I'm doing on this train – I went to the post office and paid in my share of the profits of my last trip on the *Lady Beth*, and then came back over the bridge just as the train steamed in. I couldn't believe my eyes when I saw you getting on.'

She rested her face against his coat and he held her close. When they were like this, he'd no doubts about their future together, but when they were apart, it was easy to imagine things going wrong.

'I've still not looked in the attics, Dan. I'm hoping there might be a few sticks of furniture up there I can use for the empty bedrooms. I can't let them out as they are. There's a second-hand shop in Magdalen Street and I thought to have a look there on Saturday. I'm glad you're going to be coming with me as I'll get a better deal than I would if I went on my own.'

'When's Daphne starting?'

'Not until next week. We've got the place to ourselves until then.' She looked up at him, her expression serious. 'I'm trusting you, Dan Brooks, not to take advantage of the situation. When I walk down the aisle on my father's arm next year wearing a white gown, I want it to mean something.'

'I'll respect your wishes, love; no man wants to wait but you're worth waiting for.'

She nodded and her smile said it all. 'Thank you. You'll have to sleep in what will be Daphne's room. I've managed to get together enough bedding so the sheets you use won't have to be washed and dried before she comes.'

The train lurched to a stop at Hythe station where a dozen or more passengers got on and almost as many got off. There were factories down that end of town as well as the bustling port. Plenty of work for those that wanted it as a lot of the casual labour had already been conscripted into the forces.

When they got off the train, Dan insisted on carrying her suitcase as well as his own bag and for once, she didn't argue. He tossed his ditty bag over his shoulder and held her suitcase on the same side. This meant he still had his left arm to put around her waist.

'Have you got grub in for the weekend, Nancy? I don't reckon there'll be any shops open tomorrow.'

'Of course I haven't. I thought you'd get what you needed from the grocers over the road.'

'There's a fishmongers and greengrocers near the solicitors, and a couple of bakers over the road as well; I was intending going to them.'

'I'd have thought you'd had enough fish as you spend so much of your time at sea.'

He grinned. 'We live mainly on pasties, bread and dripping, that sort of thing. Don't reckon I've had a morsel of fish on board since I started with Percy.'

'Did you eat fish when you were fishing?'

He chuckled. 'You bet, nothing like a couple of fresh mackerel done on a skewer over the fire, washed down with a mug of tea and a couple of slices of bread.'

'Sounds delicious. Mr Roby sometimes makes sardines and mackerel which he does under the grill. There isn't a modern gas cooker in my new home but I'm used to cooking on a range.'

She seemed oblivious to the attention they were attracting as they walked through Colchester. Dan was a good-looking bloke, he saw himself every morning in the mirror when he shaved, but he was pretty sure it was Nancy they were looking at. In the past few months, she'd blossomed, was even more beautiful than when he'd first fallen in love with her.

'Imagine how good looking our children will be,' he blurted out and she looked up at him, her eyes wide.

'Babies? I don't want any of those until we're married, and then not until after the war's ended.'

'Crikey, that might not be for years. It's not got started yet and the Germans have got a bigger air force than us, better tanks and more submarines.'

She pursed her lips and looked exactly like her mother. 'You mustn't say things like that; you'll get arrested for being subversive. I read about it in Dad's paper. We beat the Germans before, and we'll do it again.'

'Of course we will, goes without saying; I was just trying to point out that it's going to take a long time.'

She laughed, she had a lovely laugh, and this made more heads turn. 'Don't worry, you won't have to live like a monk for that long. My mum told me that there's no need to have a baby every year if you don't want to.'

They were now approaching Head Street; better to continue this when they were inside. He wasn't sure if he was impressed that his girl had knowledge like this or shocked that she'd looked into it. Men worked and women had babies – that's how things were.

He'd no intention of remaining in Colchester once they were married, but if she didn't fall pregnant then it might be difficult to persuade her to come to Brightlingsea. He knew about the things men used to stop babies but he wasn't going to use one of them. It wasn't natural, in his opinion.

Nancy was only eighteen but she acted as if she was lot older than him and he was twenty-one next January. He followed her down the narrow passageway that led to the back of the shop and for the first time almost wished he'd never fallen in love with her. There were lots of other girls as pretty as her who'd have jumped at the chance of being married to him, who wouldn't want to wear the trousers.

Being married to her would mean that he was always second place in the relationship – he wasn't as clever as her, didn't have her drive to succeed, and without a clutch of kiddies at her ankles, he'd have no control over the situation.

Emily hadn't felt well on the way to school and had been in the sick bay on the first floor curled up with a hot water bottle until lunchtime. Matron had given her an aspirin with a glass of water and told her to speak to Mummy as soon as she got home.

'I think it's my monthlies coming, Matron. I know all about them.'

'The correct term, Emily, is menstruation. Do you have the necessary sanitary protection on?'

'I'm not exactly sure what that is, Matron.'

The sick bay was a daybed behind a screen in the corner of an open space and the matron's room led from it.

'Come with me, my dear. I'll show you what you need and how to use it.'

* * *

Emily found wearing the sanitary belt and pad awkward and uncomfortable but she was relieved that there'd be no embarrassing accidents now. Nancy hadn't told her about these but she'd told her everything else.

She felt very grown-up, a woman almost, and couldn't wait to tell Nancy that she was now menstruating. The idea that she'd have to put up with this unpleasant and painful business every month until she was old, unless she was having a baby, didn't please her, though.

She rejoined her classmates at lunchtime and then headed up to the art room after they'd eaten. Cynthia was the only one she'd told and her friend wanted every detail. 'How ghastly – I wish I'd been born a boy. They don't have to go through all this.'

'But they have to go to war, do the dangerous things, and women don't,' Emily said.

'My Aunt Charlotte died from having a baby a few years ago; you can't get much more dangerous than that.'

Emily nodded. 'I don't think I'll have any children. I want to go to university and be a career woman. There aren't any married women teaching us, are there? They seem happy enough.'

'Miss Phillips said her fiancé was killed in the last war; I think millions of young men died which is why there are so many spinsters. Do you think that's going to happen this time?'

'Golly, I hope not. I'm so glad my brothers are younger than me; even if the war goes on for years like the last one did, they won't be old enough to fight. My daddy's in a reserved occupation. What does yours do? You never told me.'

'I don't exactly know; it's something in the city. He's too old to be called up. I've got two brothers at Eton, and two older sisters who are both married with children. I think I was a bit of an unexpected arrival as Anthony's ten years older than me.'

'I'm ten years older than Grace – it's strange to think that by the time she's my age, I'll have left home.'

'That's if your parents let you go to university. I won't be going; my father doesn't approve of educating women. If I want to leave home, I'll have to marry someone.'

'You don't have to marry unless you want to; nobody can force you to say yes.'

They'd now reached the attic art rooms and the conversation ended. There were some older girls there but they were all nice enough and didn't object to having a couple of lower fourths in with them.

* * *

Emily was disappointed that Nancy had left so unexpectedly.

'You can go and visit her next week. Annie can accompany you and the boys this time but after that, you'll know where it is and will be able to get there safely after school. An occasional visit, Nancy won't want to be bothered with you too often as she's got a business to run.' Mummy was about to take the baby upstairs to change her. 'I need to talk to you, Emily, will you come with me now?'

The last thing Emily wanted to do was watch the baby being fed or changed. Despite the fact that the infant now smiled, waved her arms around and was a bit more interesting, she still didn't want to spend time with her.

'I've got something to tell you; I'll tell you now before you go. I started my monthlies today. Matron gave me a sanitary belt and towel. Do you have some I can use, or do I have to go to the chemist and buy them?'

'That's exactly what I was going to speak to you about. It seems that, as is often the case, I'm too late. When you go into Colchester next week, Annie is going to take you to buy the new underwear that you need whilst the boys stay with Nancy.'

'I don't know Annie; I don't want to go with her. If Nancy can't come then I'll go on my own. If I'm old enough to have a baby then I'm quite sure I'm old enough to buy myself a brassiere.'

This wasn't very polite but her mummy looked more upset than cross. 'My dear, you have to get measured; you can't just walk in and buy something like that.'

Emily shuddered. 'I don't want to do that; I'll ask Nancy to measure me before I go then I won't have to undress in the shop.'

'That's a good idea. I'll put what you need in your commode. I hope Nancy told you that you can't flush the towels; you have to wrap them in newspaper and put them in the rubbish.'

This was something else that Nancy hadn't told her. Emily's eyes filled. Being a little girl had been so much easier than growing up like this.

20

Nancy gave Dan ten shillings and sent him out with her ration book to register her with the general stores on the other side of the road. Mrs Roby had kindly donated a wooden box of assorted groceries from the still well-stocked larder at Harbour House.

This meant they had the basics, including half a dozen cracked eggs that would have to be used soon or they'd go off. Mum had made a nice cake and this was what she put on the table. What they needed was bread, milk and fresh veg if there was any to be had and a nice piece of fish. Everybody ate fish on a Friday and especially tomorrow, which would be Good Friday.

She was so excited and busy putting things away that it didn't occur to her until too late that after what had happened on the train, asking him to do the shopping, which was a woman's work really, might not have been the best idea. Especially as he'd gone out with the enamel-lidded milk jug in his pocket – sometimes, they had bottles of milk for sale but often the customer had to bring their own jug.

In pride of place in the sitting room on the first floor was the sewing machine that her aunt had given her. She'd already made blackout curtains for the rooms they'd be using and was just waiting for Dan to hang them up for her. Dad had given her a toolbox with a hammer, a selection of nails and screws, and a few other odds and ends that she wasn't quite sure what to do with.

The kettle was singing on the range, the table in the kitchen laid and ready, all she needed was for him to return. It was quiet at the rear of the shop; what she really wanted was a wireless to listen to in the evening but that wasn't going to happen. Instead, she'd have the sound of her treadle sewing machine to keep her company whilst she worked.

The back gate banged and Dan came in grinning. 'Sorry I've been so long, love; I had to wait to get your name down before I could buy what I wanted. I got to talk to several of your neighbours and they seem a decent lot. Look what I managed to get for us.'

He plonked the full jug on the dresser proudly and then began to delve into his pockets. 'A smashing piece of cod and a pint of prawns; I got a good rate because I'm a seaman. Then there's spuds, cabbage, carrots and, wait for it, a whole onion!'

'You've done a lot better than I would have done. I suppose you charmed all this out of a wide-eyed shop girl,' she said with a smile.

'That's not all, love; I've also got a freshly baked loaf and some beef dripping.'

'Shall we toast a couple of slices and have it with the dripping? I'll make the tea and get the salt to go with it. Can you make toast?'

He nodded solemnly. 'I can; whether I will depends if you kiss me or not.'

She giggled as they kissed passionately and for a moment,

she was swept away by the occasion. Fortunately, Dan broke the embrace and gently pushed her towards the pantry.

His voice was gruff when he spoke. 'Fetch the salt, love; I'll get the toast on the go.'

Later, whilst she was washing up the dirty dishes, Dan collected the blackout curtains and nailed them up. They should have gone on a curtain rod but needs must. She'd asked him to put a hook on each side of the windows so she could tie them back during the day. Not ideal, but it would work until something better could be arranged.

He was upstairs banging away when she noticed that his bag was still leaning against the kitchen wall. Poor man, she hadn't even given him the chance to unpack before sending him out on errands. She mustn't let the fact that she was now in charge not only of her own life, but also of the shop, and of Daphne when she came to join them next week, go to her head.

The kitchen was spotless, everything put away, the food stored in the pantry on the slate shelf where it would keep fresh for longer. Nancy picked up the ditty bag, surprised at how heavy it was, and with it held in front of her, she negotiated the stairs to the first floor.

'Here you are, Dan: I've brought up your bag. I'll put it in your room. It's the one with the single bed.'

He'd removed his overcoat and his thick navy jumper and was working in rolled-up shirtsleeves. His arms were heavily muscled, tanned up to the elbows, but his upper arms were white. It made her wonder about what he might look without his clothes and that was a dangerous thing to think.

He'd stopped and his smile made her tingle all over. 'That's hardly fair, love. I'm twice your size; shouldn't I have the double bed? My feet will hang out of the end of that little one.'

'I'm sure you'll manage. You sleep on tiny wooden bunk on

that barge and Daphne's bed is much bigger than that. Stop complaining and get on with your work.'

She tossed her head and she heard him laughing as she left him in the sitting room where he'd almost finished attaching the second curtain to the big window that looked over the street.

There was a very small landing from which the three doors led. The single bedroom was closest to the stairs and the main room to the adjoining property. If it was going to be difficult for her sleeping soundly knowing he was just the other side of the thin wall then it would be even harder for him. Nancy didn't know a lot about men, but she did know from listening to her friends who were far more experienced that men had more urges in that direction than women and often found it hard to control them.

She poked her head into the sitting room, not daring to go in after the way he'd looked at her earlier. 'I'm going to have a good look in the attics. I don't think there's any electricity up there so I need to do it before it gets dark.'

'Okay. It'll take me another hour to finish these. If you're not back by then, I'll send a search party.'

* * *

The attics proved to be even more exciting than the ones at Harbour House. Really, she should have left Auntie Ethel to open the trunks as everything inside them belonged to her. But once she'd started looking, she couldn't stop.

There were three trunks full of books, newspapers and magazines and she couldn't wait to examine them more carefully. In another, there was a strange selection of men's garments that she thought must be at least fifty years old. What she found really surprising was there was no sign of moths and the material was good quality. The things might be old-fashioned but she could already imagine them altered to fit Dan. He would be very smart when she'd finished doing that.

At the back of the first attic there were two bookshelves, empty, half a dozen kitchen chairs that just needed a good scrub, and a pile of musty bedlinen. These would soon be usable once they'd been laundered and hung out in the sunshine.

She was just about to explore the second attic when Dan arrived. 'Crikey, this is a real treasure trove. No wonder you've been up here banging about for so long.'

'I can't go down until I've looked in the other one and I'm glad you're here. The door's stuck and I need you to put your shoulder to it.'

He ruffled her hair as he walked past. 'Have you tried pulling it rather than pushing it?'

'Of course I have, I'm not a nincompoop. It's stuck fast. It doesn't have a lock so I'm wondering if it's been nailed shut for some reason.'

* * *

Dan was about to laugh at Nancy's suggestion but when he examined the door more closely, he saw she was right. He could think of only one reason anyone would nail the door shut and that was because there was something in there they didn't want anyone else to see.

'I need my hammer to pull out these nails. Shall we leave it until tomorrow morning? It's beginning to get dark and I'm parched after all the hard work hanging up your curtains.'

'That's a good idea. I need to tidy up, wash the cobwebs and grime from my face and hands and then I'll make tea. I thought we could have an omelette.'

'Right, I've left the curtains drawn. We don't want to be getting a fine for showing a light the first night here.'

'Don't be long; your meal will be on the table in half an hour.'

He waited until she was all the way down to the kitchen before pulling out the hammer from his back pocket. He wanted to open this door when she wasn't there, just in case there was something unpleasant inside.

He hooked the nails out easily, then took a deep breath and opened the door, half-expecting to see a couple of skeletons as he couldn't think of any other reason someone would have nailed the door shut.

His mouth dropped open. No human bodies, but what was in there was almost as horrific. The previous owner of this house had been an amateur taxidermist. There were dismembered animals lying on a bench, fortunately so old they no longer stank, and at least a dozen grotesque attempts at reassembling cats, dogs and birds.

It might not be illegal to do this but it was certainly bizarre. Someone had worked by oil lamp, no power up here in the attics, but there was a large skylight which let in more than enough light for whoever had been attempting to stuff an animal.

He couldn't shine his torch on the finished animals, wasn't sure he wanted to, as the light would have broken the blackout rules. He didn't know what Nancy would make of this – most girls would run screaming but he thought his girl was more likely to laugh.

After pulling the door shut behind him, he headed for the kitchen, rolling his sleeves as he did so. He'd left his heavy sweater in the sitting room and collected it on the way past. The nights were dark and cold still; couldn't really expect anything else in March.

'I heard you banging about in the attic, Dan; what did you find?' Nancy didn't seem particularly upset that he'd gone ahead and investigated without her.

'Stuffed animals and I'm not talking about teddies or rabbits.'

To his surprise, she nodded. 'Of course, how silly of me. I did read something about that in one of the papers from the solicitors but had forgotten. It was Mrs Mortimer's hobby. Are they very bad?'

He grinned. 'Before this evening, I'd only ever seen taxidermy in a museum under a glass cover – the ones upstairs are barely recognisable, but I think Mrs Mortimer was trying to recreate domestic pets. Perhaps they were hers; did it say that in the papers?'

'No, it just said that Auntie Ethel could dispose of the animals in any way she wanted. I thought they were probably in one of the outhouses we haven't looked in.'

'I'll not be a minute. Something smells good. I've not had an omelette for years.'

He pumped enough water into the basin to dip his face and wash his hands. Nancy had been living in the lap of luxury for the past few months and he wondered if she was going to adjust to this new life as easily as she thought.

There was enough room for six or seven chairs around this table but he hoped there wouldn't be as many as that.

Over the meal, he voiced his concerns. 'If you take in lodgers, Nancy love, how are you going to find time to cook for them? Is Daphne going to do the laundry and that?'

'I've not really had time to think about the next step; I'm

going to concentrate on making a success of the shop before I consider adding to my worries by having strangers living under this roof.'

'What about getting a dog? I bet I could find you a stray, an animal that's desperate for a home and will guard the place for you in return.'

She closed her eyes and he smiled. She always did that when she was thinking seriously.

'I think that's a good idea; it's not far to the river and there's plenty of countryside down there to walk him. It needs to be a him; I don't want any puppies.'

'I think a lot of people have had their dogs put down; I think I saw a leaflet suggesting that there wasn't going to be enough food to spare to feed domestic pets. Cats can look after themselves; it would be harder for a dog.'

'I don't remember having seen any strays skulking in the streets, nosing around rubbish bins and so on, on my visits here. Maybe it's only in the big cities people have got rid of their dogs.'

* * *

It was Good Friday when Dan woke up and he wondered if Nancy would want to go to church. There was one at the top of North Hill. He'd not got anything smart to wear but he supposed God wouldn't mind as long as you came.

He knocked on the dividing wall between their bedrooms. 'Morning, love, are we going to church?'

'I am; if I want to get to know my neighbours then the best place to do it is the church. I'm ready to leave now; I don't expect you to come with me. St Peter's is a very old building.'

He stepped out into the tiny hall at the same time as she did.

'I'm not sure what the age of the church has to do with me not coming with you.'

She laughed. 'Nothing at all, it was just an observation. We both know you really shouldn't be staying here until Daphne comes next week. If I turn up with you, it'll set tongues wagging. Although I suppose they already are; someone will have noticed you coming in here with the shopping yesterday. I don't want to rub people's noses in it.'

'Fair enough. I'm not a God botherer myself, so I'm happy to stay here. I'll start bringing down the furniture we found, shall I?'

'That would be good, thank you. It's a communion service; there won't be any sermon or hymns so I shouldn't be that long.'

'You look just the ticket, love, very smart. That hat suits you; I don't think I've seen you wearing it before.'

'I haven't had the opportunity. Mrs Roby gave it to me.' Her smile slipped and she tried to hide her tears. 'I'm already beginning to think I've made a dreadful mistake coming here; I really miss the children and my family. I've burnt my boat so I can't go back as Annie has my job now. I've just got to make it work.'

Dan was tempted to tell her that she didn't have to worry about making anything work, she could marry him and then he'd take care of her, but he didn't, knowing it wasn't the time.

'You can do anything you want to, love; you'll make a roaring success of this.'

She didn't answer, just nodded and hurried out of the back door. They'd have breakfast when she got back but he made himself a pot of tea before heading to the attics to bring down the chairs and such that they'd found.

He was in the backyard scrubbing down the final chair when he heard her laughing, talking to somebody in the passageway that ran behind the houses. She certainly wasn't upset now from the sound of it. He straightened and turned to face the gate, hoping he might see who it was.

It opened and she stepped in, her cheeks flushed, her eyes sparkling – something had changed. This wasn't the same sad girl who'd left here little more than an hour ago.

* * *

Nancy had enjoyed the service, even though on Good Friday, it was a very solemn occasion. The congregation filed out and two children about the same age as Emily and George pushed in front of her and almost sent her flying.

'Jean, Ronnie, come back here. You wait till I get hold of you; you'll not sit down for a week,' a woman, obviously their mum, screeched and then did exactly the same as her children. If Nancy hadn't been alert and able to step aside this time she'd definitely have fallen.

'I say, that's not good. Are you all right, miss?' A young man not much older than herself but certainly not from the same background was smiling at her. He was definitely from a good family. His clothes had been tailored for him, his boots too, and his voice just confirmed her opinion. He was an inch or two taller, had pleasant but not handsome features, but his smile was nice.

'Thank you, sir. I'm fine. Although I doubt those two children will be when their mother catches up with them.'

They'd stepped to one side and the flow of exiting worshippers continued as they spoke. He held out his hand after removing his glove. 'I'm Philip Bannister, delighted to meet you.'

With some reluctance, she offered hers; she thought it probably wasn't a good thing to talk to a complete stranger and certainly not shake his hand. 'I'm Nancy Bates. I've just moved here and will be reopening my great-uncle's shop, Mortimer's Haberdashery, very soon.'

The words had tumbled out and she'd given him far more information than was necessary.

'I know exactly where you mean. I'm back for Easter from Cambridge; I'm in my final year. I live in Lexden Road but prefer to come to this church.'

Nancy didn't know how to get away from him without seeming rude. He was confident, must be used to talking to young ladies in the street, but apart from the redheaded lodger at Harbour House, she'd had no dealings with young men like him.

'Excuse me, Mr Bannister, I've enjoyed talking to you but I must get home.'

'I walk right past your property, Miss Bates, so kindly allow me to escort you to the door.'

She thought he would come with her whether she wanted him to or not and just prayed that Dan didn't see them together. He wouldn't take kindly to her walking and talking with anyone but him.

Fortunately, it was only a few minutes to her turning and she was able to smile, thank him politely, and hurry off before he could suggest they met again. As she turned into the passageway, she was aware that someone was following her. For a horrible moment, she thought it might be him.

'You dodged a bullet there; that Bannister boy has a shocking reputation. He's working his way around the town and you wouldn't believe how many silly girls have their heads turned and learn very soon to regret it.' The speaker was a woman about the same age as her mum.

'I really didn't want to talk to him but he gave me no choice. I'm Nancy Bates, thank you for the warning.'

'I'm Iris Turner, I'm two doors down from you at the bakers. My hubbie and I run it – our two boys are in the army.'

'That must be hard for you both. I'll be along tomorrow to buy some bread.'

'We do pasties, pies, buns and bread. First come first served but always keep something under the counter for friends and neighbours.'

Nancy laughed. 'In which case, Mrs Turner, can I place an order for a loaf, two meat pies and a couple of buns?'

'They'll be waiting for you.'

Nancy was still laughing as she opened the gate. Dan was in the yard and was tight-faced and cross.

21

Emily persuaded her parents to allow her to visit Nancy on her own. They agreed that as she travelled in and out of Colchester every school day unaccompanied, she was old enough to do this.

'Nancy won't know that you're coming today, sweetheart,' Daddy said as they ate breakfast together. The boys were still in bed, Mummy was fussing with the baby as usual, and Annie was doing the cleaning.

'I know, but I need to see her before she opens the shop which will be at the end of the week. If the shop's open then she won't be able to take me to Williams and Griffin's in the High Street to buy my necessities.' Emily didn't like to use the word brassiere when speaking to her father. Mummy had said it was all right to mention intimate apparel but only to another woman.

'I understand. I've put two pound notes in your purse. That should be more than enough for what you need to buy. Make sure that you purchase a housewarming gift for Nancy from all of us whilst you're in that department store.'

'I'll do it on the way there, otherwise it won't be a surprise. I'll have a look around whilst I'm buying the gift to see if they stock what I need.'

'That's an excellent idea, sweetheart. I still think that you're going far too early. I doubt that the shops will even be open yet. Why don't you catch a later train?'

'I'm going to explore the town; I've not had the opportunity so far. My school's really close to the castle but I've still not looked at that.'

'Then go ahead. Make sure you say goodbye to your mother before you leave. I'll see you this evening.'

He ruffled her hair, dropped a kiss on top of her head and strode off with his briefcase in his hand. Mr Stoneleigh had left half an hour ago because he was going to Brightlingsea to oversee something that was being built there.

She called goodbye up the stairs but didn't hear a response. Emily knew she should really go up and knock on the door but if she did that, she might miss her train.

Her hair was loose, plaits were for school, but she thought it was too long and floppy. A daring idea occurred to her. There was a hairdresser in Queen Street that she passed every day on the way to school – she was going to ask if they would cut her hair into one of the short cuts that she'd seen in one of the magazines that her mummy read. Once it was cut off, there was nothing her parents could do about it except tell her off.

Annie was busy upstairs, Mrs Bates was at the shops, there was nobody else to say goodbye to, so Emily stepped out into the late-March sunshine. As she walked briskly to the station, she worked out that it would be 1 April next Monday, which meant there was another two weeks of holidays, and she intended to enjoy every minute of her freedom.

* * *

Emily wandered up Queen Street, peering in the shops, enjoying her excursion, feeling very grown-up. The hairdressing salon wasn't open but Emily read the notice and saw that to have her hair cut would cost her one and sixpence if she had it shampooed and set – she wasn't exactly sure what that meant – and one shilling for just a cut.

'You looking for an appointment, ducks? I'm just opening,' a tall, thin lady, it was hard to guess her age, with very firm curls and bright-red lipstick, said from behind her.

'I am, but I can't see on any of your pictures the way I want it done.'

'Come in, you can look through the book of styles. What was you thinking?'

'I saw a picture in my mummy's magazine, I think it was a film star in America, she had it short and it looked lovely. I've got a lot of bounce in my hair so I think that sort of style would suit me.'

'I reckon it would. It'll cost you a bob; I can do it now if you like. It won't take more than half an hour and I ain't got any appointments until after nine.'

Emily hadn't been going to do it until she was on the way home as Nancy probably wouldn't approve, but this offer was too good to refuse.

'Yes, please. I don't have to be anywhere until after nine o'clock either.'

She thought she'd have to take off her jacket but the hairdresser just swirled a big cape of shiny material around her shoulders and tied it up at the back.

'There, sit yourself down. I'll just dampen your hair with

water. I know exactly what you want. Not too short, I'll cut it just to your collar and then your lovely curls will do the rest.'

The woman paused for a minute and seemed to be measuring the length of her hair. 'If I plait this before I cut it, I reckon it's long enough to go to make a wig. I'll do your hair for nothing if you agree.'

'Yes, that sounds like a good idea.'

Her hair, if you stretched it, went halfway down her back. Far too soon, the hairdresser had picked up her scissors and had snipped off the plaits. No going back now.

Emily closed her eyes; she didn't like looking at herself in a mirror anyway. The lady was singing to herself, it was a catchy tune about going to a place called Tipperary, whilst she worked.

'All right, ducks, you can open your eyes now. I think you look really lovely. You've got beautiful blue eyes and you're going to turn a few heads when you're a bit older.'

Nervously, Emily looked into the mirror and didn't recognise the face looking back at her. Her hair had been swept back and fell on either side of her face down to just below her ears. She looked like a grown-up and she wasn't sure that was a good idea after what had happened with Pete last year. He'd thought of her as old enough to be his girlfriend when she wasn't even eleven. Now if she put on lipstick – which she'd never do – she thought she'd pass for fifteen.

'Thank you. I love it.'

The cape was removed and then the hairdresser brushed the stray hair from around the collar of her blouse and she was ready to leave. She couldn't believe this transformation had taken so little time and had cost her absolutely nothing.

Not wanting to hang about in case the hairdresser changed her mind about paying, she nodded and smiled and rushed out through the door. Her head was lighter; she loved the way her curls bounced as she walked.

Williams and Griffin's was open and deserted. Emily selected a pretty gingham tablecloth with matching napkins for three shillings and sixpence for Nancy's gift. The shop assistant was young and as she was handing over the beautifully wrapped brown paper parcel, Emily whispered to her, 'Do you sell brassieres at this shop? I need to buy one.'

'We do, in the ladies' lingerie department. Girls your age must come with an adult as they have to be fitted. Is there somebody who'd accompany you?'

Emily nodded. 'Yes, I'm just going to visit them now. Thank you very much.'

She caught a glimpse of her reflection in a tall mirror as she passed it and stopped to admire her new hairstyle. She was lucky that she'd inherited her mother's looks – golden curls and bright-blue eyes.

It was only a short walk from the department store to where Nancy now lived and there wasn't time to think about the repercussions of her dramatic decision. The shop wasn't open, of course, so she headed around to the back where she'd gone in last time.

The gate wasn't locked and she stepped into the yard. As she approached the back door, she heard raised voices. Her hands clenched and she backed against the wall, not wanting to be seen. Who was Nancy arguing with?

She didn't mean to eavesdrop but knew she couldn't arrive in the middle of this row.

'If you don't like the way I behave, Dan Brooks, then you know what you can do? I'm not your possession, I don't have to do what you tell me, and I don't have to listen to you.'

Emily's stomach churned. She hadn't known that Dan was

living there too. She was sure that a couple shouldn't be living together like this until they were married. Nancy wasn't expecting her so wouldn't know that she'd come. She'd begun to sidle down the wall when Dan spoke. He sounded different, angry, not like the Dan she knew and liked.

'First, you flirt with that Stoneleigh, then that posh boy comes round here to find you. You're my girl, my fiancée, my future wife and I won't have you carrying on like that.'

There was silence for a few seconds – more terrifying than the shouting. Then Nancy replied and Emily didn't recognise her from the way she was talking.

'I just told you that how I behave is none of your business. If you think that I'm free and easy with my favours then you don't know me at all.'

There was the sound of something small clattering on a surface.

'Here, take your ring back. It's over. Get your bag and go away. I never want to speak to you again.'

Emily was paralysed by fear. Dan was going to burst out and he'd see her and that just couldn't happen. She was standing by the door of an outhouse. She flicked up the catch and slipped inside just as he stormed out.

* * *

Dan's rage carried him almost to the station before he stopped and opened his hand and gazed down sadly at the ring Nancy had thrown at him. His eyes blurred; he knew he was in the wrong, but when that posh bastard had knocked on the back door asking to speak to his Nancy, he'd completely lost his rag.

He hadn't allowed her to answer the door, had picked her up and put her in the shop before he flung the door open. The young man recoiled. Took one look at Dan's face and scuttled off. If he hadn't then he might well have left with a black eye which wouldn't have helped either of them.

After hearing her laughing in the passageway on Friday and her refusing to say who she'd been talking to, he'd been on edge. The fact that she was here and not in Wivenhoe where she should be, the fact that she no longer talked about getting married this year, the way she'd spoken about that lodger – it had all congealed in his head, making him irrational and unpleasant.

Head down, he continued to the station. The train waiting there was going to Clacton, but he decided to get on it anyway and get off at Wivenhoe. He wanted to speak to Mrs Bates, ask her to convey his apologies to Nancy and ask for advice about how to put things right.

There didn't seem much point in returning to Brightlingsea and working on the cottage – it was an unnecessary expense if Nancy wasn't going to be there with him. He'd paid the rent until October but could hand back the keys now if he wanted to. He certainly wasn't going to spend any more time and money doing it up.

He didn't find a seat. Someone might want to speak to him and he wasn't in the mood for conversation. Therefore, he propped himself against the wall by the door and stared miserably out of the window as it chugged past the river which flowed on the right of the track and steamed to a halt at Wivenhoe. He arrived at Harbour House, his head down, too miserable to acknowledge passers-by.

The huge ginger cat greeted him outside the back door. He barely acknowledged it and dumped his bag by the back door before knocking loudly. Mrs Bates answered and took his arm.

'Come in, Dan. I'm just about to have a cuppa; you look as though you need one.'

Over a mug of tea, he blurted out the whole sorry story and waited for her to condemn him for his behaviour. What she said was far worse.

'I'd a feeling it would come to this. I'm so sorry, but when my Nancy decided to move to Colchester, my Bert and I knew there'd be no wedding this year or next.'

His hands jerked, slopping the tea on the table. 'You think it's over? That Nancy had changed her mind about marrying me before this row even happened?'

'I'm afraid I do. Nancy wouldn't admit it, wouldn't have broken it off unless you gave her an excuse. I'm not saying she doesn't love you, but she doesn't love you enough to give up what she's been given by this opportunity.'

Tears dripped into his tea. Nancy was his whole world; without her, nothing made sense. Mrs Bates patted him on the shoulder and handed him a rag to blow his nose and wipe his eyes.

He swallowed the remainder of his tea and came to a decision. 'You know how I feel about her but you're right. She's too good for me. I always knew this could happen. Better now than later. I was going to write to her, but I won't bother now. She'll be relieved it's over and can concentrate on being a successful businesswoman.'

'I'll tell her you called in, that you're sorry, and that you've accepted the engagement's over and you're going to move on with your life.'

'I don't care what you tell her; if she doesn't love me then that's the end of it. I'll never love anyone else the way I love her, but one day, I expect I'll find somebody who'll do.'

'Don't do anything foolish because of this. You're a good man and Bert and I would have liked to have you as our son-in-law.'

'Ta, Mrs Bates, that's something, I suppose. I'd better get to Brightlingsea and tell Percy what I've decided. I'll also tell the owner of the cottage that I won't be needing it now.'

'Decided? Are you going to leave the barge and go back to fishing?'

'No, I'm going to speak to that naval bloke and see about joining the navy.'

Before he caught the train, he considered visiting his old home for one last time but decided against it. He had his ration book, his identity card, his post-office savings book – which could be used at any post office, not just at Wivenhoe – he was all set for his new life. Not the one he'd dreamed of, but he was going to do his best to forget Nancy and make something of himself. She was going up in the world and maybe he could too.

* * *

Dan found Percy in the cabin of the *Lady Beth* where the old man was busy polishing the woodwork, making everything shipshape.

'What's up, lad? There ain't no work for another few days.'

'That's it, Percy, I'm not coming back. My Nancy's broken the engagement. I'm going to join the navy.'

Instead of looking shocked, Percy laughed. 'You're in the blooming navy, Dan. Don't you remember I told you we've been requisitioned? From now on, this old girl is going to be working directly for the Admiralty. You don't have to be in a uniform, answering orders; you can stop here with me and still do your bit for the war.'

Dan collapsed onto the padded bench that ran along the

wall opposite Percy's bunk. 'Stop here?' He shrugged. Nothing really seemed to matter any more. 'Right, I might as well. I won't be going back to Wivenhoe, that's for sure – too many bad memories for me.'

'There's a load we can collect from Tilbury tomorrow. It's not for the navy, but the posh bloke in charge here said we're free to sail as long as we're back by next week. I'll ring them and let them know we're on our way, shall I?'

There was a flurry of wind that rocked the barge.

Dan nodded. 'Might as well. Last thing I want to do is sit around feeling sorry for myself.'

22

Nancy heard the back gate slam. Too late to call Dan back, tell him that she didn't mean it, tell him that she loved him. Her heart was pounding, her hands clammy and her legs gave way. She flopped onto the nearest chair, put her arms on the table and dropped her head onto them.

Her breathing was harsh and she waited for the sobs to start but her eyes remained dry. Slowly, she recovered her composure and sat up. Why wasn't she crying? The man she loved had just slammed off because she'd broken the engagement. If she'd really wanted him back then she'd have been on her feet calling his name, not sitting here like a stuffed dummy.

They'd not been getting on for the past few days and his jealousy and possessiveness had been driving a wedge between them. He wanted her to be something that she wasn't and she thought they'd just sit down and talk it through – she'd never expected things to end like this.

They could have made it work. He'd said he could just as easily get to Colchester as to Wivenhoe, they'd be living in this lovely house, both be making good money and she'd been certain they'd come to some compromise. However, she wouldn't have married him until he'd accepted that she had a life too. If women could be in the army, the RAF and the navy then Dan would have had to accept that things had changed – that women could be independent financially and hold down a responsible job.

She heard someone in the yard, was on her feet instantly and threw open the door, expecting to see Dan outside.

'Emily, good God, what have you done to your hair?'

The girl didn't answer, bit her lip, and before Nancy could stop her, had vanished out of the yard.

She should go after her but didn't have the energy. This was a day of disasters. Mr and Mrs Roby must have given Emily permission to come for a visit but she was quite sure they hadn't given her permission to have her lovely hair cut off.

* * *

Half an hour later, she heard the gate opening a second time but was too miserable to investigate. Nancy retreated to the shop where she was doing an inventory. She didn't want visitors so whoever it was could go away again.

'Excuse me, Nancy, I'm sorry I ran off. I was worried when you didn't answer the door,' Emily said from behind her.

'I'm sorry. Come here and give me a hug. I was just shocked when I saw you. I almost didn't recognise you; that cut makes you look so much older. I do love it; it really suits you.'

The little girl – not so little really – hugged her back and things were all right between them again.

'I did it on impulse. I don't regret it though I know my parents won't like it. Here, this is a housewarming gift from all of us at Harbour House.'

Nancy took the parcel and carefully unwrapped it. 'Oh, this is lovely; it'll go perfectly in the kitchen. Did you choose it?'

Emily nodded. 'I did. I need to ask you the most tremendous favour – I can't buy a brassiere unless I have an adult with me and I do most desperately need one.'

'Bless you, love, shall we go now?'

'I'd like that.' Emily flushed and looked away before continuing. 'I heard you and Dan arguing and hid in the shed until he'd gone.'

'I'm sorry you heard all that. Grown-ups argue; don't worry about it. We'll sort it out once he's calmed down.'

'I do hope so. I really like Dan and I think you must be the best-looking couple in Essex.'

Nancy smiled. 'I don't know about that, but I'm not letting him go that easily.' Then she found herself talking to the girl as if she was an adult and not still eleven years old. 'He wants me to be just his wife, not to have employment of my own. I think a lot of men are like that but I thought he was different.'

'Women can do anything a man can do,' Emily said fiercely. 'Well, apart from heavy physical work. Dan will understand that and agree to compromise because I'm quite certain he loves you too much to lose you over this.'

Nancy stared at her. 'When did you grow up? I really shouldn't be talking about this with you but too late to worry about that now. Shall we go to Williams and Griffin's and buy what you need?'

'I'm a woman now, I have my monthlies, so I expect that's why I sound different.'

'I'm sure it is. Now, after we've bought what you need, shall we find ourselves a nice lunch somewhere? I went to the Red Lion not long ago and it was excellent.'

* * *

Emily stayed until teatime, helping with the inventory, and Nancy appreciated her help. 'I can't believe how much we've got done today. Thank you. You can come again whenever you like.'

'I've got another two weeks of holiday. I'm going to ask my parents if they'd allow me to stay here for a couple of nights later this week and help you get ready to open. I can't help you the last week as I'll be at the farm. Mrs Peterson will be back with the children and she particularly asked me to come and help out.'

Nancy wasn't sure that having Emily staying would be a good idea.

'I'd love to have you but wait and see what your parents say. I have a nasty feeling when they see your hair that you might be spending the next two weeks in your bedroom in disgrace.'

Emily clapped her hands to her hair. 'I'd forgotten all about that. You said it suited me and that it looked lovely.'

'I did and it does. But it's not really a suitable style for someone your age. I can't believe that you dared to have it cut. I didn't think you liked to do anything outrageous.'

'I've never been called outrageous; I rather like it. I suppose it's a good thing that they don't believe in corporal punishment or I expect I'd be soundly spanked. What would your mother have done if you'd turned up with your hair short?'

Nancy grinned. 'She'd have given me a hug and said she loved it then stood up for me when my dad came home and created a scene. Dan didn't want me to have my hair cut but now I've seen yours, I think I might do the same. I know the place you're talking about and the hairdresser did a good job.'

'You don't need to get yours cut as you can wear it up. If I'd been allowed to put my hair up then I wouldn't have had it cut short. I just hated having it hanging down my back or in plaits.'

'I'll have to think about it. I don't want to do something I regret because I've been upset today. Come on, I'll walk you to the station.'

On the way down, she told Emily that she was hoping to take in a stray, something big enough to be a guard dog.

'I know just the animal for you, Nancy. There's a scruffy stray that lives in the farmyard; he's very friendly with people he knows but growls and snarls when strangers come into the yard. I'm sure that Mrs Peterson would be delighted if you took him.'

'Then I'll come and collect him tomorrow. Will there be somebody there we can speak to?'

'Jimmy and his dad will be there. What train will you come on as if I know, I will meet you and walk up to the farm and introduce you to them.'

'I don't know exactly when I'm coming. I'll call for you. Let's hope you're not confined to your room for the rest of the holidays.'

'I won't tell anyone what happened with Dan; I'm not a tell-tale,' Emily said as they exchanged a quick hug before the girl got on the train.

As soon as she got back to the shop, Nancy started to get things ready for the new arrival tomorrow. She found a couple of old blankets, a moth-eaten rag rug and two cracked dishes that would be ideal for dog water and dog food. She'd have to go to Mr Chaney's shop in Wivenhoe and see if she could buy a dog collar and lead – failing that, she'd have to buy rope and make do with that.

She went to bed feeling more optimistic about the future. Dan wouldn't give up on her, whatever she'd said. There would be a letter arriving in the morning post apologising and asking if he could visit to put things right. They'd have to have a lot to talk about, but she was confident that when two people loved each other as much as they did, they'd find a way to make it work.

* * *

Emily was tempted to sneak in through the back door and hide upstairs until she'd no option but to come down for tea. Mrs Cousins, the doctor's wife, saw her approaching the house.

'My word, Emily, I love the new hairstyle. Short hair really suits you and makes you look very grown-up. Well done.'

'Thank you, I love it. I was wondering if you'd like me to take the children for a walk sometime. I have two more weeks' holiday and don't go to the Peterson farm until next week.'

'How kind of you, yes, I'd love you to take them both for a walk when the weather's fine. Are you sure that your mother won't mind?'

'Mummy's very happy for me to go to the Peterson farm so I'm sure she won't mind me taking your two for a walk.'

'I'll check that your parents agree before we make an arrangement.'

'Thank you for liking my hair. Good evening, Mrs Cousins.'

Emily sprinted up the front path, hoping no one had been looking out of the window. She kicked off her winter shoes, slipped her feet in her slippers which were kept neatly in a wooden box by the front door, then hurried to the boot room to hang up her coat and put her shoes away.

She could hear Mrs Bates and Annie doing something in the

kitchen and thought that getting their reaction first might be sensible, prepare her for what would be coming next.

'Hello, do you like my new haircut?'

Annie was laying the table for tea, and as she looked over her shoulder, her eyes widened.

'Good grief, what have you done to your lovely hair?' Annie obviously wasn't impressed.

Mrs Bates had been stirring something on the old range and turned. She dropped the wooden spoon on the floor with a clatter. Another negative response.

Emily pinned on a brave smile. 'I like it. Nancy liked it too – after she'd got over the shock. Mrs Cousins likes it because she just told me so.' She tilted her chin defiantly.

'I was just shocked; not many girls have such long, beautiful, golden hair, like a fairy princess,' Mrs Bates said. 'That doesn't mean I don't think your new style isn't nice; it's just not the way a girl your age usually has her hair.'

'I see. I didn't want to look like a fairy princess, I didn't want to have plaits at school; now I don't have to.'

'I doubt that your parents will be pleased,' Annie said.

'I'm sure they won't, but there's absolutely nothing they can do about it. It's my hair, and I gave it to the hairdresser to send off to be made into a wig. I got the haircut for nothing because of that.'

'I'm not surprised you got a free haircut, Emily; she'll sell it for ten times more than your haircut would have cost,' Mrs Bates said.

'I don't see that it matters. I didn't want it; if I'd said no then it would just have been swept up and put in the bin. Aren't we being told all the time to "waste not, want not"?'

She hadn't meant to raise her voice but Emily wasn't used to being criticised and especially by two people at the same time.

'What's going on? Good God, you've cut your hair off.'

'Actually, Daddy, the hairdresser cut it off. I really didn't like having long hair and it was so difficult to wash and dry every week. This will be so much easier.'

Her pert reply hadn't gone down well. He was looking at her in that terrifying way. 'I don't find the situation at all amusing, Emily, and neither will your mother. I suggest you go to your room and remain there until you're told you may come down.'

He stood to one side and she scuttled past like a terrified beetle, fled up the stairs and into her room, remembering to close the door extremely quietly behind her. Slamming it wouldn't be a good idea at the moment.

Emily flung herself face down on the bed, bitterly regretting her actions. She buried her head under the pillow, waiting for the tears, but they didn't come. Slowly, the lump in her chest vanished. She sat up and went to stare at herself in the mirror. Yes. Her parents would forgive her eventually and she'd still have this lovely grown-up hairstyle.

* * *

Nancy managed to charm a couple of marrow bones from the butcher for the dog. Thinking about him kept her thoughts from straying to what had happened with Dan yesterday. She waited eagerly for the early post, but nothing arrived through her door. Maybe the expected letter from Dan would come that afternoon instead.

When she called in at Harbour House to collect Emily later, she'd decided not to tell her mum what had happened – no need to worry her as with any luck, the engagement would be restored by the end of the day. If Dan was staying at the Falcon, she'd go round and see him, be the first one to apologise even though he'd been the one in the wrong.

On arriving at Wivenhoe, she went immediately to the hardware shop on the corner of Queen's Road and the High Street. She wondered how the less agile members of the community managed to get into the shop as you had to go up several steep steps.

The bell over the door rang noisily and Mr Chaney emerged from a corner smiling and pleased to see an early customer.

'Good morning, Mr Chaney, how are you? I'm getting a dog today and I'd like to buy a collar and lead for him if you happen to have one tucked away somewhere.'

'Morning, Nancy. A dog, you say? What size of dog might that be?'

'I'm not exactly sure as I've not seen him. He's a stray that's living at the Peterson farm. Emily Roby told me about him and said that he was quite large.'

'Right you are. I've got exactly what you need – it's not new, but good as. Just a tick and I'll find it. I know it's somewhere under the counter.'

Mr Chaney vanished and Nancy could hear him rummaging about, exclaiming when he came across something he'd forgotten about, and was beginning to think he wasn't going to find what she needed.

'Here we are, I knew it was here somewhere. What do you think?' He held up a leather collar and matching lead. They'd once been blue, Nancy thought, but the colour had faded.

'Thank you, they're perfect. Lovely and supple, and several holes in the collar so I can adjust it to fit. How much are they?'

'Sixpence will do. Is there anything else I can get you whilst you're here?'

'Nothing, thank you, unless you've got any old tins of meat, ones that the labels have fallen off and nobody else wants. It's going to be difficult finding food to feed him. I expect he'll get used to vegetables and fish as there isn't going to be much meat, that's for sure.'

He chuckled. 'Do you know, I've got exactly what you're looking for. Mind you, I can't be sure that there's actually stew inside the tins as I've not opened any of them. Do you want to take a gamble? Twopence a tin – cheap at twice the price.' He pointed to a row of slightly rusty, label-less tins on the shelf behind him. There were seven of them.

Nancy was tempted to buy one and open it and then buy the rest if they were in fact a meat stew. If she did discover the contents were what she wanted then the price might treble.

'I'll take all of them. I've got a string bag in my pocket. I think it'll be big enough.'

'Good for you. That'll be one shilling and eightpence, if you please.'

With a bulging shopping bag, which weighed a tonne, in one hand and the collar and lead in the other, Nancy headed for Harbour House. She put the tins down by the back door; there was no point in carrying them up to the farm and back. She'd collect them before she went home.

Mum must've seen her out of the kitchen window as the back door opened before Nancy knocked. 'I'm so sorry about Dan, love, but it's for the best. He said he's accepted that the engagement's over and is going to move on with his life. You've got to do the same.'

For a second, Nancy was speechless. 'Did he come here yesterday? What did he say?'

'He told me that you'd broken the engagement and asked me to say he was sorry things had ended like this. He's going to join the navy. I think he always wanted to do that but didn't want to because of you. Now you're both free to follow your dreams.'

Nancy swallowed the lump in her throat. 'I was going to tell you myself, but now I don't have to. Anyway, I've come to collect Emily as she was going to take me to the Peterson farm.'

'She's in disgrace because of her hair. Mrs Roby took it even worse than Mr Roby. She's only allowed to come downstairs to use the WC. Annie's taking meals up to her and she's not even allowed to talk to the boys.'

'Oh, I'm sorry to hear that. Will you give her my love? I've left some tins I got from Mr Chaney outside the door. I'll pick them up later.'

'Why are you going to the farm, love?'

'I'm collecting a stray dog that Emily told me about. That's if I can find him and he wants to come with me. I thought having a guard dog would be a good idea as Daphne and I will be living there alone for the moment.'

'You don't know anything about dogs; how are you going to manage him?'

'The same way that I manage everything else, Mum. If I can run a shop without help from anybody then I can certainly look after a dog. I'll see you later. I want to catch the next train back to town so I'd better get a move on.'

She bit her lip as she hurried out. How could Dan have given up so easily? When he was in the navy, she'd not see him at all; there'd be no chance of smoothing things out.

23

Nancy looked up as she turned left to walk down The Cut and saw Emily standing sadly at her bedroom window. She waved the collar and lead and Emily nodded but didn't smile. The girl wasn't used to being in disgrace and Nancy hoped her parents didn't keep her cooped up for too long.

Nancy hadn't gone far when she spotted George and Sammy lurking at the corner. She smiled but didn't indicate that she'd seen them in case they were hiding from their sister.

'Are you coming to the farm with me? I'm not even sure how to catch a dog – can you help me with that?' Nancy spoke as she walked past them. As soon as they were out of sight of the house, the boys joined her.

'We can,' George said as he bounced up and down. 'Emily's not allowed to speak to us but she wrote us a note and pushed it out under her door. Daddy didn't actually say we couldn't communicate by notes.'

'How are things between her and your parents? I assume they were very angry,' Nancy said.

'If that had been me that did it, my old mum would have

given me what for. She kept a wooden spoon especially to beat us with,' Sammy said with a grin. 'Emily's lucky; she's getting fed, doesn't have to do any chores and will be allowed out tomorrow, I reckon.'

'I don't suppose she feels very lucky. Do you think your parents will allow you to come back to Colchester with me? I've got a large bag of unlabelled tins and if the dog's boisterous, I might not be able to carry them and lead him safely.'

George exchanged a look with Sammy. 'We don't have to be back until dark; we're allowed to play out. Nobody said we couldn't catch a train to Colchester so we won't be breaking any rules, will we?'

Nancy wasn't sure Mr and Mrs Roby would agree with George but she wasn't going to argue. The closer she got to the farm, the more anxious she was about taking on a dog that she knew nothing about.

'Have you met this dog? Do you know where he hides?'

'We don't go up to the farm very often; that's Emily's thing,' George said, 'but we've seen it and it's got long hair and big, brown eyes. He certainly seems friendly. We gave him a sandwich and he was ever so grateful. Have you got anything to tempt him with?'

'I'm not daft, George Roby; I've got two stale sausage rolls. There's a bakery a few doors up from me and I've become good friends with the owners.'

They walked past the Brewery Tavern and the Yachtsman's Arms, but they were silent – they only got busy in the evening when the men from the shipyards came out.

It had been several years since Nancy had come this way; she used to pick blackberries in the fields, collect sloes and rosehips from the hedgerows which her mum had made into jam, jelly or preserved in Kilner jars.

'Does this dog have a name?' she asked George as they approached the gate.

'I don't think so, Emily said she just calls out Boy and he comes immediately. Did she tell you that he's probably got fleas and that his coat's matted with mud?'

'She didn't have to; I worked that out for myself. If you two wait here, I'm going to knock on the door and let them know I'm here.'

'There won't be anybody in; they'll be out on the farm some-where,' Sammy said.

'I know that too, but I'm still going to knock, and I've already got a note written to tell them that I've taken him – that's if I actually manage to catch him and he'll come with me.'

As expected, the farmhouse was empty. Nancy pushed the note under the door and then returned to the boys.

'Here, Boy, see what I've got for you. I'm going to take you home with me if you like.'

There was a noise from a barn and a skinny, pathetic-looking dog wriggled out from under an old trailer.

Nancy called him again and waved the bag with sausage rolls in the air. The dog wagged his tail but didn't rush over.

'Look, I've got a collar and lead for you. I'm going to take you home and you're going to be very happy and well looked after.'

She held them up and the dog's ears pricked, his tail wagged harder and then he galloped across to them. He sat in front of her, his long tail sweeping the dirt, not trying to snatch the food but staring into her eyes as if he knew, actually recognised, the significance of a collar and lead.

'Quick, Nancy, put the collar on him. He wants you to,' George said.

'Good boy. I'm going to put this round your neck and click

on the lead. Then you can eat your sausage rolls and we can go home.'

He sat shivering in front of her. It was love at first sight. She'd never owned a pet of any sort – her home had been far too small to share with animals. The dog's long, pink tongue licked her hand as she was doing it; she was astonished he didn't try and snatch the food.

'Poor old thing, such a good boy, I've got you now.' Nancy wanted to hug the dog but thought it might be better to wait until she'd combed through his tangled coat and given him a good bath.

'We're going to find him some water, Nancy; there's a rain butt over there. We can bring it back in that old bucket if it doesn't have a hole in it,' George said, and he and Sammy ran off.

She offered the dog the first sausage roll and it vanished in two gulps. The second went just as quickly. The bucket of water was offered and he dipped his face into it and drank for a minute or two.

'There, are you ready to come with me, Boy?' She smiled and decided to slightly change his name. 'I'm calling him Boyd, boys: close to what he's used to but an actual name.'

Nancy wound the lead around her fist and started to walk. 'Come on, Boyd, let's get home.'

The dog fell in beside her as if he'd been walking to heel all his life. Maybe he had – she'd never know his history, but she did know that his future was going to be a happy one.

'We'll meet you at the station,' George said as they reached the turning to Hamilton Road. 'Can you manage the bag and the dog from the house to there?'

'I can; he doesn't pull at all. He must have come from a loving home to be so well trained and gentle. I wonder how he came to be a stray. It occurs to me, boys, that the guard might insist that we travel in the van with him. Passengers won't want to have this dog in a compartment with them, not the way he is now.'

'Guard's van? We'd love that, wouldn't we, Sammy? This day can't get any better,' George said. Then he and his foster brother dashed off down Brook Street, leaving her to complete the short walk to Harbour House with just the dog for company.

She looked up at Emily's window, half-expecting the girl to be there, but there was no sign of her. Nancy didn't want to speak to her mother again, not right now, so collected the tins and hurried past.

The boys were ahead of her. Sammy took the tins and George took the lead while she went into the ticket office to explain their circumstances.

The stationmaster, Mr Higgins, happened to be there too; he listened then looked out of the window at the boys and the dog.

'You're right, Miss Bates; that mongrel can't travel with my passengers. However, you're doing a good thing taking him in. You can go in the guard's van with the parcels at the end of the train.' Mr Higgins smiled and turned to the ticket clerk.

'No charge for these four going to Colchester. But the boys will need to buy tickets to come back.'

'I'll make sure they have enough money to do so. Thank you very much.'

The guard made no objection to his unusual companions and the dog flopped down on the floor as soon as the train was in motion, his big head resting on Nancy's foot. For the first time since her mother had given her the heartbreaking news that Dan wasn't going to come back, her eyes brimmed. She hid her tears with her hanky and by fussing with the dog at her feet.

* * *

Emily heard Nancy collect the tins but didn't dare go to the window. She was hating being incarcerated, not being able to speak to anybody, but what was even worse was that her parents were disappointed with her. For the remainder of the school holidays, she wasn't going to be allowed out for more than half an hour. She hoped this meant that at least she'd be allowed out of her room and to go for a walk around the village soon.

She wouldn't be able to spend time at the farm, nor take the children next door out for a walk and certainly not go to Colchester and spend any time with Nancy. Despite this, she didn't regret having had her hair cut. Every time she looked in the mirror on her dressing table, she liked it more.

She was wearing one of her new bras – it made her stick out in the front rather a lot but she liked her new silhouette. If girls her age could have a baby, then as far as she was concerned, she shouldn't be treated like a child.

George and Sammy arrived back just in time for tea and she waved to them from the window. They gave her a thumbs up. She quickly scribbled a note asking where they'd been and what had happened, what the dog was like, and how Nancy was. As she wasn't allowed out of her room, she couldn't slip it under the door but had to wait until one of them stopped outside.

Annie brought up her tray and, as before, put it on the table without comment. Emily wasn't sure if she liked Annie much; Nancy would have ignored the rule and managed to speak to her somehow.

She wasn't allowed to have her door open even a crack so it was difficult to hear what was going on downstairs. She thought that was the idea, but she didn't like it one bit. Even her brother had never been punished so harshly and she thought it all very unfair.

An hour after the boys had returned, there was a scuffle outside – they weren't allowed to knock on the door or speak to her but hadn't been told they couldn't make their presence felt. She was across the room in a flash and pushed the note out and heard them pick it up and go into their bedroom.

The time crawled by whilst she waited for an answer. Then the same piece of paper was pushed back, but this time with writing on the back. She snatched it up and opened it.

Nancy's collected Boyd, that's what she's called him, and we went with her in the guard's van with the dog. We spent the day at the shop and it was smashing. We bathed Boyd and combed his coat with a nit comb. He had a few fleas but we caught them on a piece of wet soap. He eats a lot but Nancy's friend will help her out with food. Nancy sends her love and says she's okay. I heard them talking about you and you're going to be allowed out tomorrow morning.

George's handwriting was nearly the same as hers and there wasn't a single spelling mistake in the entire note. She'd love to have had that adventure with them but was glad that her friend had the dog for company.

Just one more night and then she could rejoin the family. It was going to take a long time for her to forgive them for treating her so harshly. She'd just had her hair cut, not done anything dreadful, and it seemed very mean of them to have behaved like that.

* * *

The next morning, Emily was up and dressed in her slacks, blouse and jumper long before anyone else was up. She wanted to be ready when Daddy came in. She'd rehearsed what she was going to say. Although she didn't think she'd done anything wrong, she was going to apologise for disappointing them and promise to do better in future. That should smooth things over.

She prayed Daddy wouldn't have that angry face when he came in as it made her feel quite unwell.

He didn't knock on the door and she thought that was wrong. She might have been getting dressed and she was far too old to do that in front of him.

'Good, Emily, I see that you're ready but I'm wondering how you knew I'd be coming to see you. Have you spoken to the boys?'

She shook her head vigorously. 'I promise I didn't break any of your rules, Daddy.'

His eyes narrowed suspiciously but he didn't pursue the point. If he'd asked her outright if she'd communicated with them, she couldn't have lied – that was one thing she'd never do.

'Then your mother and I have decided you can rejoin the family. As I told you the day before yesterday, you can't be out of the house for more than half an hour at a time. Do you understand?'

'I do, and I'm sorry that I disappointed you. I'm going to do better in future.'

He smiled. 'Come here, give me a hug. We've both hated punishing you but you left us no choice. You're a child, whatever you might think, and need our permission to make any changes to your appearance.'

For some reason, her feet remained firmly planted and she didn't move. She wanted to be hugged, be his special little girl again, but needed him to understand how she felt about things now.

His smile vanished but he didn't look cross, just sad. 'Oh dear, I feared this might be the case. Tell me, sweetheart, why you're hesitating.'

'I'm really, really sorry, but I can't help it. I don't feel the same way; I don't want to be treated like a little girl some of the time and like a responsible young adult at others. If you think I'm old enough to go to the farm and look after somebody else's children, to go in and out of Colchester on my own, then in my opinion, I should be allowed to get my hair cut if that's what I want to do.'

He shook his head. 'I thought I'd have longer before you grew up. You're right; your mother and I have got this wrong.' He saw her smile and raised a hand. 'No, not about your punishment; you deserved that. If you'd wanted to get your hair cut, you should have discussed it with us first. I didn't give you that money to spend on yourself.'

Emily thought it wouldn't be a good idea to remind him that she hadn't had to pay for the haircut so stood silently.

'What happens now, Daddy?'

He shrugged and in two strides was beside her and she was in his arms. She leaned into him, loving his familiar smell of wood and the sea, wishing that things could remain the same but knowing that they couldn't, that she wasn't the Emily she'd been only a few weeks ago.

They broke the embrace and she was shocked to see tears in his eyes. She'd only been thinking about herself, hadn't realised how hard it was going to be for him.

'I love you and Mummy, and I really won't let you down again. I didn't want to grow up like this, I liked being a little girl with plaits, but my body has changed inside so I thought I ought to look different on the outside.'

He laughed and finally looked like her daddy. 'Well, you certainly have done that. Your mother said that plaits and long hair down to your waist were no longer suitable but that you were still too young to put it up like hers. To be honest, sweetheart, we both think you look quite lovely but frighteningly grown-up for a girl who won't be twelve until September.'

The lump in her chest that she'd had for two days finally left, allowing her to breathe freely and relax. She might be more grown-up, but she still wanted to be approved of by her beloved parents.

'Daddy, I don't want you to be cross with the boys but we did communicate by letter. We didn't speak and I didn't leave this room.'

He grinned. 'I guessed as much, but thank you for telling me. I'd have been very surprised if your brothers hadn't found a way to give you news. I won't say anything to them, don't worry.'

'Good. I know it's only been two days but it seems like a month. Even Mrs Bates's delicious food doesn't taste the same up here.'

'Come on, let's go downstairs and have breakfast together before I go to work. Grace kept us both awake last night so I don't think your mother will be down for a bit.'

* * *

Daddy wasn't cross when she told him about the dog and the boys going to Colchester but didn't, unfortunately, change his mind about her being unable to go to the farm or to Colchester herself.

Today, she'd eaten in the dining room but didn't want to do

so when Mr Stoneleigh was there. She thought she was probably in a sort of halfway stage, neither a child nor an adult but something in between.

'May I walk to the shipyard with you, Daddy? Then I'll go along the quay and come home again. I need some fresh air.'

'All right, I don't see why not. Are you going to wear hats now you're almost a grown-up?'

'Do I have to? I hate wearing my school hat; I really don't want to wear one when I'm on holiday.'

He chuckled. 'I was teasing you, sweetheart. No, come as you are; let's not hurry things any more than we have already.'

24

———

Dan pushed aside his misery and concentrated on getting the *Lady Beth* ready to sail. The tide would be right in a couple of hours and they needed to be away by then. The grub locker was full, his belongings safely stowed in his bunk, and when Percy returned with Fred, there was scarcely time to set sail before they missed the tide.

'We're collecting a load of rice meal and cement from Tilbury,' Percy told him once they were underway. 'Good paying trip, and we'll be back in Brightlingsea tomorrow if the wind stays fair.'

'There's a storm brewing, Percy; I can feel a change in the weather,' Dan said as he scowled up at the clear blue sky.

The skipper sniffed. 'I reckon you're right; I can smell it too. We'll get up to Tilbury easy enough but it'll be a bugger coming back.'

The wind was behind them and they flew across the sea and up the estuary. They were loaded and ready to begin the return trip by late afternoon. The weather had continued to deteriorate and Dan wasn't sure they should attempt the return today, but Percy was having none of it.

'This old girl likes a good blow; she's never let me down and won't do so now.'

The blow was what they got, closer to a gale than a storm, Dan thought. All might have been well if, as they approached Harwich, thick, impenetrable fog hadn't descended, blotting out all visibility within minutes.

Since the war began, there'd been no lit buoys allowed, not that in this fog they could have seen them, but he trusted Percy's knowledge of the sea and the coast to get them safely ashore whatever the weather. Dan could barely see his shipmate through the fog; he looked more like a ghost than a hardened seaman.

They were dragging their anchor to slow them down and Dan was about to begin lowering more sail when to his horror, the prow of another, much larger ship appeared. Too late to call a warning.

The impact was catastrophic. The barge was holed beneath the waterline.

The captain of this motor-driven ship seemed unaware that he'd caused such devastating damage. They couldn't see him but he hailed them from his deck, apologising and wishing them well.

By the time Dan and Percy had picked themselves up from the deck, the ship had gone, leaving them floundering, taking on water, somewhere outside Harwich. The new wartime regulations meant that no barge was allowed to dock at night. Either they'd have to try and stay afloat where they were or risk launching the lifeboat in this swell.

'Man the pumps,' Percy yelled as he struggled with the tiller.

'With this cargo, we'll soon become waterlogged and go down if we're not careful.'

'Fred, put your life jacket on,' Dan yelled into the fog, hoping that the lad was still on his feet after the impact.

They were fighting a losing battle. They might have managed if one of the pumps hadn't failed. They dragged it out by the light of torches and he and Percy lay flat on the deck and tried to repair it.

'*Lady Beth*'s in trouble, Dan; I can hear the water sloshing about inside every time a wave hits us. I ain't abandoning ship; I'll stop on board, pray that this old girl stays afloat until the fog lifts.'

Dan collected the watertight tins with the flares and distress rockets from the cabin which was already half filled with water. He didn't bother to collect his own belongings; there was nothing of value. He had his identity card, ration book and wallet wrapped in oilskin and safely tucked inside his clothes.

The boy crawled towards them, dragging two lifejackets behind him. Dan put his on but again Percy refused. 'No, I'll go down with her if I have to.'

'I'm going to send up a distress rocket and a flare, Percy,' Dan yelled above the lashing rain and howling wind. 'I doubt anyone will see it in this fog, but you never know. If it lifts, you let the others off. Harwich can't be far away and they have a lifeboat there.'

Percy was old school, would stay on the barge, believing that, being all wood, it would somehow stay afloat long enough for the coastguard to rescue him. He prayed the old man would somehow survive, but now he had to get Fred safely ashore.

He and Fred lowered the lifeboat into the heaving waves and then scrambled over the side of the dying barge and into comparative safety.

He was just dropping the oars into the rollocks when the boy screamed a warning. Too late. A massive wave caught them broadside and the lifeboat capsized, pitching them both into the freezing sea.

He'd tried to grab hold of the boy but failed. Dan was a strong swimmer, had the sense to keep his mouth shut as he went down, knew that with the life jacket, if he held his breath for long enough, he'd bob to the surface.

He wouldn't drown but the cold would kill him quick enough if he didn't keep moving and by some miracle reach the shore. His last thought as he plunged down into the depths of the sea was that Fred wouldn't make it and it was his fault.

Nancy rushed downstairs the following morning, expecting to find the kitchen wrecked by the dog with puddles and mess on the floor. But the kitchen was pristine, just as she'd left it. Boyd greeted her with a look that made it seem as if he was smiling, his long, plumy tail wagging furiously, and then ran to the back door and whined.

'Good boy. I'll take you out. There's a nice field five minutes from here – do you think you can hold on till then?'

The collar was still around his neck; all she had to do was click on the lead, push her feet into her shoes and she was ready to go. She already had her coat on.

There wasn't time to stop and lock the door but she thought there probably wouldn't be any lurking burglars at seven o'clock in the morning – at least she hoped not. She ran down the narrow passage and the dog loped along, somehow knowing she was taking him somewhere he could relieve himself. She smiled – at least she liked to think he did.

When she reached the field with the small wood at the end, she wasn't sure if she should let him off the lead, but he probably wouldn't want to do his business with her standing next to him.

'Off you go, Boyd, don't be long. I'll be waiting here for you.'

The dog was gone and in seconds, had vanished into the trees. Nancy watched anxiously; would he keep running when he'd finished or would he come back to her? He'd only been part of her life for a few hours but already she loved him. She didn't have Dan any more, couldn't think about him without crying, but having Boyd would make things just a little bit easier.

She was about to call his name when he burst out of the trees and galloped towards her. She braced herself, expecting him to jump up, but he skidded to a halt in front of her and looked up adoringly.

'Good boy, what a good Boyd you are. Let me put your lead back on and we'll go home and have some breakfast.'

As soon as they were back, she gave him one of the big bones she'd got yesterday from the butcher and sent him outside in the yard to eat it. She watched him fondly out of the window for a few moments as he crunched and slurped; all the time his tail was wagging.

Tomorrow, Daphne would be moving in and the shop would be opening the next day, on the Saturday. This would be the best time as the town would be bustling with shoppers as it was also market day. High Street and Culver Street – which ran parallel to it – would be packed with stalls. People came from the villages around the town to buy their weekly necessities as things were cheaper at the market. There wasn't as much new stuff for sale now because of the war, but there'd be second-hand things that would do just as well.

The cattle market used to be in the High Street but that had moved almost a hundred years ago and a good thing too. You could still buy chickens but not live ones. Nancy hadn't been to the market for a couple of years, but she was pretty sure there was usually a haberdashery stall of some sort. She'd be competing with them but was confident her stock was better quality and there would be a wider choice – at least for the moment.

The house was clean, she'd nobody to cook for, and she needed to keep busy, keep her mind away from her heartbreak. If Dan hadn't told Mum that he was moving on, not going to see her again, she wouldn't have believed it. She missed him dreadfully. Even when he'd been away at sea, she'd still felt connected to him, could still think about the future they'd have together. Now she'd nothing to look forward to; even being here, having her own home and business to run, didn't seem as important as it had before.

Then she smiled. It wasn't too late. Until she'd spoken to Dan face to face, she wouldn't believe that he'd given up on their love so easily. She came to a life-changing decision. As soon as the cottage was finished, ready to be occupied, she'd marry Dan and, if he wanted her to, she'd give up the shop and move to Brightlingsea. She hoped by then, he'd see the sense in keeping it on as they'd be able to put by enough to set them up for life.

* * *

Emily spent most of the day drawing in her room, apart from a few surreptitious visits to the sitting room to look at the baby. She couldn't even be tempted out to play a game of Monopoly with the boys.

Mid-afternoon, she decided to take another walk but before

she did that decided it might be sensible to make sure she was allowed. Mummy would be with the baby in the sitting room.

'I'm going for a walk, Mummy, just down to the quay again.'

'Emily, I thought you'd want to spend more time with us all after being shut in your room for two days,' Mummy said. 'The few times you popped in don't really count, do they?'

'I'm drawing; you know how much I love art. I decided to do a portrait of each member of the family. I've started with Grace; she's changing so quickly I wanted to capture her as she is now.'

Mummy's worried expression changed to a smile. 'That's an absolutely lovely idea, darling; if it's as good as the one you did of the two fighter planes then I'll ask Daddy to have it framed. Off you go, and don't worry about being exactly half an hour; as long as you're back by teatime, that will be just fine.'

'Thank you. I've almost finished my drawing. I'll show it to you later.'

She paused and looked out of the dining room window and, seeing that the trees were waving wildly, the sky dark, she realised that she'd better put on her boots and raincoat. This time, she went in the opposite direction, past the sewing factory, down Hamilton Road and then back up Brook Street.

The tide was high, the water almost up to the Black Boy; the poor people who lived along the Folly would have wet feet tonight. She couldn't walk along the quay as it would be underwater but thought it might be safe to go down Anchor Hill. However, when she arrived, she discovered the water was high there too.

Emily cut through the little alley at the end of the row of terraced cottages and out into West Street. She wondered if the shipyard where her daddy worked was flooded as well. He'd told her that spring tides were often the highest and if the wind was in the wrong direction, it did cause the river to overflow. This seemed more like a flood than an overflow to her.

There was water in Quay Street, but she had her wellingtons on so paddled down to the canning factory where the fishing boats landed the small fish that were going to be put into olive oil and sealed into little tins.

As she approached, she could hear people crying, loud voices, and almost stopped. Something bad had happened – it was nothing to do with her so she should go home. Then she heard Dan's name mentioned and a lump settled in her stomach. Her throat closed – it was hard to swallow – but she needed to find out if what she'd overheard meant what she thought it did.

As she sloshed to the corner, she met a fisherman. 'Excuse me, sir, I heard someone mention Mr Brooks. Has something happened to the *Lady Beth*?'

The young man gripped her shoulder painfully. 'The barge went down outside Harwich. No survivors.'

The man hurried off, possibly to let the family know. Nancy was going to be distraught; she still loved Dan even if they were no longer engaged. She had to tell Mrs Bates and the rest of the family the dreadful news.

Ignoring the water that splashed into her boots, Emily ran back along Quay Street and raced home. She burst into the house, tears streaming down her face, too distraught to explain what had happened.

'What's wrong, love, look at the state of you,' Annie said as she stepped up and steadied Emily by the shoulders. 'Here, stop still whilst I get you out of these wet things. Don't try and speak for a minute, gather yourself, and then you can explain.'

Emily took several deep breaths. Tried to think of something normal. She saw that the sitting-room door was open, Mummy wasn't in there and neither was the baby so they must be upstairs. She didn't want to speak to Annie; she wanted to tell one of her parents.

She wriggled away and, in her socks, ran upstairs and burst into the main bedroom without knocking – something she'd never done before.

Mummy was holding Grace over her shoulder and spun round in shock. She put the baby into the crib before speaking.

'Darling, what happened? Tell me at once. Sit on the end of the bed and I'll put my arms around you to make it easier.'

Emily clung on, needing the reassurance, the comfort, still unable to say the dreadful news. Eventually, she gulped to a stop. 'It's Dan, Mummy, people were crying down at the cannery and I asked a fisherman what was wrong. He told me that *Lady Beth* had sunk near Harwich and there were no survivors.'

'Here, darling, dry your eyes and blow your nose. Could you please keep an eye on your sister for a little while? I need to tell Mrs Bates and I expect that she'll want to tell Nancy herself.'

'What if she cries? I don't know what to do with a baby.'

'I haven't had time to bring up her wind. If she does cry, just pick her up, sit in my special chair and put her over your shoulder and then pat her back. Nothing difficult.'

Mummy hugged her again, kissed her and hurried out. It was as if Grace sensed this and immediately began to cry. Emily had never picked the baby up, hardly spent more than a few minutes a day with her; now she was in charge and couldn't just sit there listening to the poor little mite screaming so pitifully.

'All right, little sister, I'm coming. I expect you've got tummy ache. Our mummy told me how to help you.' Talking to Grace somehow made it a bit easier. She reached in and picked the squalling, wriggling little body up and rested her against her shoulder. The crying didn't stop but it lessened.

'There, you'll be tickety-boo when I've brought up your wind. I hope you don't fill your nappy as I really don't want to have to change that.'

Emily carried the precious bundle as if she was the most delicate china before lowering herself into the chair that Mummy used. Then she patted the tiny back whilst murmuring encouragement. To her astonishment, the crying stopped and a few moments later, a series of burps followed.

'Well done, sweetheart, you'll be more comfortable now.'

Emily wasn't sure if she should carry on patting or if she could now cradle the baby and look at her. She decided to try this but was ready to resume the patting on her shoulder if the screeching started again.

'Look at you, little Grace, how pretty you are. I've been drawing a lovely picture of you for our mummy and daddy.'

Then to her surprise, Grace smiled directly at her, then reached out and tried to touch her face. For the first time since the baby had arrived in February, Emily felt a rush of love, finally understood what all the fuss was about.

She nursed the baby, cooing and talking nonsense to her, whilst tears dripped down her cheeks. Dan, the nicest and kindest of young men, had died today and it just wasn't fair.

25

That night, Nancy didn't bother to cook, had no appetite, and after walking the dog down to the river and along the path for an hour, she headed home, strangely reluctant to return to an empty house.

She'd spoken to no one all day, not even seen anyone she knew even slightly, which just reinforced her growing dread that without Dan to support her, she didn't want to do this. Her boats were burned, she knew that, so unless she was prepared to let her aunt down and work as a seamstress at the sewing factory again then she was stuck where she was.

She could join the WAAFs or the WRENs but wasn't going to do this. She was a woman of her word and had to buckle down and get on with the life she'd chosen on her own.

On her return, she locked the back gate securely behind her as she went in. Boyd suddenly pushed past her, his hackles rose, his deep, low growl made her shiver.

'What's wrong, Boyd? What do you hear?'

He pressed against her, his sides vibrating, his eyes no longer friendly and his lips pulled back in a snarl. There must be someone in the house. Her heart thudded in her ears. Her mouth was dry. She couldn't remember if she'd locked the door when she went out.

Then Boyd stopped growling and wagged his tail. It must be someone he didn't consider a threat. 'Hello, who's in my kitchen?'

The door flew open and to her surprise, her mum rushed out. Her face was drawn, her eyes red. Something dreadful had happened, otherwise she wouldn't be here so late.

'Nancy, love, I'm so sorry, it's Dan. His barge went down and he's gone. It's all my fault. I should never have told him to go, then he'd have been safe at the Falcon waiting for you, not drowned in the sea.'

Nancy barely heard anything her mum said after, 'Dan's gone'.

Her world fell apart. If he was dead, all hope was gone along with her happiness.

Her legs crumpled and she slid down the wall onto the ground. Boyd dropped across her lap. She hugged the dog and tried to hold back her sobs.

'You can't sit out here, love, not in the cold. It's going to rain. You'll catch your death. Let me help you inside. I'll make a nice cup of tea.'

Mum meant well and leaned down and took hold of Nancy's arms. Boyd growled and bared his teeth.

'Bad dog, let me help her. She needs to be inside,' Mum said and ignored the warning.

Nancy could feel the dog's tension and feared he might bite to protect her. 'I'm coming, just give me a minute.'

Mum backed off.

'It's all right, lovely boy; she wasn't going to hurt me. My

Dan's been drowned. How can I live with that? I sent him away—'

Something her mother had said finally registered. She staggered to her feet and went in. 'Did you say that you sent my Dan away?'

'I'm sorry, love, I thought it for the best. You'd broken off the engagement and I thought—'

'You thought? It was nothing to do with you. You're right; if you hadn't interfered, Dan would have come back to me and wouldn't be dead. I'll never forgive you, never. Get out of my house, get out now and don't ever come back.' Nancy was screaming and Boyd added his growls to make sure that Mum left.

The door banged and then the gate.

'Good boy, we don't need her; we don't need anyone. I'm on my own now; I'll not go back to Wivenhoe ever again. That part of my life's over.'

She huddled on the floor by the range where it was warmer and the dog kept her company. Eventually, she crawled to her feet and staggered upstairs. The blackout curtains hadn't been drawn anywhere – she didn't care – if the Germans dropped a bomb on her, so much the better. She didn't want to go on living.

* * *

Nancy woke the following morning to find the dog lying next to her. He should have been downstairs in his own bed but she was glad of the company. It was dark outside so it must be early.

She'd cried herself to sleep, her throat was sore, eyes gritty and she ached all over. Until now, she hadn't realised grief was a physical pain as well as an emotional one. She turned over, pulling the blankets across her head. Getting up wasn't something she was capable of doing; she didn't think she'd ever move again.

She must have drifted off to sleep as she was roused by someone banging on the back door. Boyd hurtled off the bed and was downstairs, barking and growling, before she could stop him.

Somehow, she pulled herself upright, found her old dressing gown and put it on. Whoever it was could just open the door and walk in as she hadn't locked it after Mum had left last night. The fact that they hadn't done so must mean it wasn't anyone she knew.

She was about to answer this insistent visitor when she caught a glimpse of herself in the mirror. Her hair was standing on end, her face deathly pale and her eyes red from crying.

Quickly, she tipped a little water from the jug on the wash-stand into the basin and dipped her flannel in. The dog was downstairs whining and scratching at the front door. Nancy ran a brush through her hair and tied it back with a ribbon, washed her face and then headed for the kitchen.

Just descending the stairs was an effort. Whoever it was could have looked in the window but had remained behind the door so she couldn't see who it was.

'I'm sorry, I'm not well, family bereavement, please go away.'

'Nancy, it's your Auntie Ethel. I'm coming in. I won't take no for an answer.'

The door opened and Boyd wagged his tail and whined a greeting. 'Why didn't you just walk in? It's your house, after all – I'm just a lodger really, your employee.'

'You're my dearest niece, Nancy love, and this is your home until you want to leave it. Now, sit yourself down and I'll make us a nice cuppa. You don't have to talk, but you do have to listen.'

'Would you take the dog out first? There's a field out the back; Boyd knows the way. You can let him off the lead.'

Talking was exhausting and Nancy flopped onto the nearest chair. Auntie nodded, unhooked the lead from the nail by the back door and the dog trotted off with her as if she was a familiar friend.

The range was out and she didn't have the energy to light it. There'd be no tea until that was done. She might as well return to bed and come down when things were ready. She fell into bed with her dressing gown and slippers on.

* * *

She was woken by the dog licking her face. 'Get off, silly boy.'

The dog sat down next to the bed, his tail gently swishing on the boards. Auntie Ethel had sent him up to get her. This time, she didn't bother to check her appearance, just shuffled down the stairs. The kitchen was warm, a pot of tea on the table but no breakfast. She was glad as just the thought of food made her stomach churn.

'Good girl, sit yourself down and drink your tea.'

Nancy's hands were shaking and she needed both around the mug to pick it up without spilling it. If there'd been sugar put in it for the shock then she'd not have drunk it. She managed half the mug then her digestion rebelled. She swallowed rapidly and her stomach settled.

'Right, love, things you need to know. Daphne will be here this afternoon and the shop's opening tomorrow as planned but I'll be here to run things until you're back on your feet. All you've got to do is look after your dog – he's a nice enough animal but he's too big for me to handle.'

Nancy managed a nod but couldn't find any words.

'Now, you need to feed him and then you can go back to bed and take the big lump with you. I don't want him under my feet all day. You'll have to get yourself dressed later as I'm not sending Daphne out with him and I'll not have him messing in the yard.'

'All right,' Nancy said she heaved herself up. 'We'll keep out of your way, don't worry.'

Boyd padded after her; once she was under the covers, he made himself comfortable beside her. She woke a couple of times crying and the dog licked her tears away. She'd heard movement outside the door but nobody came in to disturb her.

She waited until she was sure her aunt and cousin were safely in the sitting room before stumbling out of bed. She brushed her hair and put it up, washed her face, and then, the dog silent beside her, went downstairs and collected the lead.

It wasn't fully dark but would be soon and she hadn't had the sense to bring her torch. She didn't have the energy to go any further than the nearest field, which meant Boyd hadn't had much exercise today. She'd do better tomorrow – it wasn't fair to him as what had happened wasn't his fault.

She locked the back gate and the back door. 'Let's get you something to eat; you must be starving, Boyd. I forgot to give you any breakfast.'

Whilst he wolfed down his food, Nancy put the kettle on. She'd had nothing to drink since the tea this morning and was gasping. This time, she drank two mugs and thought about making herself some toast but couldn't face it.

'You should really stay in your bed, boy, but I don't suppose you will.'

There were voices in the sitting room but she didn't want to see anybody tonight; maybe tomorrow she'd feel a bit better, but she doubted it. The blackout curtains had been drawn all day as she hadn't wanted any light in the room. She'd visited the outside WC on the way past so wouldn't have to get up again.

She didn't want to cry any more; it made her headache worse. As she'd been asleep most of the day, she couldn't drift off into welcome oblivion. She buried her fingers in the dog's long, silky fur, finding some comfort in his warmth.

Being awake meant she had to think about what had happened and she didn't want to do that. She kept imagining her beloved Dan being sucked under the waves, still thinking that she didn't love him. That she'd chosen her new life over him.

Why had her mum sent him away like that? Nancy didn't understand anything. Was it her fault too? If they hadn't had that terrible row, if she hadn't thrown his engagement ring back in his face then he'd still be alive as he wouldn't have returned to Brightlingsea until today.

The dog gave a small yelp as her fingers tugged too hard on his fur. 'I'm sorry, Boyd, I didn't mean to do that.'

She cried and went through everything that had happened again and again and eventually gave up any hope of sleeping. Her stomach growled and she sat up. 'I'm going to make myself some more tea and some toast.'

The house was quiet; she'd no idea what time it was but it had to be after midnight. It didn't matter – she could please herself.

Whilst she waited for the kettle to boil, the dog scratched the back door hopefully.

'I'll let you out, but you're not bringing that smelly bone in here.'

She took the key from the nail adjacent to the dog lead and opened the door. The dog shoved past her and vanished into the darkness.

After two mugs of tea and two slices of bread and jam, Nancy felt a lot better. She'd never be the same again, but she wasn't the only woman who'd lost her man and she had to pull herself together and get on with it like other women were doing and would have to do.

As she turned to go upstairs, she thought she'd better visit the loo again – after so much tea, this might be a sensible idea. She didn't want to trudge downstairs again and so far had avoided using the pot in the commode.

The feeble light of her torch was just sufficient to allow her to find her way without walking into anything. Boyd rushed to the back gate and started to growl. Nancy swung the beam towards the gate and to her horror, a man's head appeared over the top, rapidly followed by the rest of him.

As he dropped to the ground, Boyd attacked.

'For Christ's sake, I've just survived being drowned; I don't want to be mauled to death by this mutt.'

'Boyd, it's Dan, it's my Dan, don't bite him,' she screamed. Her legs moved of their own volition. She fell to her knees beside them both. 'I thought you were dead. I love you so much, I can't believe you're here.' Her heart was bursting with joy. Her man was alive and she'd been given another chance at happiness.

Dan pushed the dog away with one hand and pulled her onto his lap with the other. 'Percy and the lad both perished, *Lady Beth*'s gone, but I managed to swim to shore.'

'We can't sit out here like this, darling Dan; come inside.'

He surged to his feet, taking her with him. He carried her to the back door and shouldered his way in. He reached behind him and closed it and then, still holding her tight, continued up the stairs and into her bedroom.

'I'm not spending another minute apart from you, my

darling girl; I just want to fall asleep with you in my arms. Don't worry, I won't take any liberties.'

She pulled his head down so she could kiss him. 'I want you to make love to me. I thought I'd lost you. I want this.' Waiting to be his was no longer an option. Tonight, she wanted to show him how much she loved him and this was the right way to do it.

He snapped his fingers at the dog and pointed to the door and Boyd slunk out. Then he closed the bedroom door.

The room was dark. She couldn't see anything but she heard him removing his clothes. She did the same, not sure if she was shivering with nerves or excitement, then his arms were around her. For the first time, her skin was touching his.

* * *

Hours later, the bedroom door opened and Auntie Ethel stepped in. 'I've brought you a lovely cup of tea and two boiled eggs, Nancy love, I—'

Dan sat up and the tray crashed to the floor. Auntie fainted and Daphne appeared at the door at the same time as the dog arrived. Nancy couldn't get out of bed and help as she hadn't a stitch on and neither had he.

'I'll take care of Auntie Ethel,' Daphne said. 'It's a blooming miracle, that's what it is. We thought you were dead, Dan Brooks, but I'm glad you're not.'

'Not half as glad as I am, Daphne. Turn your back for a minute, I'll get decent, then I can look after your aunt.'

Before he could get out of bed, her aunt sat up, rubbing the back of her head and looking a bit bemused. 'I'm not sure if I'm more surprised at finding you in bed with my niece or that you're not dead.'

Daphne helped Auntie Ethel up. 'What a to-do – no one will believe it when I tell them.'

Nancy finally found her voice. 'No, you can't tell anyone; you must promise to keep this to yourself.'

Daphne giggled. 'Blimey, I wasn't going to tell them what you two have been up to; I'm just going to tell them that Dan ain't dead.'

The door closed behind them, leaving the mess of the breakfast on the boards. 'I'd better get dressed and clear this lot up. I doubt that my aunt will ever recover from the shock.'

Dan slid his arm around her naked waist and drew her back under the covers. 'You're a ruined woman, Nancy Bates, so it doesn't matter what we do now, does it?'

'I hope you're going to make an honest woman of me, Dan Brooks?'

'Try and stop me, but not right now; I've other things on my mind.'

His smile sent a flicker of anticipation down her spine.

They remained undisturbed in bed until lunchtime.

'I've been listening to the bell ringing in the shop. I think it's been really busy. My aunt will need to get home as she's never left Uncle Stan alone overnight before.'

Dan yawned loudly and stretched. 'I suppose I should let folks know I'm alive. The coastguard know, they picked me up, but not my mum nor brothers.'

Dan threw back the covers and was about to clamber out. 'Another thing, love: I've got nothing to wear. Those togs I came in are ruined and still wet.'

'Well, you can't walk about like that. Get back in at once. I'll get dressed and see if I can buy you something in the market. If you weren't so blooming tall and broad, it'd be a lot easier.'

'There's those togs in one of the old trunks in the attic. I'll put this lot on and go and find them.' He pointed at the heap of damp clothing in the corner.

Nancy watched him stroll, unashamedly naked, across her bedroom as if he belonged there. She smiled. It didn't matter what anyone thought or said; Dan was staying with her until he sorted himself out, until he found another berth. She'd thought she'd lost him; his return was a miracle. She'd never doubt the existence of the Almighty again.

MORE FROM FENELLA J. MILLER

The latest instalment in another emotional wartime saga series from Fenella J. Miller, *Army Girls: Operation Winter Wedding* is available to order now here:

https://mybook.to/ArmyGirlsWinterWedding

BIBLIOGRAPHY

A to Z Atlas Guide to London, 1939 reproduction
Wartime Britain by Juliet Gardiner
One Child's War by Victoria Massey
Sea Change by Paul Thompson
How We Lived Then by Norman Longmate
Growing Up in the War by Maureen Hull
The Home Front by Marion Yass
The Battle of the East Coast by J. P. Foynes
The Story of Wivenhoe by Nicholas Butler
River Colne Shipbuilders by John Collins and James Dodds
The Wartime Scrapbook by Robert Opie
Oxford Dictionary of Slang by John Ayto
Coasting Bargemaster by Bob Roberts
London Light: A Sailorman's Story by Jim Lawrence

ACKNOWLEDGEMENTS

Again my thanks to Michael Smither and James Dodds. This book owes much to both of them for its accuracy and authentic details.

ABOUT THE AUTHOR

Fenella J. Miller is the bestselling writer of over eighteen historical sagas. She also has a passion for Regency romantic adventures and has published over fifty to great acclaim. Her father was a Yorkshireman and her mother the daughter of a Rajah. She lives in a small village in Essex with her British Shorthair cat.

Sign up to Fenella J. Miller's mailing list for news, competitions and updates on future books.

Visit Fenella's website: www.fenellajmiller.co.uk

Follow Fenella on social media here:

 facebook.com/fenella.miller
x.com/fenellawriter

ALSO BY FENELLA J. MILLER

Goodwill House Series

The War Girls of Goodwill House

New Recruits at Goodwill House

Duty Calls at Goodwill House

The Land Girls of Goodwill House

A Wartime Reunion at Goodwill House

Wedding Bells at Goodwill House

A Christmas Baby at Goodwill House

The Army Girls Series

Army Girls Reporting For Duty

Army Girls: Heartbreak and Hope

Army Girls: Behind the Guns

Army Girls: Operation Winter Wedding

The Pilot's Girl Series

The Pilot's Girl

A Wedding for the Pilot's Girl

A Dilemma for the Pilot's Girl

A Second Chance for the Pilot's Girl

The Nightingale Family Series

A Pocketful of Pennies

A Capful of Courage

A Basket Full of Babies

A Home Full of Hope

At Pemberley Series

Return to Pemberley

Trouble at Pemberley

Scandal at Pemberley

Danger at Pemberley

Harbour House Series

Wartime Arrivals at Harbour House

Stormy Waters at Harbour House

Standalone Novels

The Land Girl's Secret

The Pilot's Story

Sixpence Stories

Introducing Sixpence Stories!

Discover page-turning historical novels from your favourite authors, meet new friends and be transported back in time.

Join our book club Facebook group

https://bit.ly/SixpenceGroup

Sign up to our newsletter

https://bit.ly/SixpenceNews

Boldwœd

Boldwood Books is an award-winning fiction publishing company seeking out the best stories from around the world.

Find out more at www.boldwoodbooks.com

Join our reader community for brilliant books, competitions and offers!

Follow us
@BoldwoodBooks
@TheBoldBookClub

Sign up to our weekly deals newsletter

https://bit.ly/BoldwoodBNewsletter

Printed in Great Britain
by Amazon

57845314R00165